MOON OVER KNOXVILLE

A Pharmaceutical Mystery

MIKE GRINDSTAFF

Jan-Carol Publishing, Inc

Moon Over Knoxville
Mike Grindstaff

Published August 2018
Little Creek Books
Imprint of Jan-Carol Publishing, Inc.
All rights reserved
Copyright © 2018 by Mike Grindstaff

This is a work of fiction. Any resemblance to actual persons, either living or dead is entirely coincidental. All names, characters and events are the product of the author's imagination.

This book may not be reproduced in whole or part, in any matter whatsoever without written permission, with the exception of brief quotations within book reviews or articles.

ISBN: 978-1-945619-70-0
Library of Congress Control Number: 2018954173

You may contact the publisher:
Jan-Carol Publishing, Inc.
PO Box 701
Johnson City, TN 37605
publisher@jancarolpublishing.com
jancarolpublishing.com

Dedicated to Bob, Laurie, and that one particular harbor where it began all those many years ago.

AUTHOR'S NOTE

This work of fiction was just a bucket list thing in the beginning. It took an embarrassingly-long time to complete, but it is finally finished.

I am a pharmacist (quasi-retired) who has always loved to read, and who dreamed of one day writing a book. My life, and hence the characters in this book, has been shaped and molded by pharmacy, baseball, and rock and roll.

As some of you may know, baseball is wrapped in superstitions. When a hitter gets on a hitting streak, he is likely to try to duplicate his daily routine, such as eating the same foods, wearing the same socks and underwear (unwashed, of course), sitting on the same place on the bench, etc.

I played baseball as a youth until the field size outgrew my talent level. As an adult, I coached my children in both baseball and softball until they went on to high school, where I couldn't coach any longer. Being unable to coach led me to becoming an umpire so that I could still be around the game that I love and cherish.

The point to all of this is that I am superstitious. So much so that there is no chapter 13 in this book! Please don't contact the publisher stating that your book is missing a chapter—it was skipped intentionally.

I hope that you will enjoy reading my book as much as I enjoyed writing it. I enjoyed it so much that I am considering writing another one, but I will leave that up to you, the reader, if you think it appropriate or not.

CHAPTER 1

As the first rays of light began to dawn, Marwin Gelstone sat on the dock staring off into a place only he could traverse. It was 6:15 a.m. on a crisp October Saturday. A shiver went through him and he realized his favorite sweatpants were full of holes, as was his favorite sweatshirt, which had become snug around the middle. Neither were adequate for an autumn morning on the lake in Tennessee. Marwin knew it wasn't just the 28-degree morning that sent a chill down his spine; he was thinking of his friend and partner, Jackson Montgomery, whose wife of 24 years had apparently just committed suicide. Jackson had called him on his cell phone just 30 minutes ago, waking him from a peaceful, dreamless sleep, the kind that can only occur in a place like the lake.

A female voice drifted down from the house. "Mar, coffee's ready." Destiny stood on the deck in her robe and slippers, hugging herself against the chill.

"Be right up, thanks," Marwin called back.

As Marwin entered the two-story log cabin, he stopped abruptly. He watched intently as Destiny Lawson moved through the kitchen. *She's really something*, he thought. Beautiful and sexy, yet he could sense a teddy bear underneath. Unfortunately, he had seen a different animal below the surface: a tiger. Destiny's temper could flare up in an instant and explode like an M-80, leaving destruction in her wake. With such a unique mixture of traits, she truly possessed a fitting moniker. Marwin was beginning to believe it was destiny that had brought them together. They came from two different states, hundreds of miles apart. They had both escaped small towns that held no opportunities for anyone with an ambition past cruising parking lots, smoking weed, and having sex in the backseat of the car behind a dumpster in the grocery store parking lot. Yet they were vastly different in many ways. Marwin considered himself realistic, laid-back, and level-headed, while Destiny could be impulsive, and might go off half-cocked at any moment. Still, they were drawn inexplicably to one another. They seemed to be good for one another. Marwin had calmed her down a little, and Destiny had made him slightly less pessimistic (or, as he claimed, realistic). He was beginning to believe they truly had a long-term future together. He knew he was in love with her, but he was still somewhat gun-shy after his divorce from his high school sweetheart, just three years ago. Marwin had been thinking about proposing to Destiny, but due to last night's tragedy, he pushed those thoughts aside for the time being.

"Marwin! I have been talking to you for five minutes! Are you OK?" Destiny asked.

"Yeah... Sorry, I have a lot on my mind," he replied.

"I know. Can you tell me what Jackson said?"

They had been sleeping soundly in the master suite's quaint double bed when Marwin's phone rang, startling them awake. As Marwin groggily reached for the phone, Destiny tensed all over. She checked the digital clock on the bedside table: 5:42 a.m. No call that comes at 5:42 a.m. is good news. They don't call to inform you that you won the sweepstakes or that your son has been accepted to Harvard at 5:42 a.m. Ninety-nine percent of the time, someone is dead. One percent of the time, someone is drunk or stoned and dialed the wrong number. No one calls to wish you *Happy Birthday* and tell you that you are beautiful at 5:42 a.m.—someone is dead!

Destiny knew plenty about death, from a personal as well as professional standpoint. She vividly remembered the early morning call that brought the news of her favorite grandfather's passing. As the district attorney for Knoxville, Tennessee, she had received more than her share of wake-up calls with information about a prominent dead person.

Marwin wandered over to the kitchen table. "Jackson's wife, Madeline, killed herself last night," he said wearily. "Jackson had been playing cards at Alain's house and returned home about one-thirty. He found her slumped in a chair in their bedroom. When he lifted her head up, he saw that she had shot herself with one of his pistols."

"My God, how awful that must have been!" Destiny exclaimed.

"Awful isn't the word. I can't imagine the horror of finding a loved one dead, much less by their own hand. Jesus, they were getting ready to celebrate their twenty-fifth anniversary! What in the world could have happened to make her kill herself?"

"I guess no one ever knows what makes a person take their own life," Destiny replied morosely.

"Well, I'm sorry, but I have to go back to Knoxville. You can stay if you want. Just rent a car to drive back, and I'll pay for it."

"No, it's OK. I don't mind going back with you."

"But we just got here," Marwin protested mildly.

"So what? Unless you don't *want* me to go with you, I would rather be with you," Destiny said, giving him a glimpse of that hidden teddy bear.

"Thanks, Baby. I would love for you to be with me." Marwin briefly thought of adding *now and for always*, but didn't, thinking *the time is definitely not right*. Marwin walked over and put his arms around Destiny. He laid his head on her shoulder and allowed the tears to slowly slide down his face.

CHAPTER 2

Dr. Jackson Montgomery stared unseeingly across the room from his seat in his study. He leaned back in the old leather chair and sighed heavily. He had just gotten off the phone with his son Cody, who was living in Montana at the time. Cody had been completely silent after hearing of his mother's death. Jackson was afraid Cody might go into shock, so he contacted Cody's girlfriend, Sandy. Jackson instructed her on the signs and symptoms of shock and how to handle them, should Cody become worse. Sandy was shocked as well, but Jackson thought she is much tougher emotionally than Cody. She will be able to keep him together. Jackson had already booked a flight for Cody and Sandy on Delta, arriving in Knoxville around noon on Sunday. He silently set a reminder in his iPhone to pick them up at the airport, lest he become distracted and forget.

"This is crazy," Jackson muttered aloud. A sense of bewilderment engulfed him as he sat at his desk trying to think of all the preparations that must be made. Helen, Jackson's head nurse and right-hand man for the last eight years, had arrived this morning with two trays of food, some soft drinks, and a bottle of Hennessy. She immediately started making arrangements and straightening up the house as best she could. Funeral arrangements were complete, apart from the specific casket. Jackson had an appointment with West and Sons at 4 p.m. to take care of this detail that afternoon. The house had been cleaned except for the bedroom, which was still off limits until the police finished their investigation.

Jackson's thoughts returned to the task at hand. He had notified Madeline's only sister, Teresa, who would be arriving early Monday. She was driving down from Syracuse, New York. Fortunately, the snow hadn't started yet; Teresa refused to fly. She had always been afraid to fly, but after the 9-11 tragedy, no amount of coaxing would get her on a plane. Jackson thought this was ridiculous and believed when the Man upstairs called, it mattered not where you were, you were going. Jackson silently dreaded Teresa's arrival, as she had never been very fond of him. Somehow, he was sure, he would be to blame for Madeline's death. Well, at least she won't want to stay here at the house, Jackson mused.

Checking his mental list, he had called Cody, Helen, Marwin, Teresa, and Ben Jackson down at Woodland Gardens, where he and Madeline owned plots. He hoped he hadn't forgotten anyone important. As Jackson was diligently trying to follow the necessary procedures checklist, his thoughts were interrupted by the ringing telephone.

"Hello," Jackson answered.

"Dr. Montgomery? This is Winston Browne from the Knoxville News Sentinel. Could I have a moment of your time?"

Shit, Jackson thought. "I...guess so," he said slowly.

"First, let me say thank you for taking the time to talk to me, and I want to let you know that you have my condolences on your wife's passing."

"Thank you. Not to be rude, but what can I do for you?"

"I just wanted to get your statement on your wife's suicide. I understand that she shot herself. I was wondering if she had a good working knowledge of guns, and if she had been ill."

"Look, I don't know who you are or how you got your information, but my only statement is that I have lost the only thing that I truly loved in my life," Jackson snapped. "If you have nothing further, I have things to take care of. Goodbye."

"Wait, Dr. Montgomery," Browne said hurriedly. "Just one more question, please."

"What," Jackson said flatly, with increasing irritation.

"How long had your wife been sick? Did you have any inkling that she was considering something like this?"

"Listen to me, dammit! Madeline was not sick. She was in perfect health. Don't you think I would have done something to prevent this, if I had any idea there was a chance in Hell this might happen?!" Jackson yelled, voice rising to the edge of a scream.

"If there were no health problems, how about personal problems? Were you two having marital problems?" Browne risked asking.

"Look, asshole, this conversation is over. Call me again, and I will have your job!" Jackson snarled.

Slamming the phone down, Jackson sat back in his chair, trembling. He couldn't believe the nerve of people these days. He took some deep breaths, trying to calm himself. After several minutes, his normal calm returned—but with it came the weight of the tragedy. Jackson leaned forward and cradled his head in his hands. "Why? Oh, why? Why did you leave me, Baby?" Jackson wailed to the empty house as the tears rolled from his somber brown eyes.

***

Some time later, as Jackson was trying to choke down the sandwich that Helen insisted he eat, a strange thought crossed his mind. Picking up his iPhone, Jackson searched for the number of the Knoxville police department. Tapping the number on the screen, Jackson waited impatiently for the call to be answered.

"Knoxville police, this is Sargent Whiteside," a man answered after only two rings.

"Uh, yes, this is Dr. Jackson Montgomery and I need to speak to someone regarding my wife's uh, investigation. I mean, death. Just whoever was in charge when they came out last night, please."

"Just a moment, Doctor Montgomery. I'll transfer you to Officer Blackburn."

As Jackson listened to the silence on the other end, his mind raced, trying to formulate the questions in the best way possible. "Blackburn," said a voice after a short time.

"Yes, hello, Officer Blackburn. This is Doctor Jackson Montgomery. I was just wondering, who was responsible for calling the reporters and giving them the sordid details of Madeline's death?" Jackson snarled sarcastically.

"Whoa, Doctor Montgomery! We haven't released any information to anyone. Our preliminary reports haven't even been finalized. After the reports are done, we will release a tasteful, generic account of the situation. We are especially cognizant of the sensitive nature of this incident and wish for you to be able to make all necessary calls before anything is made public."

"Well, it's a funny thing that I received a call from some asshole reporter at the Sentinel, about an hour and a half ago, and he had plenty of details. So, somebody called someone."

"Doctor Montgomery, I assure you no one here has released anything to anyone at the paper," Blackburn stated testily.

"Look, I'm sorry. I didn't mean to jump on you. I just want an explanation. It has been a very long, trying day," Jackson said mournfully.

"OK, no sweat. I understand your frustration. Let me double check around here. Give me the reporter's name, and I will place a little call down to the paper myself. I'll call you back within the hour."

"Thanks. His name is Winston Browne."

"Winston Brown at the Sentinel, got it. I will call you back as soon as I find out something," Blackburn promised.

Jackson hung up, then sat back, aggravated with himself. Twice in one day he had completely lost his cool. He was normally a very laid-back person. He'd jumped on the reporter first, then he exploded on the police officer who was trying to help him. *I'm not handling this very well. But then how often does your wife kill herself, anyway?* he thought.

CHAPTER 3

"Well, that's everything," Marwin said, as he finished loading his 2016 Toyota Sequoia. "Are you sure you want to go with me?" he asked Destiny.

"Look, I have already said I would stay with you. If you keep asking me, I'm going to think you don't want me to come."

"OK, I just hate for you to lose this time away. I know you really need it."

"Hey, everybody needs it occasionally. Besides, I wouldn't be able to enjoy myself knowing what you are going back to," she said.

"All right. Let's go, then," Marwin said, glancing toward the dock. He smiled briefly as he recalled the wonderful night they'd just shared. They hadn't unpacked anything. Instead, they took the Kentucky Fried Chicken they'd picked up on the way and a six-pack of Rolling Rock down to the dock. They watched the sun set behind the ridge across the lake. They spoke infrequently, mostly about how beautiful the place was and how much they both badly needed some time away. Long after the light faded and the chicken had been devoured, they sat close to each other in comfortable silence, finishing their beers. Neither one wanted the scene to end, but finally Destiny said, "I'm getting cold and I need to pee, so I'm going up to the house."

"Go ahead. I'll clean up down here and be right up. If you need any help in the bathroom, I can help you there, too," Marwin said sweetly, with a faint leer.

"I think I can handle that part all by myself, but I may need some assistance later," Destiny replied demurely.

Marwin watched Destiny disappear into the house, then picked up the remnants of the chicken and beer and headed up the hill to the house. After disposing of the trash, he lit a fire in the large fireplace. He poured two glasses of Mondavi Merlot, then settled onto the rustic couch. Marwin closed his eyes and felt the energy beginning to ebb away. As he became slightly groggy, Destiny cleared her throat. "Ah? Hmm..." Marwin opened his eyes to see Destiny standing in the doorway, dressed only in a merry widow. *Holy Shit*, he thought, almost saying it out loud.

"I think I'm ready for that help now," Destiny purred.

"Come on over here; the doctor will see you now!" Marwin responded.

Destiny crossed the room to Marwin's seat and leaned teasingly forward so that her 34-C breasts almost spilled out. "Like what you see, Doctor?" she teased.

"Oh, yes," Marwin murmured, leaning forward to kiss and caress the lily-white skin of Destiny's breasts. As Marwin's tongue traced a line toward a pink nipple, Destiny pulled quickly away.

"Not so fast, Doctor," she scolded.

Marwin fell back on the couch and watched Destiny walk to the stereo. She turned on the CD player, and Bad Company's "Feel Like Makin Love" immediately blared from the speakers. Marwin stared as Destiny danced and slid across the floor. She slowly slipped a thin strap from her right shoulder, then followed with the left as she danced seductively, inches from Marwin's face. As Marwin reached for her, she again pulled back, saying, "Not yet; not yet." Destiny turned away from Marwin and slowly bent over, showing him her sexy rear end. She glanced back over her shoulder and slowly began gyrating her hips. Finally, Marwin could take no more; he stood up, spun Destiny around, and pulled her tightly to him. Marwin hungrily kissed her, their tongues jousting roughly at first. Shortly, they began to slow things down and their kisses and caresses became more tender. As Marwin pulled apart the remaining snaps of her lingerie, Destiny became aware of the hardness pressing against her stomach, and their pace increased once again. They made their way to the couch and Marwin used his tongue to follow the trail that his fingers had blazed earlier. Suddenly, Destiny bucked wildly against him, then pulled his head up and drew him to her. Slowly, she guided him into her, and a moan escaped her lips. Destiny's rhythm increased rapidly; within seconds she spasmed all over, then became very still.

"Are you OK?" Marwin whispered as he continued thrusting.

"Uh, no. I mean, yes," Destiny giggled. "Are you OK?"

"Well, I'm not as OK as you, but I'm fine," Marwin answered.

"I'm sorry, Baby," Destiny said. "You can finish if you want to," she continued, moving her hips again.

"No, I think it's a little late for that now," Marwin said, withdrawing his semi-flaccid member. "It's OK; you can just owe me one. I won't let you forget, either. Grab that blanket and your wine, and come over here," Marwin said, patting the couch beside him.

Destiny covered herself with the blanket and put her head on Marwin's shoulder, feeling completely content. As Marwin stroked Destiny's hair, they both nodded off, only to wake around 1:30 a.m. and stumble to bed, where they immediately fell back to sleep.

***

"Hun, are you ready?" Destiny asked.

"Yeah, I was just daydreaming about last night. You sure surprised me."

"Thank you. If you play your cards right, there is more of that in your future," Destiny replied with a brilliant smile.

"Promises, promises," Marwin said, smiling back and climbing into the car.

Marwin and Destiny were quiet as they began their trip south on I-81. Each was lost in their own thoughts as they traveled in silence. Marwin watched the beautiful Tennessee landscape rushing past the windows and marveled again, as he did so often, at the beauty in the world. The last cold snap brought the fall colors to life. *The foliage is breathtaking*, he thought. Marwin glanced sideways at Destiny and saw that she was resting with her eyes closed, her head back against the seat. He risked studying her peaceful face briefly, then returned his full attention to the road. With Destiny asleep,

Marwin thought about Jackson's wife again. He debated calling Jackson, but decided to wait until they got back to Knoxville.

Marwin remembered Madeline Montgomery as a proper woman who at times could appear standoffish. She was always at least cordial to Marwin, even though he had limited social experiences with her. He knew Madeline was very active in the Knoxville community. She served on the board at St. Mary's Hospital in some capacity. Marwin remembered Jackson complaining that Madeline was never home because, "She's always out doing some shit for the church, hospital, school, or some other damn place." Marwin briefly wondered if Jackson's marriage wasn't quite as good as he claimed. Jackson was one of the few men Marwin knew who talked lovingly about his spouse. Other than her busy schedule, Marwin had never heard Jackson complain about Madeline in any way. Jackson had never even openly complained about a lack of sex, and they had been married for 24 years. Recalling none too fondly the decrease in sexual activity in his own marriage after several years, Marwin was impressed with Jackson. At men's gatherings, the lack of women's libido was the second most popular subject, trailing only the pathetic state of the University of Tennessee's athletic department. Yet Jackson appeared genuinely satisfied with his marriage. *What a shame*, Marwin thought sadly.

Marwin was deeply saddened for his friend and professional colleague. Jackson had been very good to Marwin. He afforded Marwin an opportunity that very few pharmacists ever receive. They met when Marwin was a first-year student at Mercer Southern School of Pharmacy. Marwin was an overly enthusiastic student, trying to devour every piece of pharmaceutical knowledge available. Jackson had recently purchased a walk-in clinic across the street from the pharmacy where Marwin was training. Upon introduction, Marwin and Jackson immediately developed a mutual respect. Marwin was fascinated with the personal, caring approach with which Jackson treated his patients. Jackson was, in turn, impressed by Marwin's drive; his past experiences with pharmacists and pharmacy students had shown little except apathy on their part. Marwin asked to attend office hours for free, just so he could observe how medicine worked. As the years went by and Marwin progressed in his pharmacy career, Jackson came to realize the incredible knowledge of drugs that Marwin possessed. During Marwin's fourth and final year, he approached Jackson with an idea for a partnership. "I want to prescribe the drug therapy for your patients," Marwin told Jackson. "You do the diagnosing, and I will do the drug selection and dosing. This will free you up to see more patients, and I can ensure the patient is getting the right drug at the right dose."

"Are you implying that they might not get the right treatment if I do it myself?" Jackson asked, trying to sound aggravated and not smile.

"Well, you do all right for a doctor, but I am the drug expert who has more training than you ever will," Marwin replied cockily.

"I don't know, Marwin... I'll think about it," Jackson hedged.

"Look, Jackson, this will work. Your patients will like it because I can spend much more time with them than you can. Nothing personal; I know you know your stuff, but I will improve their care. Your peers may be skeptical at first, but I guarantee you they will want in after they see the results. I've already thought about having a fourth-year student track the results, so we can see it on paper. Give me six months; if you don't think I'm making a difference, we'll call it quits with no hard feelings. Whaddaya say?"

Jackson studied Marwin silently, marveling at the young man's intensity and self-assurance. "Let's play some golf on Sunday and talk more about it then," Jackson said at last.

"What time, and where do you want to get your ass kicked?" Marwin asked, with his ever-present cockiness.

***

As Destiny shifted in the seat next to him, Marwin suddenly realized he was no longer traveling south on I-81. He saw an upcoming exit sign on I-40, but had no recollection of making the transition. The adage that God takes care of kids, drunks, and idiots should apparently include day-dreaming pill pushers as well. Marwin chastised himself for not paying attention, and silently prayed his thanks for still being in one piece. As Marwin finished his prayer with a promise to be more diligent in his responsibilities, Destiny woke and groggily asked, "Where are we?"

"Just about twenty minutes from home. You must have been really wiped out."

"I guess I was more tired than I realized. Thanks for letting me get some sleep."

"No problem," Marwin replied. "I got in my own nap, too."

CHAPTER 4

As the last light of the afternoon gave way to the darkness of the approaching night, Jackson sat alone in the guest bedroom. The room hadn't been used since Cody and Sandy visited in July. He didn't know what time it was, or exactly how long he had been sitting here. He remembered going in there to see if the bed had sheets on it, as his bedroom wasn't clean. *And may never be clean again*, he thought. Jackson didn't remember the last time he'd been in this room, with its simple furnishings. While Madeline liked to appear stylish to her friends, she had decorated this room modestly. The double bed was covered with an antique quilt, sewn by Madeline's grandmother, and given to her when she left home. The nightstands harbored only plain black lamps with simple white shades. An antique rocker, where Jackson was sitting, resided in the corner overlooking the pool area. Lastly, an antique dresser in front of the bed gave off a dull reflection of the dimly lit room.

Jackson was roused from his fog by the phone ringing. As there was no phone in the guest room, he wearily headed for his bedroom—but stopped mid-stride. The horror of the empty room that was once his and Madeline's came rushing at him once again. He suddenly couldn't move, and realized he was holding his breath. Somehow, the ringing finally broke through his paralysis and he was able to lurch forward again. He headed for the bathroom, where long ago Madeline had insisted upon having a phone installed. Jackson reached the phone just as the answering machine picked up; Madeline's voice emanated from the speaker, making his knees go weak. He grabbed the marble counter with one hand and the receiver with the other. "Hello; wait for the machine to quit. OK, go ahead."

"Doctor Montgomery, this is officer Blackburn from the Knoxville PD. I have some information for you, and I was wondering if it would be convenient if I stopped by tonight."

"It has been a very long day. Can you just give me the information over the phone, please?"

"I would rather not. I can be there in twenty minutes. I promise to make it quick; I won't keep you long."

"Fine," Jackson said testily. "I'll see you shortly."

Jackson sat on the counter next to the sink, confused. *What in the hell is going on? All I wanted to know was who was leaking information. I don't want to have to deal with the cops again tonight; I am too damned tired.* After a few minutes, Jackson climbed off the counter and trudged heavily downstairs to wait for Blackburn.

***

The doorbell rang loudly and Jackson glanced at his watch; nineteen minutes had passed since Blackburn called. *At least he's punctual*, Jackson thought sourly. Looking through the peephole, he saw two men on his doorstep. One was dressed in a Knox County police uniform; his name tag read Blackburn. The other man was dressed in faded jeans and a UT Vols sweatshirt. *Shit*, Jackson thought. *Who the hell is this guy? I hope it's not that asshole Browne from the paper*, Jackson thought as he opened the door. "Doctor Montgomery, I'm Officer Ray Blackburn, KCPD, and this is Detective Bradley Jinswain," said the man dressed as a cop, pointing to the one in jeans.

"Detective? I don't understand... Why is he here?"

"Can we please come in?"

"Oh, sure. I'm sorry."

Jackson led the men into his study, turning lights on as he went. "Please, sit down," he said, pointing to the two black leather chairs adjacent to his desk.

"I'll get right to the point, Doctor Montgomery. I placed a call to Elliot Rodsmith at the Sentinel. I asked him for information on your reporter, Winston Browne, and how I might be able to contact him. Mr. Rodsmith stated that there is no one by that name working at the paper."

"What do you mean?" Jackson asked bewildered.

"Apparently, someone was posing as a reporter. The question is, who was he, and how did he get the details of your wife's death?" Blackburn said, looking directly into Jackson's eyes.

CHAPTER 5

Marwin exited I-40 on Cedar Bluff Road and Destiny said, "I'm starving. Can we grab something to eat?"

"Sure, whaddaya want?"

"I really want something good, like Calhoun's, but we aren't dressed for it. Why don't we just pick up some Chinese and eat at my place?"

"OK," Marwin said, although Chinese food would usually give him the runs. As they pulled into the parking lot, Marwin asked, "What do you want? I'll go in and get it."

"I trust your judgement. Just bring me something good."

Fifteen minutes later, Marwin returns with four egg rolls, a carton of chicken fried rice, egg drop soup, an order of moo goo gai pan, and an order of sweet and sour shrimp. "Damn! You hungry or something?" Destiny asked as she looked through the bags.

"No, not really. I just know how hungry people get after sleeping the day away," he teased.

"Bite me," Destiny replied, laughing.

***

With dinner finished, they moved to the living room. "Good Lord, I'm as full as a tick," Destiny declared, falling back on the couch.

"Boy, people in Louisiana have some strange sayings," Marwin replied.

"You're one to talk, Mister 'dumb as a coal bucket,'" Destiny retorted, referring to Marwin's favorite description of anyone with an IQ lower than his own.

"Touché," Marwin said, smiling.

Destiny smiled back and Marwin asked, "What are you smiling at?"

"You. I'm getting kinda comfortable having you around," Destiny replied, patting the couch beside her. "Come here," she demanded playfully.

Marwin crossed the room and sat next to Destiny on the couch. They leaned their heads together, entwined their fingers, and said nothing more.

***

"I have no idea," Jackson stated. He had begun to feel slightly woozy; the previous 24 hours had just been too much for him. His mind and nervous system were fried from trying to process all the new information.

"OK; first, repeat the conversation you had with this man, exactly. Bradley, you take notes for us," Blackburn instructed. Jinswain raised one eyebrow and stared at Blackburn as if he had just given him instructions to flush the toilet after peeing.

"I need a drink," Jackson stated, walking to the fully-stocked oak bar. "Can I get either of you anything?"

"Well, we are both off duty…so sure," Blackburn replied. "I'll take a beer, if you have one."

"What about you, Detective?"

"No thanks. I never put poison into my body. Do you happen to have any mineral water?"

"Will Perrier do?" Jackson asked.

"That would be great, thanks," Bradley replied.

After the drinks were poured, Jackson recounted his conversation with the supposed reporter. The two men listened in silence, Bradley making an occasional note. When Jackson was finished, Bradley asked, "Was there anything special about the voice? Old, young, accented? Was it gravelly like a smoker's? Do you think you've ever heard it before?"

Jackson didn't answer. Slowly replaying the conversation in his head, he paid special attention to the man's voice. Finally, he said, "Probably an older voice. Definitely southern, but unremarkable otherwise. It could have been the voice of any Tom, Dick, or Harry walking down the street. If I have heard it before, it didn't make a lasting impression."

"OK, that's fine," Bradley said, taking the lead. "I need you to answer some questions now."

Jackson's blood began to boil. "I've already answered questions, for two hours this morning! My wife killed herself and destroyed my entire life in the process. I just found out that some jerk thinks it's funny to pour salt into a fresh wound, and now I have a detective in my den who wants me to answer more questions, or maybe the same damn ones again, when I don't have even one fucking answer!" Jackson nearly screamed.

Silence filled the room for a moment. Finally, Jinswain spoke, eyeing Jackson intently. "Where were you last night?"

"Goddammit, what does that have to do with anything?" Jackson exploded.

"Doctor Montgomery, I am just trying to gather all the facts. I am not implying that any of this is your fault. I want to find whoever is harassing you, so I just need all the pertinent details."

"I'm sorry," Jackson apologized, his voice cracking. He sat back heavily in his chair and covered his face with both hands. After several deep breaths, he finally spoke. "I was at a colleague's house playing poker until approximately one-fifteen this morning. Alain Houston is his name. Call him if you want; he or any of the other four players can vouch for my whereabouts."

"Can I have his number, please?" Bradley asked.

Jackson recited Alain's number, then rose to mix another Wild Turkey and water. That round was much darker in color than the first.

"Thanks," Bradley said. "Now, can you tell me exactly what you found when you got home?"

Jackson visibly shrank as he began to tell the story of his grisly return home. "All the lights in the house were off when I came in. I checked all the doors to make sure they were locked, then went upstairs."

"Were all the doors locked?" Jinswain asked.

"Yes. All the doors were locked, with the deadbolts in place. When I got to our room, the lights were off. So I went into the bathroom and turned on the light over the vanity. I closed the door so as not to wake Madeline. When I came out after brushing my teeth, I noticed something in the chair next to the bed. That chair is used mostly to house clothes, or books and magazines that we read in bed and then toss into the chair. I couldn't tell what was in the chair, so I went back to the bathroom and turned the overhead light on, then opened the door to shed some light on the bedroom. I was surprised to see that Madeline wasn't in bed, but was instead sitting in the chair." Jackson paused and took a long pull from his bourbon before continuing. "I went over to the chair and shook Madeline's shoulder to wake her up. Her head was kinda hanging slightly forward and to the side, and she was leaning on the arm of the chair. When she didn't respond, I leaned down to talk in her ear and shook her again. That's when I—" Jackson stopped, turning pale.

"I know this is incredibly painful for you, and I am sorry to make you relive it, but anything you can tell us may be important," Blackburn interjected.

"I'm sorry," Jackson repeated. "When I leaned down, I felt something wet on the arm of the chair and I smelled blood. I ran to turn on the light and couldn't believe what I saw. Madeline's brains were all over the chair and bed," Jackson said pathetically. "I ran back to her, but of course she was already gone. I sat holding her and crying for some time, then called 911." Jackson leaned back, slumping in his chair as if all the weight of the world had fallen on him.

"What happened after the police arrived?" Bradley prodded gently.

"They asked me a lot of questions, like you are. They wanted to know where I had been. They asked if the gun on the floor was mine, and I told them that it was. They asked about Madeline being depressed, if she had been ill, and if she had ever mentioned hurting herself. They wanted to know if she'd left a note."

"Did she?" Jinswain asked.

"Not that anyone has found," Jackson replied. "Honestly, I don't even remember all the questions that the police asked. I was completely out of it."

"That's OK; we have the interviewing officer's report. Had your wife been ill or depressed?"

"No. Like I told the officer, she was in perfect health, as far as I know. She was active in the community and church. There was never any indication of something like this. As a matter of fact, she was a devout Catholic; suicide is an unpardonable sin in the Catholic religion. That makes this even more surreal."

"Are you Catholic also?" Blackburn asks.

"No. I'm not religious, really. I was raised Southern Baptist, but now I don't really practice much of anything, I'm afraid."

"OK, I think that will do it for now," Jinswain said. "I'll be in touch. I promise I'll try to not intrude; I know you have some very difficult days ahead."

"Thanks. Before you go, no one ever answered my question. Why are you here, Detective? There is no criminal investigation to conduct, so I can't believe that Knox County sends out detectives to investigate prank phone calls."

"Well, actually, Ray called me and told me about the phone call that you got. Frankly, something doesn't smell right. Your wife was a prominent citizen of Knoxville who was known for being outgoing. Suicide seems out of character to me. The preliminary reports all agree that it was a suicide, but I need to understand why she would have done this. Call it a flaw in my character, but I firmly believe I can solve any mystery."

"Detective Jinswain, I don't believe we'll ever know what caused Madeline to do this," Jackson stated tiredly.

"Don't give up hope, Doctor Montgomery. We will be in touch soon," Blackburn said, rising to leave with the detective.

CHAPTER 6

Marwin pulled into his three-car garage, which has only contained one car since the divorce. He leaned back in the seat and sighed wearily before exiting the vehicle. He carried his suitcase, bathroom bag, and the food inside, dumping it all on the kitchen counter. Walking to the fridge, Marwin took out an ice-cold Sam Adams, then trudged into the den and turned on the TV. Without much thought, he searched for and found a West Coast football game: Oregon State Beavers vs. Fresno State Bulldogs. Marwin silently thought of all the jokes the students of Oregon State must endure for a moment before his mind returned to Jackson's plight. He knew he should call Jackson, but convinced himself it was too late. In reality, he was only prolonging the inevitable uncomfortable feeling of sharing his partner's pain. Marwin had never been good in emotional situations. His ex-wife always said he would have made a good woman, with his propensity for wearing his emotions on his sleeve. While this appeared in stark contrast to the cocky pharmacy student of years past, Marwin had never had much self-confidence in any other area. Maybe this began at birth; his name was originally supposed to be Marvin, but his father had poor penmanship and the entry was read as Marwin. After the mistake was discovered, his parents decided to keep the name and began calling him Marwin. So, he was Marvin for the first month of his life. After that, he became Marwin. Surely, this negatively affected his personality.

Marwin was never much of a ladies' man, either. This was mostly due to lack of effort on Marwin's part. While not ugly, he was not someone women would look twice toward. His sexual activity, excluding Rosy palm, consisted of his high school sweetheart, Lindsey, whom he had married and later divorced, and Destiny. He was always introverted until pharmacy school, when he found something to truly excite him; he became completely engrossed in the material.

Marwin retrieved another beer and glanced at the clock on the microwave above the stove. Ten thirty-eight. *I guess I'd better call Lindsey and let her know I'm back in town,* he thought. Knowing Lindsey had always been a night owl, he dialed the number. After Lindsey answered, Marwin said, "Hey."

"What's wrong?" Lindsey asked, alarmed.

"I'm back in town. Jackson's wife died last night," Marwin stated, not knowing how to get into the details.

"Oh, God. I'm sorry."

"Yeah, me too. I just wanted to let you know that I am in town, in case something comes up with the kids."

"OK, thanks. The kids are fine. Bogie has a friend spending the night, and Morgan has been working on an Odyssey of the Minds project that is due this week."

"Who is spending the night with Bogie? I hope it isn't that little jerk Tyler."

"Yes, Tyler is spending the night, and he is fine. Bogie really enjoys his company."

"Bogie needs to stay away from him. He is a little thug who idolizes that hip-hop rap shit he sees on MTV!" Marwin said loudly.

"Relax, Marwin. Bogie is a good kid. He's just going through a teenage rebellion phase. And there are worse things than rap music and baggy pants," Lindsey reminded him.

"I know, I know. I just don't want him influenced by the wrong people," Marwin said.

"Bogie's fourteen now. He is going to be influenced by his peers to some degree. I believe that you and I have instilled the important beliefs in him. We'll just have to watch him make some mistakes along the way, and hope that none of them are catastrophic. You know what they say, 'God looks after kids, drunks, and idiots.'"

"Yeah, and daydreaming pill pushers. I gotta go. Give the kids a hug for me, and I will see you tomorrow night."

Returning to the football game, he saw Oregon State was blowing Fresno out. He silently kicked himself for not selecting the Beavers when he made his weekly football wagers. As Marwin sipped his beer, his mind began to whirl. He thought of his son Bogie, who was named for Lindsey's love of golf. At fourteen, Bogie had been increasingly hostile toward Marwin of late. The apparent hormonal surge of puberty was quickly changing the smiling young boy who lived for baseball into a surly, foul-tempered little shithead who listened to rap music and wore his pants so low that his boxer shorts were in plain view. Marwin sadly shook his head as he thought of Bogie playing baseball. From the time Bogie was a year old, he could hit a baseball. Of course, it started with a giant yellow bat and wiffle ball, then progressed to recreational baseball, All-Stars, and finally travel baseball, made up of only elite players. Bogie had played travel ball for three years and always excelled, until recently. He appeared to have lost interest and didn't want to practice anymore. He had become generally apathetic about everything except rap music and old reruns of Cribs on MTV. Marwin fumed; he was afraid Bogie was wasting his baseball talent, and for nothing. Marwin reflected on Lindsey's words, deciding she was right—Bogie is a good boy. As far as Marwin knew, Bogie didn't drink, smoke, or use drugs. He had rarely even heard Bogie utter a curse word, which was ironic since Bogie's very name produced many curse words on the links. Marwin vowed to spend more time with Bogie. Maybe he'd even try to listen to some of that crap Bogie called music.

Marwin turned his mind to his other child, Morgan. Morgan had turned eleven and was also going through puberty. Lindsey had informed Marwin the previous week that Morgan had started her period and would need to see a gynecologist. Marwin gave her the name of a female gynecologist who had a large adolescent practice. Marwin silently wondered where the time had gone. It seems like just yesterday when Lindsey had Bogie, and then shortly thereafter, Morgan. They were so happy then, and had bought this huge house that Lindsey thought she couldn't live without. Now, fourteen years after their first child was born, they had been divorced for three years. The divorce was amicable enough; Lindsey just fell out of love with Marwin.

She said she loved him like a brother, but not like a husband. Marwin was crushed at first, but later wrote it off to Lindsey's youth and immaturity. Three years later, he and Lindsey were best friends again, much to the chagrin of Lindsey's new husband, Adam. They tried hard to raise their children together. Marwin held no thoughts of reconciliation with Lindsey and wished her nothing but happiness. He was ready to move on with his life, including bringing Destiny entirely into his world.

Marwin returned to thoughts of Morgan. He worried about how she would handle puberty and all the changes that go with it. She was pretty, but not yet gorgeous. He had recently caught glimpses of the woman she would become. Morgan was shy and mostly introverted, like Marwin. She spent most of her time reading and playing educational games on the computer. Marwin had tried to get Morgan interested in softball, basketball, gymnastics, and other sports, but to no avail. Morgan had recently joined an Odyssey of the Minds group and was currently engulfed with the competition. Marwin didn't even know what OM, as Morgan referred to it, was about. He made a mental note to ask Lindsey for more details.

Marwin's eyelids started to droop, due to the late hour (past midnight), the events of the past 24 hours, and the beer. As his head lolled to one side, he jerked himself awake. He rose unsteadily to his feet, cut off the TV, and trudged slowly up the stairs toward his bedroom, feeling lonelier than he had in years.

CHAPTER 7

Jackson was awakened by the *tink* of something hitting the guest bedroom window. Moaning, he rolled toward the window and tried to get his eyes to focus. Unable to determine the source of the continuing noise, Jackson climbed out of bed and stumbled to the window. "Shit," he muttered, pulling back the drapes to see ice pellets bouncing off the window sill and falling to the roof below. *It can't be sleeting this early; it's only the middle of October*, Jackson thought, as he pulled on a robe and padded downstairs to check the weather on TV. As he descended the stairs, the antique grandfather clock began to chime. Jackson absently counted the number of chimes and frowned when the clock stopped at eleven. *What the hell? It can't be eleven. That damned clock must be broken*, he thought. He turned on the light in the den, then the TV, scanning quickly to the Weather Channel. Across the bottom of the screen, a banner read 11:02 a.m. "Holy shit," Jackson said aloud. I've got to pick-up Cody and Sandy in less than an hour, he remembered.

"What kind of language is that to start the day?" said a voice behind him.

Jackson turned to find Helen standing in the doorway with a cup of coffee in her hand. "How long have you been here?"

"Since about eight-thirty or so, I guess. I didn't want to disturb you; I know you need your rest."

"I guess so. I don't even remember sleeping. I tossed and turned all night, I think. I guess I was sleeping better than I thought. I've got to go get Cody at noon," Jackson said, starting back up the stairs.

"No, you don't. I've taken care of that. Cody and Sandy are being picked up by a limo service when they get in, and they will be dropped off here."

"How did you know when they were coming?"

"Uh, I took the liberty of looking through your phone to see if I could help you and I found your note about their arrival. I hope you're not mad," Helen said sheepishly.

Jackson stared directly into Helen's eyes and said, "Of course not. I don't know what I would do without you." He walked over and placed a hand on her shoulder. "Thank you," he said.

"You're welcome," Helen said, giving him a long look. "You might want to catch a shower before Cody and Sandy get here," she said as the strange moment passed.

"You're right. I'll be right back. Make yourself at home," Jackson said, turning away.

"I already have," said Helen, watching Jackson climb the stairs.

***

A short time later, Jackson returned to the kitchen, hair still wet from the shower. Helen had been making sandwiches. "Hey, you don't have to do that," he protested.

"Yes, I do. You only had coffee for breakfast and you need to keep your strength, so eat," Helen instructed. She handed him a Cajun roast beef and turkey on pumpernickel.

"Thanks, once again," Jackson said, taking the plate to the table. Despite the emotional turmoil, Jackson suddenly realized he was ravenous. Without saying a word and only pausing to wipe his hands a couple of times, he consumed the sandwich quickly.

"That was great. We rarely ever have sandwiches because Madeline doesn't—didn't—like them."

"I'm glad you liked it. Would you like another one?"

"God, no. I am stuffed." The phone rang, interrupting their chitchat. Jackson momentarily hesitated, remembering the imposter reporter, then made his way to the phone. "Hello," he said cautiously, gripping the receiver too tightly.

"Hey, Jackson, how are things going?" Marwin asked.

"Hi, Marwin. They are...going," Jackson replied sadly.

"I just wanted to touch base with you and let you know that I am back in town. Is there anything I can do?"

Bring back my wife, Jackson thought, but he said, "No, most everything is taken care of, but thank you. Cody will be here shortly. We're receiving friends at West and Sons Monday night from seven to nine. The funeral will be Tuesday morning at eleven, with the burial right after at Woodland Gardens."

"OK. I'll call Sam and get him to cover the next few days at the store. Do you feel like company? I'll buy you lunch," Marwin offered.

"No, thanks. Helen came over and brought me lunch. I don't know what I would do without her. She's been great through this whole mess. You know, she's been with me for over eight years," Jackson said, beginning to ramble.

"All right, call me later when you feel like some company."

"I will," Jackson agreed. "See ya."

***

"They're here," Helen called, startling Jackson out of a daydream that he immediately couldn't recall.

Jackson rose and walked to the door, watching Cody and Sandy climb from the limo and approach the house. Jackson marveled at Cody's good looks, which he undoubtedly got from Madeline. He was 6'2", with blond hair and sturdy shoulders. Cody held Sandy's hand as they walked up the sidewalk. Sandy could be mistaken for Cody's sister; she also had blonde hair that reached just past her shoulders, and was tall with a shapely figure that turned many heads, both male and female. They walked with a shared comfort and appeared to be perfectly in love. Cody's face became solemn as he saw Jackson standing in the doorway. The light conversation that he and Sandy were having quickly evaporated.

"Hey, Bud," Jackson said lightly, tears threatening to choke him.

"Hey, Dad," Cody replied.

They embraced for a long moment. Sandy wrapped her arms around both men. They remained this way for quite some time. Finally, Jackson broke the three-way embrace, saying, "Come on; let's get inside, out of this weather."

"You call this weather?" Cody joked. "We had ten inches of snow last week."

"Better you than me," Jackson responded, showing his ever-increasing dislike for winter weather.

After the bags were carried in from the limo, Jackson told Cody, "You guys can take the guest room, and I will sleep in your old room."

"We can grab a hotel, Dad. It's no big deal."

"The hell you will. You are staying right here. I think I'm going to need you," Jackson rasped, again choking back tears.

Seeing his father's face, Cody replied, "Sure, Dad, whatever you want."

"Good, that's settled. You guys hungry? Do you want something to drink? I've got beer, wine, soft drinks..." Jackson said, trying to be a good host.

"Thanks, Dad. We can take care of ourselves. You don't need to try to wait on us."

"Hello, Cody," Helen said, coming out of the kitchen with a tray covered in pepperoni, summer sausage, Muenster, pepper jack, and two types of crackers. A look of surprise quickly crossed Cody's face as he saw Helen doing something his mother had always done.

"Hello, Helen. What are you doing here?" Cody asked cautiously.

"I'm just trying to help your dad during this terrible time," she answered innocently.

Cody looked at Jackson, who said, "Helen has been a godsend. She has helped with the arrangements, straightened up, and even cooked for me. She was also the one who arranged for you two to be picked up at the airport."

"Looks like she's moved right in," Cody spat bitterly.

"Cody! Helen has been nothing but a help," Jackson said sternly.

"I'll bet she has," Cody murmured.

"That's enough! You apologize, right now!" Jackson demanded, his anger rising.

Cody looked from his father to Helen and back again, then said, "I'm sorry. I guess I'm just a little stressed out. I think I'll go up and shower, try to clear my head."

"It's OK, Cody. I know you didn't mean anything by it," Helen responded, eyeing Cody. "You take a shower, and I'll help Sandy get settled in."

Cody stared at Helen for several seconds, then turned and ascended the stairs without another word.

CHAPTER 8

Cody was awakened by the sound of voices coming from downstairs. He turned toward the clock to see the time and noticed Sandy sleeping peacefully on her side. He settled back and watched her sleep until she at last opened her eyes. "What are you doing?" she asked, in a voice that was much too clear for someone who just woke up.

"Staring at the love of my life," Cody said sweetly. They moved close together and snuggled until the voices from below again penetrated their room.

"I'm going to see who is here at this hour," Cody declared, nodding toward the clock, which read 7:45 a.m. He climbed out of bed and pulled on boxer shorts, sweatpants, and a t-shirt before padding down the stairs.

"Well, hello, Cody," Teresa greeted him.

"Hi, Aunt Teresa. How are you doing?" he asked, hugging his mother's sister.

Pushing back from the hug, Teresa said, "I'm devastated. I can't believe this has happened. I don't understand any of this. What in the world would cause your mom to do this?"

"I know. I don't understand it, either," Cody said, tears forming once again.

***

Jackson, Cody, and Teresa were in the kitchen having coffee and bagels when Sandy walked in. "Good morning, Dad," she said, planting a kiss on Jackson's cheek.

"Good morning, Sandy," Jackson replied with amusement.

"Sandy, this is my Aunt Teresa. She is mom's sister who lives in New York. She just got in this morning," Cody explained, introducing the two women.

"Nice to meet you," Sandy said, extending her hand.

"And you... Did I hear you call Jackson Dad?" Teresa asked.

Sandy's cheeks turned crimson, and she answered more boldly than she really felt. "Yes. I thought I would see how it sounded."

"Thank you. It sounded great to me," Jackson said, hugging Sandy.

***

Jackson and Teresa sat at the kitchen table talking after Cody and Sandy returned to their room upstairs. Jackson sadly recounted the events of Madeline's death. "It doesn't make any sense! Madeline loved life. Look at all the activities she was involved with. Plus, she was a devout Catholic; she would never take her own life," Teresa declared, mirroring Jackson's own thoughts.

"I know. None of it makes any sense."

"Is there any chance that it wasn't a suicide? Could someone have killed her and made it look like a suicide?" Teresa asked, grasping at straws.

"What? Who would have killed her? The house was locked up tight, and there was no sign of a struggle. I'm afraid she did it."

"Have the police ruled it a suicide?" Teresa asked, continuing to chase a fleeting hope.

"I don't know. I'm not sure if they've finished everything yet, but no one has mentioned anything except suicide," Jackson replied weakly.

"Well, I'm just trying to make some sense out of this insanity. Not that someone killing Madeline would make any more sense," Teresa said wearily. "I have to go get some rest. Where is the closest hotel?"

"There's a Radisson Inn a couple of miles from here. Do you want me to go with you, to help get you settled in?" Jackson offered.

"I think not. I just drove eight hundred miles by myself. I think I can check into a hotel on my own," Teresa snapped.

"Fine. Would you like me to pick you up tomorrow to go to the funeral home?"

"No, just give me directions. I'll find my way."

"OK, would you like to eat with us tonight?" Jackson offered.

"No, I don't think so—but thanks anyway," Teresa said, with a little less bite. "I think I'll just order room service. I'll call you after I get settled in to let you know which room I am in."

Seeing Teresa head toward the door, Jackson started to get up and walk her out, then thought better of it and settled back into his chair.

***

Marwin walked to the door and opened it to peer out at the front lawn. He looked left, then right, and finally located what he was looking for: the Sunday newspaper. The jerk of a paper boy had managed to lodge the paper deep into the holly bush at the far end of the sidewalk. Marwin silently cursed the boy and went back inside to throw on some clothes and grab his shoes, as it was far too cold to go dig in the shrubbery barefoot and in boxer shorts. Marwin took his paper to the den, where SportsCenter was emanating from the TV. He opened the paper to the Sports section, which was his daily custom. He skimmed the lead story on the Vols squeaking by Alabama Birmingham, 20-14, shaking his head as he thought of all the crazed Big Orange supporters who probably lost their collective asses on Tennessee, a 22-point favorite. Continuing to the back page, he checked the final scores of the day before against the games he had bet on. "Fuck," he said to the paper, TV, and empty house. After tallying up the damage, Marwin realized he'd lost $320 on college games. He quickly turned the paper to that day's pro match-ups and began to make his prognostications. His ciphering was quickly interrupted by the phone.

"Hey, Marwin, it's Jackson."

"Hey, how ya doing?" Marwin asked, having already forgotten his sports predictions.

"I'm OK, I guess. I just wanted to call since I kinda blew you off yesterday."

"Hey, no sweat. You certainly don't have to apologize to me."

After an awkward silence, Jackson asked, "Did I give you the arrangements?"

"Yeah, you did. I'll see you at the funeral home at seven tomorrow night. Is there anything you need?"

"No, I'm OK. I'll see you tomorrow night."

"OK, but I want you to promise me that you'll let me know if there's anything you need. Anything," Marwin said pleadingly.

"Sure, no problem; I will."

Marwin hung up and returned to the paper, but he was unable to concentrate. After several wasted minutes of reading about the same games over and over, he decided to give up and take a shower.

***

With his shower complete, Marwin hastily picked his games and called his bookie. He knew if his picks didn't pan out, he would have to pay up on Monday. The money didn't bother him, but the losing did. He wished he had been able to concentrate better. He picked up the phone and dialed Destiny, but only got her answering machine. He left a message about having dinner with him and the kids, then returned to the TV in the den to watch NFL GameDay. He silently hoped Hammerin' Hank wouldn't pick the same games he had, as Hank was seldom right.

***

Destiny closed the door behind her and walked directly into her bedroom, pausing only to rub the head of her Persian cat, Gabby. As she stepped out of the green dress that she wore to church, she saw the message light blinking on the answering machine. Hoping it was Marwin who called, she hit play and listened to his message. Wearing only her bra, she smiled as she heard his voice. After going to the bathroom, she returned to her room to get dressed but decided to return Marwin's call first. She unhooked her bra as she waited for him to answer, and was slipping into her panties when he finally picked up.

"Hey, Babe. Where have you been?" Marwin asked.

"I went to church. I didn't realize I had to get permission," Destiny said teasingly.

"You don't. I didn't even think about you going to church. Good for you."

"Well, I felt like I really needed it today, especially after what happened with Jackson's wife," Destiny stated.

"Yeah, I need to get back into church. I mostly only take the kids occasionally," Marwin admitted.

"So, what's up with dinner?" Destiny asked, changing the subject.

"I thought I might throw some ribs on the grill and make some baked beans. Sound good to you?"

"You know me; I will eat anything that doesn't eat me first," Destiny said, laughing.

"What happens if it does eat you first?" Marwin asked suggestively.

"I don't know, why don't I come over and we'll find out," Destiny purred.

***

After hanging up with Destiny, Marwin went to Kroger to pick up supplies for dinner. He purchased spare ribs, garlic bread, and beans. He also grabbed a bag of salad, some tomatoes, and a cucumber, debated getting croutons, then decided against the extra carbs. As he headed toward the wine section, he noticed the lights were off and realized it was Sunday; he couldn't purchase alcohol. He hoped he still had wine in the rack at home.

After returning home, he boiled the ribs, brushed them with a thick layer of barbecue sauce, and placed them in the oven. He dug out his grandmother's recipe for baked beans and got them ready to put in the oven later. Salad and bread would be done right before they ate, so Marwin capped some strawberries. He had also bought a can of whipped cream and had plans for the strawberries once Destiny arrived. With dinner preparations complete,

Marwin remembered the wine. He found a bottle of Mondavi chardonnay and put it in the freezer for a quick chill. With everything done, he turned on the TV and reminded himself to get the wine out in a few minutes. As Marwin watched the Falcons and the Bucs game, his mind drifted—surprisingly not to Destiny, but instead to Jackson's wife, Madeline. While trying to make sense out of the senseless situation, the doorbell rang. Marwin opened the door to find Destiny hugging herself against the cold wind.

"What took you so long? I rang the bell twice."

"Sorry, I guess I didn't hear the first ring," Marwin said, stepping aside to allow Destiny inside.

"Man, it is freezing! What is up with this crazy weather?" Destiny asked.

"Beats me. You want me to make us a fire?"

"You know me well enough that I don't even need to answer that," Destiny replied.

When Marwin had the fire roaring, he and Destiny settled down on the floor in front of the hearth. "Wait here," Marwin said, rising. He left the room and returned with pillows, a blanket, and a large down comforter. Marwin spread the blanket out and arranged the pillows. They snuggled under the comforter, not speaking, just enjoying the moment. They remained this way for a while, until Marwin felt Destiny's hand reach expertly behind her to find his crotch. As she slowly rubbed her hand between his legs, he rolled slightly away to allow her better access. Destiny felt his response and turned toward him. They stared into each other's eyes, and Marwin leaned in to kiss her. Just before their lips touched, Destiny pulled back teasingly. She dropped her lips below his chin and kissed his neck, traveling around his neck to his ear, where her tongue darted quickly in. A soft moan escaped Marwin and he tried to pull her to him. Their lips locked and tongues darted for a moment before Marwin pulled back and mirrored Destiny's actions. Destiny tossed her head back to allow Marwin better access to her throat. Slowly tracing an outline on her throat, he suddenly opened his mouth and kissed her neck deeply. Destiny moaned and began to squirm. Marwin reached under Destiny's shirt and let his fingers explore, working softly at first, then becoming more urgent. As he roughly caressed her breasts, Destiny began to grind her pelvis against Marwin. Suddenly, Destiny rose and pushed Marwin back. "Raise your arms," she commanded. Marwin did as he was told, and Destiny pulled his shirt off.

"Leave your arms up," she said. Destiny teasingly kissed Marwin's lips, pulling away as he tried to kiss her back. She then drifted down to his nipples, where she kissed, licked, and playfully bit each one. She continued downward until she reached his jeans. Looking into Marwin's eyes, she unbuttoned his jeans and ran her tongue into his belly button. "Lift up," she ordered. Destiny slid Marwin's jeans and underwear down together, then continued her exploration with her tongue. She gently licked the inside of Marwin's thighs and flicked her tongue quickly across his scrotum. Marwin was lying back and thrusting his hips toward her by this time, trying to get her back where he wanted her. However, Destiny quickly resumed her descent and traveled down to his feet. She traced each toe with her tongue before slowly inserting each one into her mouth. Marwin was writhing on the blanket then, practically begging her to move back up. Destiny stood up and looked into Marwin's eyes as she slowly undressed. Marwin was mesmerized and couldn't look away. He felt her foot against his erection and immediately grabbed it, rubbing it back and forth.

Completely undressed, Destiny commanded, "Lie back." As Marwin complied, Destiny straddled his face facing the opposite direction. Marwin immediately plunged his tongue into her wetness as she engulfed his shaft with her mouth. Destiny allowed this to continue for a short while, then climbed off to the side and began to ravish Marwin's member. Marwin began to buck and thrust and Destiny's mouth kept pace. "You better stop!" Marwin said breathlessly, trying to pull her head up. At his words, Destiny attacked even more fiercely, with renewed vigor. Shortly, Destiny sensed that the end was near and made one final deep plunge, which finished Marwin off instantly.

Afterward, as they lay cuddling on the blanket, Marwin said, "Thank you; that was great."

"Thank you," said Destiny, smiling.

"I didn't do anything," Marwin replied.

"Oh, yes you did!" she said, grinning.

"You mean... you did?" Marwin asked incredulously.

"Yes, I did," Destiny admitted.

"Cool," Marwin said finally. "I guess you still owe me one then!"

Destiny playfully slapped Marwin and snuggled even closer.

***

A while later, Destiny walked to the door that led to the back deck, where Marwin was busy grilling. She watched as he stared at the smoke rising from the Big Green Egg ceramic smoker. "Penny," she said, walking out into the cold October air.

"Nobody pays good money for garbage," Marwin replied, turning to greet her.

"If you were thinking it, it can't be garbage," she said, folding into his arms.

Hugging her tightly, he kissed the top of her head and said, "The egg is ready. I'm going to put the ribs on. Lindsey should be here any minute with the kids."

"OK, what do you want me to do?" she asked.

"You mean you're ready to do something already?" Marwin replied playfully.

"I swear, you only think about one thing. I meant can I do anything to help with dinner?"

"How about making the salad and opening the wine?" Marwin suggested.

"I'll make the salad; you open the wine," Destiny said.

"Deal," he replied, re-entering the house.

***

Marwin and Destiny were enjoying the wine, listening to a Meatloaf CD while she prepared the salad. The doorbell rang and Marwin opened the door to find Lindsey, Bogie, and Morgan on the front steps. "Why didn't you use your key?" he asked Bogie.

"Mom wouldn't let me," Bogie answered snottily.

"I saw you had company," Lindsey said, pointing to Destiny's car in the driveway.

"Oh, OK," Marwin said, nodding to Lindsey. "Do you guys need any help with your stuff?"

"No, Sir," they replied in unison.

"All right, take your stuff to your rooms and put everything away. Go ahead and get your clothes ready for school tomorrow, then come down for dinner. It should be ready in about fifteen minutes or so."

"What are we having?" Bogie asked.

"Ribs, baked beans, salad, and bread," Marwin responded.

"Cool," Bogie said, but Morgan complained, "Ah, Dad! You know I don't like meat. Why do we always have to eat meat?"

"Because meat is awesome, ya turd head! What kind of moron doesn't like meat?" Bogie sneered.

"That's enough, you two. You're home less than five minutes, and already fighting. Go get ready for dinner," Marwin directed sternly.

After the kids trudged upstairs, Marwin said to Lindsey, "Come on in the kitchen and have a glass of wine with us."

"Thanks, but I don't want to intrude," she said, turning toward the door.

"Come on, Linds; I wouldn't invite you if it was going to be an intrusion."

Hesitating briefly, Lindsey said, "Thanks, but I'll take a raincheck. Adam is waiting for me."

"OK, a raincheck it is," Marwin agreed as he studied Lindsey's face, detecting a hint of sadness.

***

After dinner, Marwin sent the kids upstairs to shower while he and Destiny cleaned up the kitchen. "Are you working tomorrow?" she asked while loading the dishwasher.

"No, not really. Sam is going to cover for a few days. I need to go in for a little while in the morning, just to make sure everything is OK, but I'm not staying."

"Don't go in. Just call him. If you go in, you will end up staying all day."

"Yes, Dear," Marwin said sarcastically.

Just then, the kids returned downstairs and began to forage for something to eat. "Didn't you just eat?" Marwin asked incredulously.

"That was a long time ago," Morgan said. "Ooh, strawberries!" she cried. "And whipped cream!" she continued, leaving the kitchen with the can and berries.

Marwin glanced at Destiny and shrugged sheepishly.

CHAPTER 9

Monday morning dawned chaotic. Marwin sleepily tried to ensure that both kids were ready for their individual buses. Morgan eventually dressed and made herself some oatmeal for breakfast. With the time to leave quickly approaching, Marwin realized Morgan hadn't yet brushed her hair or teeth. However, she apparently thought she had plenty of time to watch TV.

"Why do you still have to be told to brush your teeth at eleven years old?" Marwin yelled, exasperated. "Cut that TV off and get your butt ready for school." With an entire minute to spare, Morgan headed outside to greet the bus.

"Love you. Have a great day," Marwin called.

Morgan stopped and blew a kiss toward Marwin before boarding the bus.

Marwin retrieved the paper from the driveway and headed to the bathroom, skimming through the headlines on his way to the Sports section. Wife of area doctor found dead caught his eye. Marwin quickly read the article, which described Jackson and Madeline as prominent citizens who were active in the Knoxville community. Without going into detail, the article stated that Madeline apparently took her own life. *Seeing it in print must be awful*, Marwin thought, worrying about Jackson. He made a mental note to call his friend, then turned to the Sports section to see how his wagers of the previous day had fared. After scanning the scores, he was pleased to see he'd won $200. He smiled thinking *all I have to do is win*

Monday Night Football tonight, and I'll be even. Maybe this would be a good week after all.

***

Marwin showered, shaved, and finished his second cup of coffee. He called Sam next to check on things at work. "Everything going OK?" he asked.

"Yep, everything's good. I just got a call from Alain about a patient, though. Apparently, there's a difference of opinion between Alain and the patient's psychiatrist."

"Imagine that. A shrink who won't listen," Marwin mused.

"Alain wanted you to look it over and set everyone straight," Sam continued.

"OK, just fax over all the info and I'll take a look at it. I'll give you a call after I review everything."

Marwin hung up and leaned against the counter, waiting for Sam's fax to come through. Looking down, he saw his pooch, which had grown noticeably larger lately. He briefly thought about starting an exercise regimen, for what he admitted was about the hundredth time. Silently vowing to work on his stomach, Marwin decided to start right after he reviewed the case for Sam and Alain.

Marwin pulled the pages from the fax machine and took them, a blueberry bagel, and his third cup of coffee to the kitchen table. The patient was a 64-year-old female with degenerative bone disease of the spine. She also had hypertension, dyslipidemia, and depression of recent onset. Her meds included losartan 50mg twice daily, atorvastatin 20mg at bedtime, estradiol 1mg daily, medroxyprogesterone 2.5mg daily, and oxycodone sustained-release 30mg every 12 hours.

The psychiatrist wanted to start fluoxetine 40mg every morning. Alain, who was her primary care physician as well as her cardiologist, refused to let her take the fluoxetine due to the interaction with the atorvastatin. He recommended paroxetine as a substitute.

Shit, Marwin thought after reading the case details. He went to the phone and called Alain's office. "Hey, Jody, it's Marwin. Can I speak to Alain?"

"Well, you know it's Monday and we are swamped. Can he call you back?"

"Sure, I was just calling about a case he sent over. Just have him call me at home when he gets a second."

"Hold on, he just came out of a room. Let me see if he can talk now," Jody said.

Van Halen suddenly filled Marwin's ear as he waited for Jody or Alain to return. As "Running with the Devil" ended, Alain's voice suddenly burst through. "Qué pasa?"

"Not much," answered Marwin. "I just want to talk about the patient you sent over."

"OK, shoot," Alain said.

"I read your comments and suggestions, and you are right that we can't use fluoxetine. Not only will it increase the atorvastatin levels and possibly lead to muscle toxicity, it will also render the losartan completely ineffective."

"No shit?" Alain offered.

"Yes shit," Marwin returned. "Losartan isn't active when taken. It must be converted to an active metabolite first, and the cytochrome P450 system is responsible for the conversion. Specifically, 2C9 and 3A4 are the isozymes involved. Fluoxetine inhibits both, so the losartan would remain inactive. Your suggestion of paroxetine is OK there, since it only inhibits 2D6 and not the other two. However, this patient is maintained on oxycodone. Oxycodone is activated via 2D6, so paroxetine could prevent her pain medicine from being effective."

"Damn, I'm glad I sent her over to you," Alain said after Marwin finished his explanation. "So, what do we do?"

"Well, let's start escitalopram 10mg every morning for a month, then re-evaluate. There is a slim chance that this could hinder her oxycodone response, so let's just watch her and see how it goes."

"All right, sounds good to me," Alain agreed.

"So, you think the shrink will go for it?" Marwin asked.

"Screw him. She'll do what I tell her to, anyway. She's already said she doesn't like him and doesn't trust him."

"Cool. Let me know when you re-evaluate. I'll let Sam know what we discussed, and he'll cover everything with her."

"Will do. Thanks for your help."

"No problem. Uh, are you going to the funeral home tonight?" Marwin asked hesitantly.

"Yeah, but I dread it."

"Me, too. It really sucks," Marwin sighed.

"Yeah, it does. See you tonight."

Marwin called Sam to discuss everything with him, and instructed him to text if he needed anything else.

***

Marwin spent the rest of the day cleaning toilets, tubs, and sinks while silently cursing himself for allowing Lindsey to talk him into buying such a huge house. The day was again unseasonably cold; Marwin hoped for warmer weather for Madeline's funeral. After cleaning, he showered and tried to find a suit to wear to the funeral home. In the very back of the closet, he spied a dark navy jacket hanging over a pair of navy slacks. Wondering if they would still fit, he stripped off his sweatpants and pulled on the slacks. Sucking his gut in, he finally made the clasps catch. His pooch hung over the beltline of his pants, causing Marwin to renew his vow to begin exercising. Picking out a yellow shirt and blue paisley tie, Marwin dressed and headed for the funeral home.

***

West and Sons funeral home was established in 1942. Woody West, the current manager, had inherited the business from his father, who had inherited it from his father. The Wests had a good reputation and prided themselves on providing a quality service. Jackson, however, had immediately developed a distrust for Woody upon first meeting him. While discussing caskets and vaults the previous day, Woody had pushed strongly for Jackson to buy the most expensive ones available. He provided at least ten reasons why Jackson should buy the $15,000 version. While money was no real object to Jackson, he couldn't justify blowing it on bells and whistles that would just be buried in the ground. After much discussion, and a great deal of frowning on Woody's part, the funeral arrangements had finally been completed.

Jackson, Cody, and Sandy arrived at the funeral home shortly after 4 p.m. They finalized the details and spent some quiet time saying their last goodbyes. When the first people arrived a little before 7 p.m., they were already drained. The next two hours passed in a blur, with Jackson only occasionally remembering someone passing through the receiving line.

Marwin and Destiny arrived separately. Marwin arrived shortly before 7 p.m. and stayed until everyone was gone, around 9:15 p.m. Destiny came after Marwin, stayed about a half hour, then left to work on a big case she had going to trial on Wednesday.

Teresa didn't arrive until after 7:30 p.m., as she had become lost on the way. Upon her arrival, she immediately tore into Jackson for giving her the wrong directions. Jackson simply slumped a little lower and apologized.

As the last people were leaving, Jackson noticed Marwin standing in the room with Madeline's closed casket. Marwin was standing in front of an easel holding pictures of Madeline and her family. "I wish I knew what happened," Marwin said sadly.

"You and me both, Bubba," Jackson said, putting an arm around Marwin's shoulders. "Why don't you come by the house for a drink?" Jackson suggested.

"It's getting kinda late and I need to let the sitter go home..." Marwin said hesitantly.

"Please," Jackson said, his voice cracking.

Looking into Jackson's face, Marwin was stung by the pain and need he saw there. "OK, sure. Just one, though. I'll let the sitter know I will be home by eleven."

"Thanks," Jackson responded gratefully.

***

Drinks in hand, Jackson, Cody, Sandy, and Marwin sat around the kitchen table. Cody discovered the remaining meat and cheese tray and brought it out. As they talked, Jackson wandered aimlessly around the kitchen. A stack of mail on the end of the counter caught his eye, and he opened it without really reading any of it. He put the bills in one pile and the junk in another. Suddenly, the color drained from his face as he opened yet another envelope. As he unfolded this piece of paper and began to read it, his hands started shaking and his knees became weak.

Sandy, who had been talking to Marwin about pharmacy, noticed Jackson's expression. "Dad, are you OK?" she asked.

At this, everyone stopped talking and turned to look at Jackson. "What is it, Dad?" Cody asked, rising from the table.

Jackson didn't answer, instead slowly sinking to the floor with his back against the wall. "Oh my God!" Cody exclaimed, having taken the paper from Jackson's hands. "It's Mom's suicide note," he announced to the group before returning to his seat.

"Cody," Jackson said, starting to come out of the shock, "let me have the note."

Cody hesitated. His eyes darted from his dad to the letter and back again. "Sure, Dad. Here you go," he said, handing the letter back to his father.

They all watched in horrified silence as Jackson read the letter completely through, twice. At last, he spoke incredulously. "I cannot believe this. What kind of person kills herself and then mails a letter to her surviving spouse?" When no one answered, Jackson continued expressing his disbelief. "Not only did she hurt me once, she is stabbing me again!" his voice rose rapidly as he lost control. "Jesus Christ, this can't be happening," he said. Jackson laid his head on the table and sobbed.

As the others tried to comfort him, he slowly calmed down. With tears still wet on his face, he began to read: "Dearest Jackson—"

"Dad, stop!" Cody interrupted.

"It's OK, Cody. Everyone here is family," Jackson said giving Sandy a faint smile.

"Are you sure?" Marwin asked. "I can go, if you guys need to be alone."

"The hell you will! You're like another son to me," Jackson said.

"Please, no one interrupt or ask any questions until I finish reading the entire thing," Jackson requested.

"Dearest Jackson," he started again, voice shaking. "I never imagined writing a letter like this, much less what I am about to do. However, as they say, 'Never say never.' I feel that I have no choice but to end my life. I've been unhappy for months, and you haven't noticed—or didn't care. I am sick of doing for everyone else and no one doing for me. I guess you will have to learn to do for yourself now, or maybe some other woman can help you. I feel that you have used me for years. I made all the appearances with you so that you could look like the happy doctor, but then you ignored me when we got home. You haven't wanted sex in months—I guess you're being taken care of somewhere else. You never worried about my wants or needs, but you sure expected me to take care of yours. I know my death will be an embarrassment to you, but not as embarrassing as being the trophy wife of a local doctor. Well, your trophy is broken. Goodbye, Madeline."

They all sat in stunned silence, mouths agape. Cody was the first to speak. "This is bullshit. Mom would never have written this letter. Nothing in this letter is true. Let me see that letter, Dad."

Jackson handed the letter to Cody and slumped back in his chair, the look of devastation now total. No one said anything as Cody silently re-read the letter, then slammed his hand on the table. "Bullshit! This is total bullshit! I know my mom, and she didn't write this."

"Cody," Jackson finally said. "Of course she wrote it. Who else could have written it?" he added rhetorically. "Obviously, she was very unhappy and I was too blind to see it. Dear God, how could I have been so stupid? How could I ignore her pain?" he asked miserably.

Sandy walked behind Jackson and put her arms around his neck. "Dad, Cody is right. There is no truth to any of that letter."

"Dammit, don't any of you see? It doesn't matter if it is true or not. It only matters how she perceived it to be."

"Jackson," Marwin said, "I've known you and Madeline for over fifteen years, and I have never seen anything to make me believe one iota of that letter."

"Well, she apparently believed it with all of her heart. So much so that she..." Jackson trailed off, unable to continue.

"Look, I'm with Cody. Something is wrong here," Marwin tried again.

"Yeah, something is wrong, all right. My wife of twenty-four years thought I was cheating on her, and that I only kept her around as a trophy. She was apparently in tremendous pain, and I'm so self-centered that I didn't even notice. I will never forgive myself," Jackson said, rising.

"Where are you going?" Cody asked.

"I'm sorry. I need to go to bed. Please forgive my rudeness."

"Don't worry about us, Jackson," Marwin replied. "Get some rest. We'll find out what is going on here."

"All you're going to find out is that I am a worthless piece of shit," Jackson replied morosely as he climbed the stairs.

***

Cody, Sandy, and Marwin sat in stunned silence for several minutes before Marwin said, "Something isn't right, but we're not going to figure it out tonight. You guys make sure he's OK, and that he doesn't do anything stupid. We'll work on it tomorrow."

"OK. Thanks, Marwin," Sandy answered.

"I'll see you tomorrow. I'll let myself out," Marwin said, turning to go.

CHAPTER 10

The morning of the funeral dawned grey, punctuated with intermittent sleet and rain. Cody sat bleary-eyed at the table, sharing bagels and coffee with Sandy. Neither of them had slept much the night before, as they had taken turns looking in on Jackson. Each time they checked, Jackson appeared to be sleeping soundly. He had gone to bed immediately after the letter incident and hadn't come downstairs yet.

"I've got to wake Dad up. We have to be at the funeral home by ten," Cody said.

"I know. I just hate to disturb him if he's sleeping," Sandy replied.

As the two debated the issue, the phone rang. "Hello," Cody answered.

"Uh, Doctor Montgomery?" a male voice asked.

"No, this is his son, Cody. What can I do for you?"

"This is detective Bradley Jinswain, of the Knox County Police Department. I was wondering if I could speak with your dad, please?"

"Well, actually, he isn't up yet. Can I have him call you when he gets up?"

"I guess," Jinswain said, after a short hesitation. "Have him call me at this number as soon as he can."

As Cody wrote the number down, he asked, "Is something wrong, Detective?"

"No, I just have some information for him, so have him call me."

"OK, I will," Cody said, preparing to hang up.

After a brief pause, Jinswain asked, "He doesn't have anything new for me, does he?"

Cody's mind whirled as he thought of the letter that came the day before. "What kind of information?" he asked, realizing he had paused too long.

"Anything. Another call from the imposter from the paper, a note, or anything that might explain what happened," Jinswain said evenly.

"Well, uh...maybe... I'm not...really sure," Cody said, fumbling for the right words. "I think you should talk to my dad. I'll have him call you later."

Cody hung up, visibly shaken. "Shit, I hope I didn't blow it for Dad."

"Relax, Baby. How could you blow it? You didn't do anything wrong. Your dad is going to tell them about the letter, right?"

"I guess, but I don't know for sure. It was a very hurtful letter. I'm sure he doesn't want it broadcast to everyone—especially since it implies that he was having an affair," Cody concluded angrily.

"No one was having an affair," Jackson stated wearily, entering the kitchen.

"I know that, Dad! How long have you been down here?"

"Long enough to know that the detective called. I appreciate your silence, but Sandy is right; I am going to tell the police about the letter. I learned long ago not to worry about what people think. As long as I am honest, especially with myself, everything will be fine."

Cody eyed his father, his heart swelling with pride and respect. "I didn't mean to imply that you were going to be dishonest," he protested weakly, averting his eyes.

"I know, Son. You were just trying to protect me, and I appreciate it." Jackson walked over to Cody and wrapped his arms around him. "Thanks for being such a great son," he murmured against Cody's ear.

Jackson pulled back, ending their embrace. "We better get moving; we don't have much time."

As the three headed up the stairs to get ready, the phone rang again. "Damn, what is with this place?" Cody said, to no one in particular.

"Hello," Jackson answered.

"Hey, Jackson," replied Marwin. "I was just calling to check on you."

"Thanks. Were you afraid I would follow Madeline's lead?" Jackson asked, trying to joke lightly.

"I wasn't worried about that, per se, but you were pretty down last night."

"Yeah, I know. But I was in good hands with Cody and Sandy. They kept checking on me all night long," Jackson said, smiling weakly at them.

"Good. Tell Cody I'm proud of him. I guess I'll see you shortly."

"Yes, we're getting ready now."

***

Jackson sat stoically beside Cody in the first pew, both men staring at the bronze coffin holding their loved one. Sandy, sitting next to Cody, entwined her fingers with his and rested her head on his shoulder. Jackson stared, alternating between the coffin and the picture of Madeline sitting on top. As his mind traced through thousands upon thousands of memories, Marwin placed a hand on Jackson's shoulder, breaking his reverie.

"Marwin," Jackson said, extending his hand. "Please sit here with the family."

Marwin's eyes began to sting and a lump quickly formed in his throat. "OK, but I'm waiting for Destiny."

"Please, I want both of you to sit here with me," Jackson repeated weakly.

"All right. It looks like she just walked in. I'll be right back."

People continued to file in as the service began. Jackson heard the first few lines about God putting us on Earth to serve Him until He calls us home. He was then told that he shouldn't be sad, but should instead rejoice in the fact that Madeline had gone to live with the Father. The preacher's voice soon faded to an indistinct drone, and Jackson's thoughts returned to happier times. He recalled countless dinner parties, summers at the lake, and the vacation to Switzerland. He smiled as he remembered the Christmas party when Madeline had too much wine and fell down the steps, only to proclaim, "It's OK, I just dropped my drink." He reminisced about their days in college, thinking of the parties, the sex. He remembered their first kiss and the sweet taste of her lips like it happened days ago, not years. As the preacher droned on, Jackson continued down memory lane—but soon tears leaked from his eyes. Sobs quickly followed the tears, and Jackson collapsed in on himself as the preacher led the closing prayer.

The funeral procession wound slowly through the midday traffic on I-40 before finally arriving at Woodland Gardens. Jackson, Cody, Sandy, and Teresa were led to a line of folding chairs in front of the casket underneath the green canvas awning buffeted by the wind. With the temperature hovering in the mid-30s, Jackson was chilled to the bone. He sat numbly as the preacher said a few more banal words and ended the service with a short prayer. As the prayer concluded and the people gave their final condolences, the finality of Madeline's death struck Jackson. *Memories are all I have now*, he thought. He murmured his thanks to the faceless people as they passed and was finally left sitting alone with Cody and Sandy, Teresa apparently having already left. As he struggled to stand, he noticed Detective Jinswain standing in a black overcoat near the hearse. This stirred Jackson to get moving, and he walked over to Jinswain.

"Doctor Montgomery, my condolences again on your loss."

"Thank you. I was going to call you later today. Cody said you needed me to call you." As a gust of wind hit the pair, Jackson said, "It's too cold to talk here. Why don't you come by the house tonight?"

"Actually, I was wondering if I could come by sooner than that, like maybe in an hour or so? I don't want to intrude. I know this is a difficult day."

"That's the understatement of a lifetime," Jackson declared sourly. "Sure, come on by whenever. I need to show you something anyway."

***

After Marwin and Destiny settled in for dinner at their table at Applebee's, Marwin told her about Madeline's suicide note.

"Oh, my gosh. How terrible for poor Jackson," Destiny responded. "He must be hurting so badly."

They stopped talking when the waitress brought their French onion soup and salads. After she had gone, Marwin said, "I don't know what it is, but something just isn't right here. The letter seems crazy, completely out of character. If you knew Madeline well, you'd think so, too. She wasn't a hurtful person. She was loving and giving, a woman who loved life to the fullest. It just doesn't make sense."

Destiny sat quietly as Marwin talked, then suggested, "Why don't you look into it? See if you can come up with an explanation."

"What would I look into? I'm a pharmacist, not Sherlock Holmes or Kay Scarpetta. I know drugs. I don't know shit about suicide."

"Was Madeline ill? Was she taking any medications that could have contributed to it? Can't some medicines cause depression or suicidal thoughts?" Destiny prodded.

"I don't know if she was on anything or not. As far as I know, she was perfectly healthy." Marwin reflected for a moment, then said, "There are medications that have been linked to suicide, but it's kind of a dicey connection. Most of the time, it's impossible to tell if the drug caused it or if the person's underlying condition became so severe that they just gave up and ended everything."

"But if Madeline was healthy, there is no underlying condition. Maybe a drug did contribute to it," Destiny said.

"True, but if there is no condition, then there would be no medication treatment," Marwin reminded her.

"Well, can you at least ask Jackson if she was taking any medications, please?"

"OK. Sure, if it will make you feel better."

***

Jackson sat solemnly as people meandered through his house. Employees, as well as patients and friends, had come to pay their respects. Helen tried to coordinate all the food that was arriving. She had started a notebook with names and a description of what each person brought so that Jackson could send thank-you notes later. Jackson had spoken to everyone, but remembered none of the conversations and few of the faces. As the afternoon passed to evening, Jackson finally saw the one face he had been looking for. He opened the door just as Bradley Jinswain pressed the doorbell.

"Come in, Detective. I've been waiting for you." Jackson directed Bradley to the study and closed the door.

"Thanks for seeing me today, Doctor Montgomery," Bradley began.

"It's fine. I needed to see you too, so it might as well be sooner rather than later."

"I'll get right to the point. The call that came from the person impersonating the reporter came from a pay phone on the east side of Knoxville. Obviously, whoever is harassing you doesn't want to be discovered," Bradley announced.

"Well, I'm not surprised. Are you?" Jackson replied, taking the information in stride.

"Actually, I am a little surprised. Most crank callers don't go to the trouble of using a pay phone. They usually call from their home or office, or even their cell phone, because they know nothing is really going to happen to them, even if they do get caught. So, it is a little odd for someone to go to this much trouble," Bradley explained.

"Well, the world is full of crazies these days," Jackson replied. He walked to his desk and pulled the letter from the top drawer. Handing the letter to Bradley, he said, "This came in the mail yesterday."

Bradley took the letter gingerly by the corners and read it slowly. Once finished, he re-read it twice more. "I'll be right back. I need to get something out of the car," he said.

Minutes later, Bradley returned with a box that resembled a fisherman's tacklebox. He opened the box and removed latex gloves, tweezers, and a resealable plastic bag. "What are you doing?" Jackson asked, bewildered.

"Collecting evidence," Bradley replied. "Do you have the envelope, too?"

Handing the envelope to Bradley, Jackson asked, "Evidence of what?"

"I'm not sure," Bradley conceded. "Something smells funny here. I want to get these to the lab for fingerprints."

"I'm afraid several people handled that letter last night," Jackson admitted.

"I expect to find several sets of prints, including mine. However, I will be shocked if your wife's prints are among them. I'll get in touch with you tomorrow. Please let me know if anything else odd happens."

Jackson stared, Bradley's implication beginning to sink in as the detective left, driving off into the cold October evening.

CHAPTER 11

After returning home from Jackson's house, Marwin sifted through the mail. He had not stayed long at Jackson's; he couldn't take the mass of people with their fake reassuring smiles. He had returned to his car and spent the next hour or so just driving around aimlessly, letting his thoughts run free. He eventually returned home to find Bogie and Morgan screaming at one another over who could use the phone. The stress of the last week led Marwin to ground both of them from the phone for the remainder of the week. This caused them to retreat to their respective rooms, both slamming their doors.

After sifting the junk mail out and briefly considering adding the bills to it, Marwin trudged wearily to the den. He started to turn on the TV, but decided he should go upstairs and talk to the kids. As he passed the phone, he saw the message light blinking. Wondering how he'd missed it with the kids fighting over it, he pressed the play button. "Hey, it's me," Sam's voice began. "Nothing urgent. Just have two cases for you to look over. I took care of everything else. Call me at home, and I'll give you all the info. See ya."

Already forgetting the kids' drama, Marwin dialed Sam. "How did the funeral go?" Sam asked.

"Lousy, but what do you expect at a funeral?" Marwin answered.

"You want me to fax them over, or just read them to you?" Sam asked.

"Just read them to me for now. If I need to see them later, you can fax them over."

"OK. The first one is a fifty-eight-year-old white male with a history of severe arthritis. His allergies are positive for aspirin. He has reacted with severe breathing difficulties requiring epinephrine on naproxen and sulindac. Previously maintained on acetaminophen one gram QID and tramadol fifty milligrams three to four times daily as needed. Alain says he usually only takes about two tramadol per day on average. His wife was diagnosed with uterine cancer three weeks ago, and he isn't handling it too well. Alain started him on paroxetine ten milligrams daily to try to help him cope. Ten days later, his wife called and reported that he was very agitated and was complaining that his knees and back were killing him. He has increased his tramadol up to eight per day without any relief. Alain says this guy is not an abuser, and he has never had any problems with him. I know the agitation is likely from excess serotonin from the tramadol and paroxetine, but what has caused the sudden increase in pain and loss of effectiveness of the tramadol?"

"Yeah, did you know about the serotonin or did you look it up?" Marwin asked.

"I actually remembered that," Sam said.

"Great. You may turn out alright after all. Now, for your lesson. Tramadol has to be activated to its active metabolite, M1, to produce analgesia."

"Damn, paroxetine inhibits the conversion, doesn't it?" Sam asked.

"Yep. Tramadol is activated by 2D6 and paroxetine inhibits 2D6, so he isn't receiving any benefit from the tramadol."

"Should we change the paroxetine to citalopram?" Sam suggested.

"Citalopram, escitalopram, or sertraline all have less effect on 2D6 and should be OK. If he goes back to PRN tramadol, the agitation should subside, too. Does he have any history of seizures?"

"No, none is listed here."

"OK, if he goes back to only a couple per day, he should be fine. Tell Alain to warn them about the risks of seizures with this combination. Since the SSRI is low-dose and the tramadol is PRN, I think we should be OK. Just counsel them and have them sign a waiver. What else you got?"

"The second one is a lady who called asking if we carried drugs for myasthenia gravis. I told her we carry Mestinon. She said she was allergic to Mestinon and all drugs like it. I told her that would be a problem. She said her doctor told her there were other options, but didn't give her the names. I did some research and couldn't find anything. You got any ideas?"

"Yeah, ambenonium. It's the chloride salt, rather than the bromide. She probably has an allergy to bromides. I don't know if they still make ambenonium or not. Tomorrow, look up Mytelase and see if we can get it. If so, let her know and contact her doctor so we can get her set up. If it isn't available, they may have to try donepezil or rivastigmine," Marwin advised.

"OK, thanks. I'll let you know if I need anything else," Sam said.

Marwin hung up and finally went upstairs to talk to the kids. He opened Morgan's door first and saw she was sound asleep, Christina Aguilera still coming from the stereo. He turned off the music, then bent down to kiss her head and whispered, "I'm sorry, Kiddo. Daddy loves you."

He backed out, quietly closing the door while thinking what a shitty father he had become. He could hear rap music coming from Bogie's room and cautioned himself to have patience. Bogie was lying on his bed with his feet on the wall, staring at the ceiling. Marwin wondered how long he had been like that. "Hey, Bud. I wanted to say I'm sorry for blowing up at you guys earlier."

"Forget it, I'm used to it," Bogie said glumly.

Ignoring the jab, Marwin said, "I guess I'm not doing too well in the dad department right now. All I can do is promise to try harder. If there's something you need from me, let me know. I can't fix things if I don't know they're broken."

"Yeah, OK. Whatever, Dad," Bogie said, looking back up at the ceiling.

Marwin fought the urge to grab Bogie and shake him until he snapped out of this shithead stage he was in. As he was leaving, he turned back to Bogie and said, "I love you, Son." Marwin then walked slowly to his bedroom, wondering if he was losing his kids.

***

Dusk gave way to darkness as the dark blue Mercedes pulled to the curb in front of Jackson Montgomery's house. The sleet had ended and the skies had cleared, leaving only a cold northwest wind and sub-freezing temperatures. The car's driver remained seated for several minutes, staring at Jackson's house. Finally, he climbed out, shivered, and made his way to the front door. Pressing the doorbell with a sense of dread, he heard Jackson call, "Coming."

Jackson opened the door with a quizzical look. "Can I help you?" he asked, vague recognition dawning.

"Jackson, hi. It has been a long time," the visitor replied.

"I'm sorry, but I'm not sure I know you," Jackson said.

"I'm Dr. Ernie Shoehorn. We were in med school together."

Jackson's mind rapidly searched for and found the memory of Ernie Shoehorn. He did vaguely recall the man from his classes at Duke University, but could remember little except for the fact that he didn't really care for him. He remembered the man being a mediocre student who thought he was smarter than he actually was. Another memory began to form, but refused to come into focus.

"May I come in?" Shoehorn asked, breaking Jackson's search of his dusty mental database.

"Of course, forgive me. I'm not myself right now."

After taking Shoehorn's coat, Jackson led him into the study and offered refreshments. "Do you have any natural spring water?" Shoehorn requested.

"No, I'm afraid all I have is some tonic water or Perrier."

"That's all right; that stuff has some pretty nasty preservatives in it. I prefer to consume only natural, preservative-free things. Thank you, anyway," Shoehorn stated.

The lightbulb in Jackson's brain started to flicker again. He strained to recall more about this man, but couldn't.

"What can I do for you Dr. Shoehorn?" Jackson finally asked bluntly.

"I know this is a difficult time for you now, with Madeline's passing and all. I just wanted you to know how sorry I am for your loss."

"How did you know Madeline?" Jackson asked, mind spinning with the realization that Shoehorn had used Madeline's first name, like he knew her well.

"She was a patient of mine, as I am sure you know," answered Shoehorn.

"Uh, no... I didn't know she was a patient of anyone's," Jackson said slowly. "What kind of doctor are you? How long have you been treating her, and what for?"

"I'm an OB/GYN, and Madeline was referred to me about three months ago."

Jackson tried to remember Madeline telling him that she'd changed gynecologists, but nothing registered. Maybe they weren't communicating, after all. Suddenly, a connection clicked into place. Shoehorn was a local gynecologist with political aspirations. He was running for some political office recently, but Jackson didn't recall which one. Shoehorn was also a "weed lover," as Jackson often called his peers who promoted only "natural" medicine, shunning traditional medications. Jackson remembered attending some dinner program where Shoehorn was the speaker. He couldn't recall specifics, only that it was some mumbo-jumbo about herbal remedies. He probably paid more attention to the prime rib and Dewar's than he did Shoehorn. As with most programs, doctors just attended to eat good food and drink premium liquor for free. Seldom did the attendees care about the content of the program. Jackson was sure this was the case the night Shoehorn was the speaker. Even without food or drink, Jackson knew he wouldn't have been listening to anything about herbs. He didn't believe 90% of the claims about herbal remedies stating they can cure everything from zits to hemorrhoids to cancer, without any clinical data to support their claims.

"I wasn't aware that Madeline had changed doctors," he said slowly.

"Yes. Apparently, a patient of mine referred her to me about three months ago. Madeline said it was time for her check-up, so she made the change."

"Was everything alright? PAP smear?" Jackson inquired.

"Physically, everything was fine. Her PAP was clean. No sign of infection or inflammation. She was perfectly healthy," Shoehorn pronounced.

"That's ironic. That is exactly how I described her to someone recently," Jackson responded.

"Well, I just wanted to pay my respects. I will be going now," Shoehorn said, rising.

"Thanks for coming by," Jackson responded numbly. He stood at the door and watched Shoehorn's taillights dim as he drove away. He couldn't help but feel that something significant had just occurred, but was unable to determine what it was. Long after Shoehorn's lights had faded, Jackson sat at the kitchen table eating cold chicken and potato salad, left over from what Helen brought yesterday, feeling lonely and confused.

CHAPTER 12

Wednesday morning dawned crystal clear and beautiful. The sunshine displayed the beauty of an October morning in Tennessee; the maple and poplar leaves had erupted in bright red, yellow, and everyone's favorite, orange. Jackson had just returned from a pre-dawn walk and sat at the table sipping coffee. He had slept fitfully the night before, finally giving up and crawling out of bed a little before 5 a.m. He'd dressed slowly in sweatpants and a sweat shirt to head out for a walk. Upon returning, he'd made coffee and waited for the morning paper to be delivered. Cody and Sandy were still sleeping upstairs, and the eerie quietness was unsettling. Jackson had spent his walk thinking about what Detective Jinswain had said the night before. He was unable to fathom why anyone would write a note pretending to be Madeline. *How would anyone else know that she was planning to commit suicide? The forensic reports were 100% positive for suicide, yet someone apparently suspected that Madeline was planning to kill herself. Could someone have forced her to do it?* Jackson wondered. Dismissing this crazy thought, Jackson saw Cody enter the kitchen.

"Have you been up long?" Cody asked.

"I got up around five or so. I hope I didn't wake you guys up."

"Not me; I didn't hear anything after I went to bed. I guess I was exhausted."

As Cody got a Danish and poured himself a cup of coffee, Jackson recounted his conversations with Bradley and Shoehorn from the previous night. At first, Cody sat quietly, but then exploded. "What the hell does he mean, Mom's fingerprints won't be on the letter?!"

"He is implying that someone else sent the letter," Jackson answered evenly, with some effort.

"But why? Who would send a letter like that?!" Cody exclaimed, exasperated.

"I don't know. Maybe that asshole who posed as a reporter the other day. Maybe some other sick person who scans the obituaries and then sends prank letters. I just don't know. Maybe…"

"Maybe what, Dad?"

"Maybe someone who knew your mom was planning this."

"How could anyone know that?" Cody asked incredulously.

"I don't know. I have been racking my brain since last night," Jackson said gloomily. Looking up, he saw Sandy standing in the doorway. "How long have you been standing there?"

"Long enough," she replied, wrapping her arms around him.

The three of them talked, trying to find solutions to impossible problems. Eventually, the subject of Madeline's sister Teresa came up. "Have you told her about the letter?" Cody asked.

"No, I've barely spoken to her since she left here the other day. She left right after the funeral…didn't even come by here. I guess I'd better check to see if she is still in town."

Jackson dialed the number for her room at the Radisson Inn. When she answered, he said, "Teresa, it's Jackson. I just wanted to make sure you were still in town, since I haven't seen or heard from you since the funeral."

"Well, actually I'm packing now. I will be leaving within the hour."

Feeling his ire rising and struggling to contain it, Jackson asked, "Are you planning on stopping by here on your way out of town?"

"No, I don't see any need for that. I'll just leave straight from here," Teresa said.

"All right," Jackson said, biting his tongue. "Before you go, I need to bring you up to date on a few things."

Teresa listened as Jackson informed her about the suicide letter and Jinswain's suggestion of a fake author. When he finished, Teresa said, "What is going on, Jackson? None of this makes any sense. I keep hoping this is a nightmare and that I'll wake up, but I'm trapped."

"I know," Jackson replied softly. "I wish I had an answer for you, Teresa. I promise you that we are going to find out the whole story. And I swear, I have never been unfaithful to Madeline in mind or body."

"She obviously thought you were!" Teresa snapped.

"What if she didn't write the letter?" Jackson snapped right back, voicing this possibility for the first time.

Teresa remained quiet for a moment, then asked, "Do you really believe that?"

"I'm not sure what to believe any more," Jackson responded sadly.

"I need to get on the road... Call me if you find out anything new," Teresa instructed.

"I will," Jackson replied. Almost as an afterthought, he added, "Be careful."

Teresa didn't respond, instead hanging up.

***

Marwin sat at the table in a t-shirt and boxer shorts. The kids had just left for school, and he was trying to plan his day. He debated going to work but decided to call Sam and tell him that he would be in the next day... maybe. Ever since Madeline's death, his life had turned to shit. He was constantly in a grumpy mood and feared his kids were slipping into an abyss. His dour thoughts continued until he thought of Destiny. This caused a smile to form despite his mood. If not for Destiny, his life would have been completely in the crapper. He recalled their last conversation, and how she said she wanted him to "do something." Marwin decided to go to Jackson's house and see if he could do something productive, instead of just feeling sorry for himself.

He dressed in jeans and a short-sleeved, collared golf shirt, over which he pulled his orange Tennessee jacket. As he drove down I-40, he marveled at the beauty of the day and chastised himself for the pity party he'd indulged in earlier, vowing to be more thankful.

Pulling to a stop in front of Jackson's house, Marwin tried to formulate a plan. He was still running different scenarios through his head when Jackson opened the door. "Hey, Buddy. What are you doing out so early?" Jackson asked.

"I thought it was time I started being productive again. I've started liking this unemployment too much, I'm afraid."

"Yeah, me too," Jackson agreed, laughing. "Well, how do you propose to be productive here? Are you going to rake leaves, wash clothes, or paint my house?"

"None of the above. If I was going to do anything like that, I would have stayed home and done my own shit. I want to go through Madeline's medicine cabinet," Marwin stated matter-of-factly.

"Wh-what? Why?" Jackson stammered. Recovering slowly from his surprise, Jackson asked, "Do you really think you'll find anything important? She didn't take any medication, to my knowledge."

"Well, you didn't know she was seeing a new doctor, either," Marwin said gently.

"How did you know about that?!" Jackson exploded.

"Easy, now. I called Cody before I came over, and he told me that Madeline's new doctor had stopped by last night. And that you didn't know Madeline was seeing him."

Jackson sat down heavily and sighed. "Maybe I wasn't as close to her as I thought. Maybe she was miserable, and I was too involved with my own life to notice. Maybe I'm to blame for this mess."

"Stop it. No one is to blame. I'm sure most husbands don't know who their wife's doctor is," Marwin said.

"I bet you knew who Lindsey's gynecologist was, didn't you?" Jackson challenged.

"Well... Yes, I did. But that's just me. I'm anal that way."

"No, you were a caring, concerned husband," Jackson replied.

Marwin stared at Jackson for several seconds, then said, "Look, if you don't want me to go through her stuff, I understand. I just wanted to try to help."

Rising from his chair, Jackson clasped Marwin's shoulder and said, "I know you do, Son, and I appreciate it. Come on, let's go see what we can find. I need to start cleaning some shit out of here anyway. May as well start today."

CHAPTER 14

Destiny sat behind her desk, which was covered in a mountain of legal files. She was trying to concentrate on the case of a 34-year-old male going on trial for molesting and abusing his ten-year-old daughter. This was the second time that piece-of-crap individual had been brought up on charges of abuse. His first wife accused him of abusing their twelve-year-old daughter, but dropped the charges just before the trial. Destiny was determined to nail the sick bastard this time. Her phone rang, interrupting her concentration.

"Hey, Des, it's Brad," the voice greeted her.

"Brad," Destiny replied, shocked to be hearing from Bradley Jinswain. "What can I do for you?"

"I was wondering if you wanted to catch up over lunch somewhere."

"I'm not sure I'll be going to lunch today. I have a million cases to plow through."

"Well, you still gotta eat. How about I bring some subs by your office? That way you won't have to go out and waste time."

"You know, Brad... Honestly, I'm seeing someone now. I wouldn't feel right about having lunch with you," Destiny stated.

"I see," Bradley said slowly. "It's just lunch. I wasn't planning on attacking you or anything. What would it hurt for two old friends to have lunch together?"

"OK, I guess it wouldn't hurt anything, but it will have to be a quick one."

"OK, great. I'll see you in about thirty minutes. Any special requests?"

"No, whatever is fine with me," Destiny replied.

"That's right, I remember; you will eat anything if it doesn't eat you first."

***

Exactly thirty minutes later, Destiny's secretary buzzed her and announced Bradley's arrival. Destiny braced herself for Bradley's appearance at the door. She and the detective had dated off and on for a little over a year, but eventually decided to go their separate ways. Almost a year had passed since they'd gone out. They had still enjoyed each other's company, but just had too many differences in lifestyles and personalities. Destiny had no patience for Bradley's stick-in-the-mud attitude and she definitely didn't understand the "only natural ingredients" philosophy that Bradley tried to live by. On the other hand, Bradley was unable to come to grips with Destiny's explosive nature. In the end, they stopped seeing each other after one of Destiny's explosions following dinner one night. Destiny had not seen or heard from Bradley in over six months. Initially, he had called a few times, but she blew him off. Finally, he stopped calling altogether.

A sharp knock on the door interrupted Destiny's recollections. "Come in," she directed as she rose from her chair.

Bradley Jinswain entered with a smile, wearing faded jeans and a grey sweatshirt. He carried a plastic bag bulging with subs and chips. "Hey, Des, you look great," he said, giving her a quick peck on the cheek as if nothing had happened since their last date.

"Thanks. I see you dressed for lunch," she said coolly.

"Sorry; I am working. I don't get to dress up to go to work, like you do," Bradley replied in a slightly bitter tone.

Changing the subject, Destiny asked, "What's for lunch? I'm starving."

"I've got a meatball sub, a Philly steak and cheese, and a vegetarian; take your pick."

The two talked idly until the conversation turned to her current relationship. "So, who is this new lucky guy?" Bradley asked innocently.

"Look, Brad, I really appreciate you bringing lunch, and it's nice to see you again—but I really don't want to talk about my relationship. You and I just aren't made for each other. I still enjoy your company, so let's just try to be friends and leave it at that."

Bradley eyed her, then said, "Fine. That's all I want, anyway. I was just curious as to who you are seeing. I just wanted to see what kind of guy it takes to get and keep your affection, that's all."

After a brief pause, Bradley added, "I just want you to be happy. I guess I'm not the right one for you, but you are a special lady and deserve to be happy. Be careful who you get hooked up with, because in general, guys are assholes."

"Thanks," she said softly. They stared at each other for a few seconds, then resumed eating awkwardly.

When the sandwiches and chips had almost disappeared, Destiny said, "His name is Marwin. He's a special type of pharmacist, and I think I am falling in love with him."

Destiny's answer to his long-ago asked question startled Bradley, but he managed to say, "I never pictured you with a pill-pusher in a white coat and glasses."

"I know how you pictured me—naked and in your kitchen!" Destiny said, referring to the fact that they had never had sex.

Laughing and blushing simultaneously, Bradley admitted, "Well, actually, you're right. I suppose I did do that. I just meant that I picture pharmacists as cranky old farts who lead boring lives, and that is not who you need. You already had that in me."

"Marwin is not like that, at all. He is fun-loving and enthusiastic. He also has a different pharmacy practice, not anything like what you see when you walk into Kroger. I think you two might actually like each other if you met."

"Why do you say that?" Bradley asked.

"Because Marwin's son is a great baseball player, and Marwin loves all sports."

"Oh, well. You know I don't have anything to do with baseball anymore."

"I know," Destiny responded softly. She knew Bradley was a great baseball prospect just four years ago. Then in one night, his career ended. He was playing AAA, just one step below the big leagues, when he was hit in the face with a 93-mph fastball. His orbital bone and left cheekbone were shattered. Doctors were originally concerned that he might lose his vision in his left eye, but eventually he regained his vision. However, with the loss of acuity and confidence that ensued, his career was finished. He tried to come back the next year, but just couldn't cut it any longer. His family wanted him to take a corporate job, but Bradley detested the white-collar crowd. So, much to the chagrin of his family, Bradley became a detective. His vision was adequate to pass all the tests, including the shooting ones. He had worked the previous two years as a detective for the Knox County Police Department. He had ascended rapidly, due to his father's powerful influence on the mayor, but also seemed to have a knack for seeing things that even the veteran detectives often overlooked.

"Des, are you OK?" Bradley's voice interrupted her thoughts.

"Yeah, sure. I was just thinking how you never know what life is going to deal you."

Looking at her oddly, Bradley said, "Uh, yeah. I know what you mean. I guess I'd better go. I'm sure there is a bad guy out there just waiting for you to catch him."

"Thanks again for lunch," Destiny said, lightly touching his arm.

"Be careful and stay in touch," Bradley said, turning away.

***

Sunlight was trying to break through the cracks in the blinds to illuminate the dark room. Jackson turned on the lights and was immediately rocked by visions of Madeline slumped in the chair, the gun beside her on the floor. He could see the pool of blood on the chair and the small pieces of grey material that once contained her thought processes. As he pictured the gruesome scene, Madeline seemed to raise her head and look into his eyes with her own dead, black eyes. She said, "You did this to me, you bastard. If only you had been there when I needed you, instead of out fucking that whore, Helen! I hope your eyes rot!"

Jackson recoiled and staggered back toward the open door.

"Jackson, what's wrong?" Marwin asked worriedly.

The sound of Marwin's voice caused the mirage to vanish, and Jackson halted by the doorway. Visibly shaking, he leaned against the wall and said, "I could see her there. She was dead, but she was talking to me. Blaming me for what happened. Jesus, it was so real."

Marwin, unsure of what to say or how to proceed, finally suggested, "Maybe we should wait a little longer."

"No, I've got to go in eventually. May as well do it while someone is here to slap me out of my wild imagination. Come on, before I lose my nerve."

Jackson re-entered the bedroom and walked purposely to the bathroom without so much as a brief glance toward the spot where Madeline killed herself. Marwin followed closely behind, and Jackson wordlessly closed the bathroom door behind them.

"Where do you want to start?" Jackson asked.

"I don't really know. I guess let me see her medicine cabinet, if she had one," Marwin replied.

"Her stuff is on the left side and mine is on the right," Jackson explained, pointing to the cabinet below the marble countertop. "I don't think there's much in there, but help yourself."

Marwin opened the left side, revealing four drawers. In the top drawer, he found base make-up, several eyeliner pencils, mascara, makeup remover, and a dozen tubes of lipstick. "I guess she really liked lipstick," Marwin mused.

"Hell, she had to match all the way down to her panties and bra, "Jackson replied. "I never did understand why she needed four different shades of red lipstick."

Closing the first drawer and moving to the second, Marwin saw toothpaste, dental floss, and mouthwash. There were three tubes of toothpaste, a couple of boxes of dental floss, and three bottles of mouthwash, two cinnamon and one mint. Thinking it odd to have that much dental hygiene material, Marwin said nothing and moved to the next drawer. This drawer held tampons, pads, and panty liners, as well as two disposable medicated douches, some mineral oil, and a box of bisacodyl suppositories. Moving to the last drawer, Marwin finally found some medications. The fourth drawer contained a variety of herbal products, including goldenseal, black cohosh, gingko biloba, ginseng, and lecithin. There was also a bottle of multivitamins and several individual bottles of vitamins, including E, C, and B-complex. Boxes of antihistamine allergy medications also littered the drawer. Unlike the first three drawers, which were neat and tidy, this drawer was jumbled and cluttered. Digging through the contents, Marwin pulled out a book titled Herbs for Tomorrow, by Dr. Ernie Shoehorn.

"Holy shit," Jackson said, looking over Marwin's shoulder. "That's her new gynecologist. He's the one who stopped by the other night. He must have really fed her a line of crap; she has never taken vitamins and herbs before."

Marwin examined the bottles of vitamins and herbs, checking the expiration dates. "She must have bought these recently; the dates are all several years down the road," he offered.

"I can't believe she was taking all of this shit," Jackson said with irritation. "You know as well as I do that most of this shit is worthless."

"Yeah, I agree for the most part," Marwin said, beginning to look back through the bottles a second time. Noticing the antihistamines, he asked, "Did she have a lot of allergies? Or, did she have a cold lately?"

Jackson thought for a minute, then replied, "I don't remember her being sick recently, but I also didn't know she was taking all kinds of herbs or had a new gynecologist. Maybe I am not the best source of information on Madeline's habits. Maybe we should ask her new doctor, 'Doctor Weed.'"

"OK," Marwin agreed, standing with knees popping. "I'm not much of an authority on herbs, but I didn't see anything in there that would explain her behavior. Unless she had an idiosyncratic reaction to one of the herbs... Let me do some research and see what I can come up with."

"All right," Jackson said dejectedly. "I was hoping for a miracle: a simple explanation."

"I know, me too," Marwin said, patting Jackson on the shoulder. "If you come across anything else while you're cleaning, let me know. Even if it is just more vitamins. Maybe there is some link between all of this junk and what happened. Then again, it is highly unlikely, I'm afraid."

"Yeah, I know," Jackson said.

As they left the bathroom and re-entered the bedroom, Jackson said, "You know, now that I think about it, Madeline was sick about six weeks ago. She was sneezing and coughing up a ton of mucus. One night, she threw up and it was mostly just clear mucus. I think that must have been when she bought the allergy medicines. I originally thought she was just reacting to ragweed, even though she had never had a problem with it in the past."

Marwin nodded and said, "Probably ragweed. That shit wears me out every fall. I have to get on the Zyrtec and Flonase a couple of weeks before it starts, just to survive."

"She really had it bad," Jackson continued. "Her breath was horrible—I guess from all the mucus draining down her throat."

Marwin nodded again, recalling the drawer full of oral hygiene products. "Did it clear up eventually?" he asked.

"Yeah. I guess it lasted about ten days or so, and then it just cleared up, almost overnight. All her symptoms cleared up, including the halitosis."

"Hmm, that's odd for it to just resolve overnight," Marwin said.

"I know, but it was gone that morning. I didn't think any more about it until right now."

"I guess she was just lucky," Marwin opined.

"I wouldn't say that," Jackson protested sadly.

***

Marwin left Jackson's house driving mindlessly, his thoughts full of sadness and frustration. He had come to Jackson's mostly on Destiny's urging, not really expecting to find anything meaningful. However, once he began his research, he felt the old familiar fire begin to glow. This fire was common during his fourth-year rotations, when his goal was to impress and show up every physician that he rounded with. As he got older, the fire had not flared up nearly as much. As a matter of fact, he'd wondered not too long ago if the fire had indeed gone out entirely.

As he had told Jackson, he was no authority on herbal medicine. He thought most of it was un-tested rubbish that did very little good and only occasionally provided more than a placebo effect. Marwin detested the fact that vitamin and herb manufacturers could make health claims for their products without having to provide any clinical data to support the claims. Secretly, he was hoping to find some literature that would show the herbs were at least partially responsible for Madeline's suicide. Realistically, however, he didn't think vitamins and herbs played any part in her demise.

Feeling more depressed by the mile, Marwin reached for his phone to call Destiny. He dialed her office only to find out that she was in court and wasn't expected back until after 5:00. "Shit," he said dejectedly. "She is never there when I need her!" he complained to the empty seat beside him. Knowing that he had just spoken the furthest thing from the truth only made him feel worse. He thought of calling her back and leaving a message, but decided he didn't want to talk to a machine. He drove the rest of the way home under a deepening dark cloud.

Marwin went into the kitchen, tossed his keys on the counter, and grabbed a Heineken out of the fridge. Realizing he hadn't eaten lunch yet, he made himself a sandwich with roast beef and Muenster and proceeded to the living room. Noticing the flashing light on the answering machine, he punched play and listened to the four messages. The first two were from salesmen—one selling vinyl siding, of no use on Marwin's brick house, and the other promoting steam-cleaning services. The third message was from Sam, asking politely when the hell he was coming back to work. The last message was from Destiny, suggesting they have dinner that night. Marwin's mood improved instantly at the sound of her voice; he thought, and not for the first time, *I am truly in love with her.* Already formulating a menu in his head, Marwin reached for the phone to leave Destiny a message about dinner. Before he could pick up the phone, it rang.

"Hello, Mr. Gelstone?" the voice asked.

"Yes, this is he," Marwin confirmed, ready to rip into the would-be salesman.

"This is Margie Kubrick at Hull High School. I'm Bogie's calculus teacher."

With a sense of dread rapidly spreading through him, Marwin asked, "Yes, Ma'am, what can I do for you?"

"Well, I'm afraid I have some disturbing news for you. Bogie has not been doing well this nine weeks. I have offered to let him come in early for some one-on-one help, but he isn't interested. He had another test yesterday and failed, badly. I had asked him to come in early today, so we could go over the test and review the material that he did poorly on, but he wasn't in class at all today. So, I thought I'd better call to see if anything was wrong."

Having only been half listening, Marwin jolted awake at the mention of Bogie not being in class. "What do you mean, he wasn't in class today?" he asked stupidly.

"I checked with his history teacher and he was in that class this morning. Apparently, he left school sometime around lunch," she explained.

His mind racing and anger rising, Marwin said, "Thank you for calling. I will find out where he is and where he has been. He will also be in early tomorrow, if your offer still stands. I will bring him myself. I apologize for his actions. He has been very distant and angry lately, and his mother and I aren't sure why."

"I understand. It isn't uncommon at this age, but..." she paused, then asked, "could he be in with the wrong crowd? Maybe doing drugs? He seems like a good kid, but you never know nowadays," she added hurriedly.

"He better not be!" Marwin snapped. "Look, thanks again. I will start tracking him down, and we will both see you in the morning."

Marwin hung up, then started to dial—but realized he didn't know who to call. His mind whirling with anger and worry simultaneously, he tried to decide what to do. *How could he have skipped school?* he thought angrily. Grabbing his jacket, he started toward the door, but realized Bogie was due home in twenty minutes. It would be pointless to go out looking for him when he should be home so soon, so Marwin settled onto the couch and waited for the bus to arrive.

CHAPTER 15

Jackson was seated at his mahogany desk in the study, staring blankly at the bookcase. He had spent the previous three hours going through Madeline's closet full of clothes and shoes. Originally, he had taken everything out of the closet and sorted it all into different piles. He made piles for suits, dresses, blouses, and pants. He intended to call the Salvation Army to come pick it all up. After finishing the clothes, he moved on to the shoes. He stacked all 32 pairs of them next to the bed. With her side of the closet completely empty, the finality of the situation slammed into Jackson once again. Sitting on the edge of the bed, exhausted, Jackson recalled the last time he and Madeline had made love.

They had attended an especially boring dinner for one of Madeline's many charities. Both had a couple of glasses of champagne, which was on the cheap and fruity side, while nibbling on caviar and crabmeat. After an hour of listening to the brown-nosers, Jackson pulled Madeline to the side and whispered, "How 'bout we leave these snotty suck-ups and go get some real food?"

Madeline started to reprimand him but thought for a second, then replied, "Hell, I could use some real food to fill me up."

"I've got something to fill you up," Jackson said, smiling with a wink.

Madeline's cheeks immediately flushed, but she smiled and said mischievously, "Come on, Doctor; show me what's in your bag."

They begged off the party by saying that Madeline wasn't feeling well, then immediately drove to Sonny's Barbecue and got pulled pork sandwiches with fries. After returning home, Jackson grabbed four Sam Adams from the fridge and they took their dinner to the back deck, where they ate and drank under the moonlight. As they ate, they talked lightly about the world's problems, the weather, upcoming Christmas presents, and other meaningless items. The only serious conversation came when Jackson said, "We have got to make more time for ourselves."

"I know," Madeline replied with a sigh. "It seems like everyone else takes precedence over us," she continued.

"You're right. We make time for everyone except ourselves. It's hard after twenty-four years, because we become so involved in things that we sometimes forget to make time for each other. I guess we kinda take each other for granted sometimes."

Reaching over and taking his hand, Madeline said, "Starting tonight, let's do this at least once or twice a month." She had moved over next to Jackson and was still holding his hand. Madeline moved Jackson's hand inside her blouse and held it tightly to her breast. They sat like this for several minutes, neither one moving. Finally, Madeline rose and walked to the door. Looking back over her shoulder, she said, "I'm making time for you right now. You interested?"

Jackson rose and followed her to the bedroom, where they explored long-forgotten areas. Their lovemaking was clumsy at first, but soon turned passionate. They had lain in bed afterward, whispering and wondering why they didn't do this more often, both vowing to make changes in the future. They talked of making more time for each other and putting their relationship first, then discussed their upcoming 25th anniversary and how the time had gone by so fast. After a while, each one drifted off to sleep feeling happier and more content than they had in months.

With the memory of their recent tryst still fresh in his mind, Jackson realized he couldn't part with Madeline's clothes just yet. He slowly put the shoes and clothes back in the closet as tears slid down his face. Just as he was finishing up, Cody knocked on the bedroom door.

"Hey, Son. Come on in," Jackson said.

"Whatcha doing?" Cody asked.

"Uh, I started to clean out your mom's closet, but realized I just couldn't do it yet," Jackson said in a shaky voice.

"Dad, it's OK. You don't have to do anything until you're ready. There's no hurry. We will do things at your pace," Cody reassured Jackson, placing an arm around his shoulder.

After a short silence, Jackson asked, "What are you doing? How long are you and Sandy going to stay?"

"I'll stay as long as you want me to, Dad. Sandy needs to get back soon, so I think she may be heading out tomorrow."

"Well, then you need to head out tomorrow, too, Son. She is a special woman and has been here for you when you needed her. Now, you need to go and be there with her. Take care of her." After a brief pause, Jackson added, "Marry her."

Cody looked at his dad sheepishly, then smiled and said, "I've been thinking about it seriously. Now isn't the right time, though."

Shaking off the oblique reference to Madeline's death, Jackson insisted, "Son, if you two are in love, then it is the right time. You not marrying Sandy will not bring your mom back; it will only hurt you two. If you guys are ready, then do it. You have my full support."

Eyes beginning to water, Cody responded, "Thanks, Dad. You're the best."

"I doubt that, but I'm the only one you've got." Changing the subject, Jackson continued, "How about something to eat?"

"OK, sure. But the real reason I came looking for you was to see if you have Brett's phone number."

"Brett Wallace, your old playmate?"

"Yeah, I thought I'd see if I could get together with him before I go back."

"I have no idea if we have his number or not, but if we do, it will be in your mom's computer. I don't know anything about computers, but maybe you can look through your mom's stuff and find her address book."

"Cool, let's go see what we can find."

CHAPTER 16

Marwin paced back and forth through his living room, alternating between telling himself to calm down, so that he could discuss Bogie's truancy rationally, and telling himself not to worry. *Bogie is a good boy*, he thought. As he passed the window for the fourth time, he saw the large, yellow number eighteen school bus, and his pulse immediately quickened. He quickly rehearsed the confrontation in his head and silently wished there was a parenting book to cover such dilemmas. He realized his relationship with his son was hanging precariously in the balance. He didn't want to tip the scales the wrong way but wanted to react firmly. As the front door opened, Marwin reminded himself one more time to stay calm.

"Hey, guys," Marwin greeted them just inside the door. "How was your day?"

"Great," said Morgan. "We're reading this really cool story called Great Expectations."

"In the sixth grade?" Marwin asked, astonished. "I didn't read that until I was in high school."

"Well, Ms. Dansby sent me to a special group today. The group was mostly eighth graders, but she said she wanted to challenge me. She was afraid I might be getting bored with the other material."

"How could you be bored in six weeks?" Marwin asked.

"I didn't know I was bored. I just thought the class was super easy."

"OK; that is awesome, Honey. If you start struggling, don't hesitate to let your teacher know so she can help you."

"I will, Daddy. I have a ton of homework to do, so I'm going to go get started," Morgan said, heading toward the stairs.

After watching Morgan climb the stairs out of sight, until he was reasonably sure she was in her room, Marwin turned to Bogie. "So, how was your day?"

"Fine. I've got homework, too," Bogies replied, turning toward the stairs.

"Wait just a minute!" Marwin commanded.

Bogie turned and saw the look on Marwin's face. He immediately knew he was busted.

"Mrs. Kubrick called this afternoon," Marwin stated simply.

When Bogie offered no response, Marwin said, "You do know Mrs. Kubrick, don't you?"

"Yeah, I know her," Bogie answered sullenly.

Seeing that Bogie wasn't going to elaborate, Marwin said, "Do you know why she called?" Not waiting for an answer, he continued, "She called to let me know that you weren't in class today. Apparently, you went to lunch and never came back. Is that about right?"

Bogie stood staring at the floor, a red flush rapidly covering his face.

"Answer me, Son," Marwin directed, trying to keep his anger in check.

"Yes," Bogie answered in a barely audible whisper. Before Marwin could continue to pry the story out, Bogie spoke. "I'm sorry, Dad. I hate calculus, and I didn't want to go to class. I don't get it, and I don't see the point of doing integrals and all that crap."

Surprised by Bogie's honesty and mild manner, Marwin's anger subsided a little. Recalling his own high school days, Marwin remembered cutting classes, too—although mostly as a senior, not while still a freshman. While Marwin liked all kinds of math, he was not an attentive student until pharmacy school. He always made As and Bs, though—except for English, where he usually scraped by with a C.

Realizing that Bogie was looking at him and expecting him to say something, Marwin said, "All right, I can understand not wanting to go to a class when you don't understand the material, but cutting that class is not going to help. It will just make things worse as you fall further behind. You should have come to me if you were having problems."

"Ha! Come to you? Since when can I come to you?" Bogie asked with surprising venom.

"You know you can always to come to me any time you have a problem," Marwin replied, much more loudly than he would have liked.

"Oh, bullshit, Dad! You are always working, gambling, or with Destiny. You never have time for us anymore," Bogie said with tears forming and his quavering voice starting to betray his emotional state.

"You know that's not right..." Marwin began, but seeing the pain on Bogie's face, Marwin's anger faded. His heart ached for the boy, and he rapidly tried to decide which path to take. He wanted to go to Bogie and embrace him, apologizing for failing as a father. For some unknown reason, Marwin pushed this thought aside. He said, instead, "You know, this is what's wrong with today's society. No one takes responsibility for their actions. You are failing calculus, cut the class, got caught, and suddenly it is my fault! How about just fessing up? Just say you messed up. Learn from your mistakes. Don't blame them on someone else."

Marwin's words stung Bogie. Bitterly, he said, "OK, Dad. I was wrong. I screwed up again. I'm a loser! Are you happy now? I'm sorry I troubled your day."

Bogie ran up the stairs, taking them two at a time. At first, Marwin started to go after him, but decided against it. As he listened, he heard Bogie slam his door and wondered how the situation escalated so quickly.

Morgan descended the stairs and entered the dark living room. "Dad?" she called tentatively.

Morgan's voice startled Marwin; he realized he was sitting in his living room in complete darkness. "Over here, Baby," he answered, clicking on the lamp. Marwin checked his watch to see it was after six; he had been sitting there for over two hours. He had been lost in thought, trying to understand what was happening to his family. He had played and replayed several different scenarios for how to handle Bogie in his mind. Each solution his mind had suggested, his heart rejected. Apparently, he had lost track of time.

"Are you OK?" Morgan asked.

"Yes. I'm fine, Baby. I lost track of time and haven't made anything for dinner. Is pizza OK?"

"Cool, pizza! Can we have mushrooms on it?"

"I guess, but are you sure you want to eat something that a frog has pooped on?"

"Dad, that's gross!" Morgan replied, giggling.

"The number is on the fridge. Order two mediums: one with whatever you want, and one with lots of meat for your brother and me. I'll be back in a minute. I gotta go talk to your brother."

"Dad?" Morgan called as Marwin climbed the stairs. "Try to stay cool. Bogie is a really good kid; he's just hormonal right now."

"What do you know about hormones, Little Bit?"

"We learned about them in health," she replied matter-of-factly.

"OK, that sounds like pretty good advice. I will try to stay as cool as the other side of the pillow," Marwin said, giving her a grin and a wink.

During dinner, the conversation lagged. Bogie had requested to eat in his room, but the request was denied. Marwin informed him in a relatively calm voice that he was grounded for a week. He was not allowed to play with friends, watch TV, or have his computer. Marwin also stated that there would be no early parole. Bogie listened quietly and didn't appear surprised. He seemed almost relieved that the punishment wasn't more severe. After he'd finished doling out Bogie's sentence, Marwin said, "Bogie, I need to know where you were today and who you were with."

Watching Bogie closely for signs of deception, Marwin was surprised when Bogie calmly replied, "I was with Emily. We walked to the Circle K, then went to the park and hung out until school was over."

Not sure if he should believe Bogie or try digging deeper into it, Marwin finally asked, "Was there something bothering you that you needed to talk about? You know you can come to me when you need to talk. Contrary to what you said earlier, I am here for you and Morgan. Always."

Marwin watched as Bogie struggled internally, trying to decide if he should confide in his father or not. Bogie's hard features dissolved and tears formed in his eyes as he visibly slumped. When Bogie finally spoke, his voice was quiet, almost timid. His earlier rage was gone like the leaves from a tree in a mid-October thunderstorm. "I don't know, Dad. Everything seems so crazy right now. Things I used to be good at, like baseball, tennis, and math,

I suck at now. My best friends, Laney, Michael, Reed, and Josh, don't seem to have the same interests as I do."

His voice beginning to shake, Bogie continued, seemingly unable to stop the flood of misery that had been unleashed. "Like I said before, you don't seem to have time for me anymore. You don't even seem like you like to be around me anymore."

His heart breaking, Marwin stared at his son for a moment before replying. He tried to recall his own adolescence, without success. Marwin put his arm around his 14-year-old son and said, "I'm sorry, Buddy. Maybe you're right. Maybe I haven't been paying enough attention lately. You don't suck at baseball, tennis, or school. You are a very good athlete, and a good student, too. You just haven't wanted to work at anything recently. The other kids have been working hard on their game and schoolwork, and they're catching up to you. You have always been advanced over most kids, but they are outworking you now and catching up to you. If you don't like that, you better get your butt in gear and get to work. If you want some private instruction, we will get it. I will be glad to get you the extra help if you need it. But you know if your grades drop, sports get dropped with them."

Seeing that Bogie appeared to be calming down, Marwin continued, "Your friends are going through the same crap as you are. You are all teenagers, experiencing common teenage problems. Your friends are still your friends until you do something to hurt them or alienate them. Try spending some more time with them. Talk to them about some of the feelings you have been having. They will be able to relate to you way better than your old man. You can always, always come to me—but unfortunately, I may not be the best source of information. However, I will always listen, and I will promise not to judge you. I just want you to be honest with me, OK? No more cutting classes. We are going in early tomorrow to get you back up to speed in calculus."

Waiting for and expecting a rebuttal but seeing none, Marwin finished with, "Thank you, Son. Thank you for telling me the truth."

Bogie said nothing but allowed Marwin to hug him. After a brief hesitation, Bogie hugged Marwin back fiercely.

CHAPTER 17

Jackson and Cody entered Madeline's office, located just off the master bedroom. She used the office to coordinate the many projects that she was involved in with her various charities. Sitting atop her oak desk was a two-year-old desktop computer, with a flat-screen monitor. Jackson, who was computer-illiterate, said, "You give it a try. You know I don't know anything about computers."

"I don't know much, either. If she doesn't have her addresses and phone numbers in a regular program like Excel or Word, then I won't be able to find them," Cody replied.

Cody booted up the computer and quickly found a document labeled Addresses. When he opened the file, over 250 lines appeared. "Damn, I think she has the address of every person she has ever met," Cody remarked.

"Well, you know your mom was anal about organization. She has receipts and canceled checks from ten years ago, and they are all crammed in boxes up in the attic."

Scrolling through the alphabetized list, Cody found his old friend's number and jotted it down on a sticky note. "I wonder if his mom and dad still live there, and if they will even remember me. It's been over ten years since I last saw them," Cody mused.

"Chances are good that they still live there. This is Knoxville, you know," Jackson opined.

As Cody closed the addresses document, Jackson saw a file labeled Calendar. Realizing he had no idea of Madeline's upcoming commitments, he instructed Cody to open the file. "I guess I need to go through the calendar and cancel her upcoming dates," Jackson said.

The file opened to the October calendar, the dates littered with various appointments. "God, Mom was busy," Cody stated the obvious.

Taking a notepad from the drawer, Jackson wrote down the upcoming dates and times. "Go ahead and pull up the November calendar, too, please," he instructed Cody. As Jackson continued writing names and dates down, he saw that Madeline had another appointment with the gynecologist during the first week of November. Thinking this odd, he asked Cody to return to the October calendar. Just as he thought, Madeline had seen the gynecologist on October 7th and October 21st, just two days before her death. Alarm bells going off in his head, Jackson said, "What the hell?"

"What is it, Dad?" Cody asked.

"I don't know. Can you go back to September, so I can see that, too?"

Jackson watched with growing alarm as the September calendar popped up. Quickly scanning the many appointments, Jackson found what he was looking for; September 23rd and 9th also listed appointments with Dr. Shoehorn. "Damn," Jackson said solemnly.

"Dad, what's wrong?" Cody asked.

Not answering, Jackson instructed, "Go back to August."

Counting backwards in his head, Jackson looked at August 26th to find Shoehorn's name. Knowing it would be there, he looked at August 12th and was not disappointed. "Go to July now," he told Cody.

"Dad, what is going on?" Cody said with alarm.

"Just keep going back, and I will tell you in a minute," Jackson answered.

Cody quickly pulled up the July calendar. Three more appointments with Shoehorn's name were listed. Upon his father's request, Cody searched the June calendar and found two appointments with Shoehorn. The month of May was void of any appointments with the gynecologist, as were the previous months.

"Your mom had a gynecologist appointment every two weeks starting in June, all the way up 'til two days before she died," Jackson stated.

"Why? I...I don't understand. Sh-she wasn't ill, was she?" Cody stammered.

"No, not to my knowledge. Her doctor told me that she was fine. 'Perfectly healthy' is how he described her."

"This doesn't make any sense," Cody complained, clicking through the calendar. "Why in the hell would she be seeing a gynecologist every two weeks if she was perfectly healthy?"

With a bitter taste rising in his mouth, Jackson said, "I'm not sure, but I know a certain weed lover who does."

***

Destiny pulled her car into the garage and trudged wearily inside, her mood as dark as the fast-approaching night. She'd had a miserable day listening to testimony in the child molester case. It was all she could do not to rip the bastard's face off. Seeing the pain that the child was going through as she recounted the story had made Destiny physically ill. Furthermore, she had hoped to have dinner with Marwin, but had not been able to reach him all day. Hopefully, he left a message. After hanging her keys up, Destiny went straight to the answering machine, where the red message count flashed 5-5-5 at her repeatedly. After listening to two hang-ups and two telemarketers, she listened hopefully to the fifth message. However, her mother's voice came whining out of the machine, causing Destiny to swear out loud. Vowing to call her mother back later, Destiny deleted the messages before the last one even finished. Kicking her black pumps off, she padded to the kitchen and retrieved a bottle of Kendall Jackson chardonnay from the fridge. With glass of wine in hand, she re-opened the fridge and stared disinterestedly inside, looking for something to eat. After several moments, she closed the door without withdrawing anything except another glass of wine. Deciding on a liquid diet tonight, she picked up the phone and again called Marwin. Listening to the unanswered rings, her ire increased. She was about to hang up when Marwin finally, breathlessly, said, "Hello."

The fact that he hadn't answered on the first ring had only pissed her off more. "It's about time; I was ready to hang up."

Hearing her voice, Marwin remembered he'd never returned Destiny's call from earlier. He had completely lost track of everything else, dealing with Bogie's issues. "Hey, I'm sorry. I was upstairs and I couldn't find the phone. I'm sorry I didn't get back with you about dinner. I had some, uh, problems here, and I completely lost track of time."

"Well, I had my own problems, but I found time to call you because I needed you," Destiny replied coldly, the implication clear.

The stress of Madeline's death, along with Bogie's stunt, caused Marwin to snap, "What the hell does that mean?"

"It means that you are not the only person in the world. Other people have needs, too."

"I don't know what's wrong with you, but I didn't do it. Don't jump on me for no reason! If you would like to talk, I will be glad to listen."

"Well, I wouldn't want you to go out of your way! Just forget it. Call me when you are problem-free."

"Dammit, Destiny! I was looking forward to seeing you tonight, especially after the day that I had, but maybe that's not such a good idea. We don't seem very compatible tonight."

"Maybe we are not compatible at all!" Destiny yelled, not really knowing why.

"OK, look, I will call you tomorrow and we can work through this," Marwin said, trying to remain somewhat calm.

"Great, just push our problems to the side until you are ready to solve them!" Destiny snarled, on the verge of tears.

Marwin sighed, exasperated. "What do you want, Des? Do you want me to come over? Would you like to come over here? What do you want me to do?"

Destiny didn't respond for a long moment, then finally said, "I don't know. I don't know what I want. I don't know why I'm yelling at you. Look, I'm sorry. I had a rotten day, and now I am having a rotten night. Just let me go, and we'll talk tomorrow."

Realizing she was about to hang up, Marwin hurriedly said, "Des? I love you."

After a long pause, Destiny responded, "I know. I'll talk to you tomorrow."

***

After closing Madeline's computer calendar, Jackson walked rapidly downstairs with the intention of phoning the gynecologist. In the middle of dialing, he abruptly hung up and started back upstairs.

"Dad, what are you doing?" Cody asked.

"I want to have the exact dates in hand when I call him," Jackson replied, without knowing exactly why.

Jackson and Cody return to Madeline's computer, and Jackson jotted down the exact dates of Madeline's appointments with Shoehorn. After going through the previous six months again, they were ready to close out the calendars once again, when Cody spotted a single word written on a date in September.

"Dad, what do you think this means?" Cody asked, pointing to the word START written on September 10th.

Following Cody's finger, Jackson replied, "I have no idea. It's right after one of her doctor's visits, but I don't know if it is related to them or not. I'll ask Shoehorn when I call."

Jackson added September 10th to his list of dates and headed back downstairs to call the gynecologist.

Listening to the phone ring, Jackson rehearsed his conversation with Shoehorn in his head. Interrupting his rehearsal, a voice said, "Doctor Shoehorn's office, this is Mary. How can I help you?"

"This is Jackson Montgomery. I would like to speak to Dr. Shoehorn, please," Jackson responded.

"I'm sorry, the doctor is seeing patients right now. Can I take a number and have him call you when he is finished?"

"No, you can go get him and tell him that Madeline Montgomery's husband is on the phone. You do know my wife—or should I say, my recently-deceased wife—don't you?"

The line went silent for a few seconds, then Mary replied, "Hold on, Mr. Montgomery. I will see if I can get Dr. Shoehorn on the line."

"Thank you. And, it is Doctor Montgomery, by the way."

"Yes, of course, I'm sorry. Please hold for just a moment."

The line clicked and Britney Spears was singing in Jackson's ear. Jackson's anger rose with each chorus of "Oops, I did it again." Finally, Shoehorn picked up.

"Dr. Montgomery, what can I do for you?" Shoehorn asked.

Having decided on his strategy, Jackson said, "I need to see you. I have some questions about Madeline."

"OK, I'll be glad to help in any way that I can. What would you like to know?"

"Not over the phone," Jackson replied. "I want to talk face-to-face. I'll be happy to come to your office, say, in about thirty minutes or so?"

"Uh, no, I'm afraid I have patients scheduled all afternoon," Shoehorn replied. "I could meet you somewhere after work, though, if you would like."

"Meet me at Ruby Tuesday's at six," Jackson said flatly.

"All right, I'll see you around six," Shoehorn agreed, with a slight tremble in his voice.

Jackson arrived fifteen minutes early and picked a booth facing the door. He ordered a Johnnie Walker Black on the rocks and waited impatiently for Shoehorn's arrival. He had spent all afternoon trying to come up with plausible reasons for Madeline to see Shoehorn every two weeks. He went through various scenarios, including breast cancer, uterine cancer, menopause, and even an extra-marital affair. None of them made any sense, though. Shoehorn had described Madeline as perfectly healthy. Jackson didn't believe Madeline would have had an affair, much less carry it out in a doctor's office and list it on her calendar. Jackson finished his drink but refrained from ordering another, in hopes of staying calm when Shoehorn arrived.

As Jackson looked toward the door yet again, Ernie Shoehorn entered and immediately shrugged out of his top coat. His grey suit jacket hung open, and his bright blue necktie had already been loosened. He glanced casually around and quickly spotted Jackson. Jackson gave a slight wave of his hand and Shoehorn slid into the booth across from him.

"Dr. Montgomery, it is good to see you, again," Shoehorn said.

Before Jackson could say anything, the waiter arrived and took Shoehorn's order for natural spring water. Jackson, against his better judgment, ordered another Scotch. After the waiter left, Jackson bluntly asked, "Why were you seeing my wife every two weeks?"

A look of surprise briefly flashed across Shoehorn's face, but was quickly replaced with an unconvincing smile. "Well, actually, I was working with her to become a healthier, happier person," he finally answered. "I had gone over her diet and medications and started her on an intense vitamin and herb regimen designed to boost her immune system, as well as improve her mental status," Shoehorn continued.

"What makes you think she needed her mental status improved?" Jackson retorted.

"Dr. Montgomery, I know you have been through a terrible ordeal recently, but you need to realize that Madeline wasn't a very happy person. I was trying to help her cope with some issues, as well as improve her well-being with vitamins and herbs that she was deficient in."

"Listen to me, you fucking quack!" Jackson exploded, reaching across the table to grab Shoehorn, knocking his water glass over in the process. "I don't know what kind of bullshit you are into, but I know that my wife was far from unhappy. If she had issues and was unhappy, why in the hell didn't you refer her to a psychiatrist or counselor? Why would you pump her full of a bunch of shit that wasn't going to help her?"

Shoehorn had recoiled from Jackson and scrambled out of the booth, clearly afraid. "I'll be going now, Dr. Montgomery. I am not going to sit here and listen to your barbaric mouth and subject myself to physical violence. If it weren't for your recent tragedy, I would be calling the police."

Shoehorn turned to leave. Only a few steps away, he stopped and said, "I'm sorry about your wife."

Jackson fought the urge to go after Shoehorn and strangle him in plain sight of everyone. Instead, he sat back heavily and drained his drink in three long swallows.

CHAPTER 18

Marwin rolled over and glanced at the digital clock on the nightstand for what seemed like the hundredth time since he'd gone to bed. 2:46 a.m. *Shit*, Marwin thought. He had been unable to get the day's events out of his head, so he hadn't been able to get any sleep. First, it was Bogie skipping class and flunking calculus, then Destiny went berserk for no apparent reason. Finally, most bothersome of all, was Destiny's response when he had professed his love: "I know you do," she'd said. He was sure she loved him—or he had been sure. Why would she say that? Why didn't she say those four magic words that every man wants to hear after he has taken the plunge? "I love you, too," was all she would have had to say, and Marwin would probably have been snoring for hours. Instead, she'd said, "I know you do," and he was reducing the thread count on his sheets with every passing hour of restless tossing and turning. Disgusted, Marwin climbed out of bed and went down to his study.

Marwin sat down to work on his computer, then remembered he needed something and went into the kitchen in search of it. Finding his notes on Madeline's medications, he returned to the study and poured a small amount of Hennessy in a snifter. He then tapped into Medline and searched for information on suicide, relating to each of the herbs and vitamins on his list. After an hour of fruitless research, he finally came across an abstract suggesting that black cohosh might have been to blame for a woman's suicide. Pulling up the full article, Marwin's hopes faded; the woman had a 25-year history of mental illness with two previous unsuccessful suicide attempts. She had been taking large doses of black cohosh prior to her last, successful attempt, but she had also stopped taking her antipsychotics and had been on a three-week alcoholic binge before she either fell or jumped onto the subway tracks, meeting the death that she had long been seeking.

Marwin closed the article and sat back, frustrated. After drinking half of his cognac, he decided to take a different approach. He began researching each herb once more, but this time from an allergic perspective. While he knew there was no link between allergies and suicide, he decided to try to expand his knowledge of herbs, since he had never paid much attention to them. As he scrolled through hundreds of articles involving herbs, something began to bother him. It was just out of reach of his consciousness, nagging him. Like trying to remember the name of the grade school bully, but unable to put a name to the ugly, contorted face. He pressed his mind further but was unable to come up with the nagging thought. Frustrated and tired, he drained his drink, then trudged back upstairs in search of a little rest.

The alarm on the clock radio sounded way too soon, and Marwin slapped sleepily at it. On the third attempt, he finally found the snooze button and returned immediately to sleep. Fifteen minutes later, the alarm sounded again. Cursing, Marwin stumbled out of bed and downstairs only to realize he'd neglected to set the automatic timer on the coffee pot. Emitting another curse, Marwin made coffee and went back upstairs to roust the kids out of bed. Both children appeared to be moving at the same slow pace as their father. After getting everyone quickly through the shower and stopping at McDonald's for biscuits, Marwin dropped Morgan off at a friend's house to catch the bus. He and Bogie headed to school early to meet the calculus teacher. The meeting went surprisingly well; Bogie had a better understanding of the material than he'd originally thought, and Mrs. Kubrick gave Bogie some assignments to help bring his grade up.

As Marwin left the school, he felt more upbeat than he had in days. He made a mental note to try to work with Bogie on his baseball skills that night, if possible. Marwin dialed Destiny's home number, but she had already left for the office. He left her a message, telling her that he was going into work and that he loved her. After hanging up, he tried her at work, but her secretary told him Destiny would be in court all day. He again left a message that he would be at work and that he loved her. His previous dark mood threatening to return, Marwin pulled into his space at the pharmacy and tried to steel himself against the mountain of problems that likely awaited him after a week off. Checking the time and seeing that he still had half an hour before he had to open, he decided to check on Jackson.

Jackson answered on the second ring with a weary voice. "Hey, Marwin. You're up early this morning."

"Yeah, I decided I couldn't bum around at home any longer, so I finally came in to work."

"I know; I'm just not ready for that," Jackson stated matter-of-factly.

Failing to change the subject, Marwin said, "I did some research last night on all those herbs that Madeline was taking. I'm afraid I didn't find anything useful, but I will keep digging."

"Thanks for looking into it for me. Since you mentioned it, I need to let you know what we found here." Jackson told Marwin about finding all the appointments with Dr. Shoehorn, then went on to describe his phone conversation with the gynecologist, as well as their face-to-face meeting. When Jackson finished, Marwin asked carefully, "Did you ever find out what the word START meant?"

"Hell... No, the little weasel left before I even got around to that. I'm guessing it was when she started taking all the crap that he gave her."

"Yeah, you're probably right. Let me know if you find anything else, and I will let you know if I find anything with the herbs."

"OK, I will. Why don't you come by tonight for a beer? I'm sure you'll need one, after working for an entire day," Jackson said sarcastically.

"Uh, let me check with Destiny. We had a fight last night, so I need to find out what's going on with her. I'll call you later."

"OK, no problem. Thanks again."

***

Destiny exited the courtroom carrying her black attaché case, stuffed with documents. She was physically as well as mentally drained from the long day in court on the child molester's trial. As she walked to her car, her thoughts turned to Marwin and the fight they'd had the night before. She was angry at herself for treating him so harshly and wasn't even sure why she'd jumped on him the way she had. She tried to remember if she was about to start her period, then realized that she had no idea when her last period was, or when it was due again. *Oh, well. I guess I'll just write it off as me being a bitch for no good reason*, she thought. Having already formed a plan to make up with Marwin, she called her office to collect her messages. None were of any importance, except for Marwin's. Destiny decided to surprise Marwin, and as she drove off toward his pharmacy, she smiled for the first time all day.

As Destiny entered the pharmacy, a bell above the door announced her arrival. A technician glanced up, then returned his attention to his computer screen. Destiny walked down the aisle between blood glucose monitoring devices and bowel prep products. She didn't immediately approach the counter, instead silently watching Marwin work from a distance. He was counseling a man about his prescription, going over the side effects and actions of the medication. After five minutes or so, the man stood up and shook Marwin's hand before gathering his medication and paperwork. As Marwin was turning to return to his workstation, he saw Destiny smiling at him.

"Hey, Doc. How's it going?" she asked, approaching the counter.

Turning to the next patient in line, Marwin said, "Joe, I will be right with you. I need to speak to this lady for just a minute."

Eyeing Destiny, the man laughed and commented, "I'd see her before me, too. Take your time."

"Thanks, I'll be right back," Marwin replied, heading around the counter.

Reaching Destiny, Marwin took her hands and kissed her softly on the lips.

"Thanks," she stated simply.

"What for? For kissing you? Anytime; no thanks necessary," Marwin said happily.

"No, for not telling me to get the hell out of here after the way I acted last night."

"No problem. I know how you can get when it's that time of the month," Marwin teased, grinning.

Destiny laughed out loud and said, "Is it that time? I was trying to figure it out on the way over here."

"Well, I think you're due to start tomorrow or the next day. You know, we men keep up with those important events."

"I knew I kept you around for some reason," Destiny replied, with a gleam in her eye.

"Look, I've got to get back to work, but why don't we go get dinner tonight?"

"I've got a better idea. Why don't you come over? I'll cook dinner, and maybe we can kiss and make up."

"OK, that sounds great to me. What do I need to bring?"

"Wood. You bring some wood. We might want to have a fire," Destiny purred seductively as she turned to leave.

Smiling, Marwin watched her shapely figure walking away.

Later, just before closing, the phone rang. Marwin looked apprehensively at the clock on the wall. 5:58. *Shit*, Marwin thought. Hoping it wasn't a doctor or patient that he would have to stay late for, Marwin hesitantly answered, "Professional Pharmacy, this is Marwin."

"Hey, Marwin, it's Jackson."

"Crap. I'm sorry I haven't called you back. It's been kinda wild here today," Marwin explained.

"You're probably just out of practice after taking a week off. Maybe Sam needs to retrain you. You coming by tonight for that beer?"

"Actually, Destiny just invited me to dinner. Can I get a raincheck on the beer?"

"Sure," Jackson said, instantly dejected. "I found something else that I wanted to show you, but it can wait, I guess."

"What is it?" Marwin inquired.

"I'm not really sure, but I would rather show you than talk about it over the phone. Maybe you can come by tomorrow night."

Marwin paused, thinking about the night ahead with Destiny. His mind and conscience struggled briefly with his heart and penis, then he said, "I'll be right over. Let me close up here and call Des, then I'll come over. I should be there in about forty-five minutes or so."

"Hey, don't make things harder for you and Destiny. I don't want to piss off a beautiful district attorney."

"It'll be all right. Destiny is a very understanding woman. I'll see you shortly."

After hanging up, Marwin dismissed his employees for the day and locked up the pharmacy. He returned to the phone, disappointment already setting in, and dialed Destiny's number.

"You better hurry. Dinner is almost ready, and so am I," Destiny greeted him.

"Uh, hey Des. I guess your caller ID is working—or do you greet everyone like that?"

"I only say that to hot pharmacists who are bringing wood to put in my fireplace," Destiny replied throatily.

"Yeah, about that... Jackson wants me to come over tonight. He apparently found something related to Madeline's death and he doesn't want to talk about it over the phone. I'm sorry. I was really looking forward to tonight, especially after our fight last night."

"Apparently, you weren't looking too forward to it," Destiny fired back. "I guess our fight wasn't as important to you as it was to me."

"Des, I'm sorry. Of course our fight bothered me. I didn't sleep a wink last night. Remember, you're the one who suggested that I try to help Jackson figure out what happened. Can we please reschedule for tomorrow night?"

"I don't know. I'll have to check my calendar." She paused to take a deep breath. "Actually, I think I am busy tomorrow night. An old friend came by to see me recently, and I think I'll look him up tomorrow night," she said bitterly.

Marwin gasped quietly; her implication was clear. Finally, he said, "What is going on with us?"

Initially, Destiny didn't answer. Eventually she said, "I'm not sure. Call me if you figure it out."

Marwin sat there holding the receiver, stunned, the dial tone ringing in his ear.

CHAPTER 19

Jackson pulled into the garage, returning from a trip to Kroger. He had picked up steaks, baking potatoes, and salad fixings for dinner. He also had grabbed a 12-pack of Sam Adams to help wash it all down. Just as he was putting the beer in the fridge, the phone rang. Cursing silently, Jackson finally managed to answer on the fourth ring.

"Hello, Dr. Montgomery, this is Winston Browne from the Sentinel again."

A chill ran through Jackson. He was instantly ready to explode and expose the imposter—but thought better of it at the last second. "Yes. Hello, Mr. Browne. What can I do for you?" he asked with what he hoped was the proper tone.

"I'm sorry to bother you. I just wanted to follow up on your wife's death."

"Look, like I told you before, there is no story here! I have no statement to make," Jackson replied, allowing a degree of anger to creep into his voice.

"I just thought you might be interested to know that at least twenty-nine other women in the Knoxville area have committed suicide in the last six months. Even in a town the size of Knoxville, that number is a bit large. Wouldn't you agree?"

Stunned into silence, Jackson eventually said, "I don't know anything about suicide rates here. I just know that my wife is gone. I warned you before not to call me again. There will be no more warnings. Do not call me again!"

Jackson hung up forcefully and sat there a moment, perplexed and angry. *Who is this asshole harassing me? Have there really been that many women who com-*

mitted suicide here recently? His mind whirling, Jackson tried to evaluate the imposter and his involvement in this mess. The doorbell rang, jarring him from his thoughts.

Entering the foyer, Marwin immediately noticed Jackson's pallor and anxiety-laden face. "Hey, what's wrong?" Marwin asked.

Jackson went to the fridge and pulled out two beers before answering. "I just got a call from Winston Browne." Seeing the blank look on Marwin's face, Jackson continued, "Remember the jerk posing as a reporter from the Sentinel who called right after Madeline's death?"

"Yeah. You mean he called again?" Marwin asked in disbelief.

"I'm afraid so," Jackson replied. He then quickly described his conversation with the imposter.

"It was probably wise not to divulge that you know he is a fake. We need to call that detective and let him know this jerk is still bothering you," Marwin suggested.

"Maybe," Jackson said. "I can't understand why this guy is harassing me. But on the other hand, I have to wonder if there is any truth to what he said. Have there really been that many suicides lately?"

"Let's call that detective now. Maybe he can answer that question, too," Marwin suggested again.

"Wait. I want to show you what I found, first. You can help me decide if I should share that with the detective, too."

"All right; what did you find?" Marwin asked.

"Later. Let me get the steaks on and dinner fixed. Then we can look at it after dinner."

***

Bradley Jinswain sat at his desk drinking mineral water and eating raw vegetables. His desk looked like a paper bomb had gone off. It was littered with paperwork from a variety of cases that he was working on, almost completely covering its surface. He had come to work early that day in hopes of catching up on the mountain of paperwork but had accomplished very little.

His mind kept returning to the recent lunch he'd shared with Destiny. He hadn't realized how much he missed her until he saw her. Since their lunch together, he couldn't get her out of his mind. He knew they had no future together, but he longed for her anyway. She had affected him more than any woman he'd ever known. She was everything he wasn't, and everything he wanted to be. He thought fondly of the dates they'd had and the kisses they'd shared. Especially the kisses they'd shared. He remembered her kisses being both passive and aggressive, and how her body felt next to his during an intense embrace. Even as he felt a small stirring in his groin, his phone rang and interrupted his reverie.

"Hello," he said disinterestedly. When no one responded, he repeated the greeting angrily.

"Uh, hey, Brad, it's Destiny."

Bradley's pulse rose to double-time and he immediately broke out in a sweat. "Oh, hey, Des. How are you?" he asked automatically, and immediately kicked himself for asking such an inane question. He'd just seen her two days before and knew she was fine. Destiny surprised him by saying, "I'm not sure. I was wondering if I could come over."

Bradley's mind exploded in a thousand different thoughts. He was about to answer with an enthusiastic yes when he realized that something in her voice didn't sound right. "Sure, Des. Would you like me to cook you some dinner?"

"No, I don't want anything to eat. I just need to talk, that's all," she said slowly.

"Have you been drinking?" Bradley asked bluntly.

"Well, yes. I've had a couple of glasses of wine."

"OK, you stay there and I will come to you. I'll be there in twenty minutes."

Holy shit, Bradley thought. He grabbed his jacket and ran for the door, leaving the stacks of paper just as unfinished as they were before.

***

Marwin pushed back from the table and exhaled loudly. "Man, that was a nice piece of cow," he declared, referring to the large medium-rare NY strip steaks that he and Jackson had just devoured.

"Thanks. They weren't bad, even if I did cook them," Jackson responded.

"The only thing that would have made them better is if you had cooked them on my Big Green Egg," Marwin said, boasting about his ceramic smoker.

"Well, I'm just a poor doctor. I can't afford fancy things like you rich pharmacists," Jackson said.

"Shit, I wish. I'm just proud to get invited into this swanky neighborhood. I hope my car doesn't get you in trouble with your homeowners' association. I know a Mercedes is usually the least expensive car allowed in," Marwin said, laughing as they fell into their poor-mouthing routine.

"Come on, you poor slob. Help me clean up this mess so we can get down to business."

"Damn, what kind of restaurant makes you clean your own dishes?" Marwin complained, trying to sound put-out.

"The kind where you get to eat for free," Jackson replied with a grin.

***

Bradley paused outside Destiny's door, his hands sweating and pulse skipping along. After taking a few calming breaths, he rang the doorbell. Time seemed to stretch endlessly along, and he began to wonder if he'd actually pressed the doorbell. Just as he almost convinced himself that he didn't ring the bell after all, Destiny opened the door.

"Hey, Brad, come on in," she said, slightly slurring. She was dressed in a red flannel shirt that was at least two sizes too large, grey sweatpants with the UT insignia on the upper left thigh, and woolly socks with rubber tread on the bottoms. Her hair was disheveled and her eyes appeared slightly glassy. Her cheeks were flushed and her mouth was stuck in a pseudo-grin.

Taking this picture in, Bradley still marveled at Destiny's beauty. He felt the knot in his stomach tighten as he sat down on the couch.

"Would you like something to drink?" Destiny asked.

"Uh, no thanks, not right now," Bradley replied.

Destiny went to the kitchen to pour another glass of chardonnay. She started to place the bottle back in the fridge, changed her mind, then carried the bottle and glass into the living room where Bradley was seated. "This way, I don't have as far to walk," she explained with a chuckle.

"Des, what is going on? You aren't usually a boozer."

Destiny didn't reply. Instead, she walked over to the couch and plopped down beside Bradley, spilling wine all over the floor. Ignoring the spilled wine, she pulled her legs up on the couch; they touched and settled against Bradley's, and Destiny silently laid her head on his shoulder.

Bradley stiffened, unsure of what to do next. Finally, he put his arm around her and quietly whispered, "Tell me what's wrong, Honey."

"Not now," she murmured, nuzzling against him. Her right arm had reached across him and she was clinging for dear life. "Don't say anything. Just hold me. Please," she implored.

Bradley's feelings swirled in his head and the knot tightened in his stomach. A flutter also began slightly south of his stomach. At first, he sat stiffly with his arm awkwardly around his former flame. Gradually, he began to relax as she molded herself closer to him than he would have ever thought possible. Bradley slowly stroked Destiny's auburn hair and whispered, "Everything will be all right." Lost in his consoling, Bradley didn't notice the tears sliding slowly down Destiny's face.

***

With the dishes loaded into the dishwasher and the kitchen cleaned up, Jackson and Marwin grabbed two more beers and retired to the study. "I'll be right back," Jackson said.

Marwin watched Jackson leave the room and a wave of pity washed over him. He couldn't imagine how difficult it would be to be in Jackson's shoes. Yet Jackson appeared to be handling Madeline's death fairly well. Much better than Marwin would handle Destiny's death, anyway. As Destiny entered Marwin's mind, he felt another pang of guilt for the direction their relationship had taken lately. *I've got to figure out what is going on with her*, he thought. Crossing to Jackson's desk, Marwin was reaching for the phone when Jackson re-entered the room.

"Need to make a phone call?" Jackson asked.

"Nah, it can wait. What have you got to show me?"

"This," Jackson replied, holding out his hand. In Jackson's palm was a small white packet. Marwin inspected the outside of the packet, but it was devoid of written or printed information, except for the number 2. Shaking the packet, Marwin heard what sounded like powder or tiny beads inside.

"Where did this come from?" Marwin inquired.

"I found it in Madeline's purse when I was looking for our checkbook," Jackson explained, slightly defensive. "It was actually inside a pouch with her make-up."

"Relax; you have every right to look for answers anywhere you can find them," Marwin said.

"I know. It's just that I've never gone through her purse before. I felt kinda dirty, like I was trying to catch her in something."

Hesitantly, Marwin asked, "Were you?"

"No, not really. Like I said, I was trying to find the checkbook. Then I saw all her stuff, and it was like something came over me; I just dumped everything out and went through every scrap. I felt sort of ashamed when I'd finished," Jackson admitted, sitting heavily on the corner of the desk with a look of sadness on his face.

"You have absolutely nothing to be ashamed of. Besides, you found something," Marwin offered.

"Yeah, but what is it? It's probably just some vitamins or some other shit that quack Shoehorn gave her to take," Jackson said dejectedly.

Marwin started to open the packet, then stopped and asked, "Has anyone else touched this?"

"No, just you and me. Oh, and I guess Madeline. Why?"

Without replying, Marwin went to the kitchen and returned quickly with a resealable baggie, into which he dropped the packet.

"What did you do that for?" Jackson asked, perplexed. "I want to open it and see what it is."

Again ignoring Jackson's questions, Marwin asked, "Did you find that detective's number?"

"Yeah, I have it," Jackson replied. "So, you think we should give it to the cops?"

"Yes, we need to find out what is in it," Marwin responded.

"Well, what if it is just vitamins, like we suspect?" Jackson asked.

Having not really thought it through, Marwin paused to ponder Jackson's question. Not waiting for Marwin's answer, Jackson said, "Besides, what difference does it make? Madeline committed suicide. She didn't die from some poisoning. I say we just open it and see what's in there."

"No!" Marwin said a little too harshly as Jackson reached for the baggie. Continuing carefully, Marwin said, "It won't do us any good to open it. It sounds like a powder inside and we have no way to discern what the ingredients are. It will have to be sent to a lab." After a brief pause, Marwin added, "I have a feeling this might be really important."

Jackson opened his mouth to reply, but something stopped him. He looked at Marwin intently and recognized the sincerity of his last statement. Finally, Jackson said, "I have his number in my wallet."

"Damn, I don't think he is home," Jackson said, counting the rings in his head. Finally, Bradley Jinswain's oddly hollow voice stated what Jackson had already surmised; he wasn't home, or couldn't answer the phone for some reason. Jackson left a brief message, then slumped into a chair.

"I was really hoping to get in touch with him tonight," Jackson stated sadly.

"Did his machine leave a pager or cell phone number?" Marwin asked.

"Yeah, his recorder left a pager number for emergencies, but I don't think this qualifies," Jackson replied.

"Who gives a shit? Page him. That's what he gets paid for," Marwin said boldly.

"Hey, you and I both hate to get called when we're off-duty. I'm sure he isn't too fond of it, either. Especially when this is not an emergency. Besides, what am I supposed to say? 'We found some vitamins. Could you drop everything and rush over to look at them?'"

"Fine, give me the number. I'll call him." Marwin said in his not-to-be-denied voice.

"I didn't write the pager number down," Jackson responded innocently.

"Shit. Give me his home number and I'll get the pager number myself."

Studying his young friend, Jackson was touched by Marwin's desire to help. Finally, seeing Marwin was only becoming more agitated, Jackson said, "His pager number is on his card. He told me to page him if I ever needed anything."

Hand out, Marwin said, "Gimme."

"I'll do it, I'll do it! Damn, you should have been a woman, you know that? The way you bitch and boss everyone around, you remind me of Madeline's sister, Teresa."

"Well, you know my mom and dad only missed having a daughter by half an inch anyway," Marwin mused. "You got anything else to drink? I'm about beered out."

"Yeah, in the bar. Why don't you get us a couple Turkeys while I page Columbo?" Jackson suggested.

Jackson dialed the number and waited apprehensively to enter his number. After Marwin returned with the bourbon, they chatted idly about the Vols and waited for the detective's call. Barely three minutes had passed before the phone rang. Glancing at the caller ID, Jackson handed the phone to Marwin. "It's for you."

Marwin looked at the name and number on the display with puzzlement before answering, "Montgomery residence."

"Yes, this is Bradley Jinswain. Did someone page me from this number?"

"Hello? Hello? Is anyone there?" Bradley said into the silence.

"Uh, yes. Just a moment," Marwin replied, startled. Marwin handed the phone back to Jackson, who was looking at him strangely.

"It's the detective," Marwin finally managed, his mind struggling to put the pieces of the puzzle together. Rapidly going through all plausible and some not-so-plausible explanations, Marwin finally arrived at the correct one. His stomach rolled over and his heart raced at the realization that

Bradley Jinswain was calling from Destiny's house. A sour taste joined the cotton in his mouth. Marwin fell numbly into a chair and drained half of his drink in one long swallow.

Jackson stared worriedly at Marwin and said, "This is Jackson Montgomery."

"Hi, Dr. Montgomery. This is Bradley Jinswain. What can I do for you?"

"Oh, hey. Thanks for calling back so quickly," Jackson said. His mind tried to assemble the same pieces Marwin had just put together. Alarm suddenly arose as Jackson reached a different conclusion.

"Are you calling from Destiny's house?"

"Uh, yes, I am," Bradley replied coolly.

"Is she OK?" Jackson asked. Marwin rose from his seat with a terrified look on his face.

"She's fine. We're old friends," Bradley explained.

"Oh... OK, good," Jackson said, relieved that his conclusion was incorrect. "She's OK. They're old friends and he's just over visiting her," he explained to Marwin.

Marwin's face relaxed, then almost immediately returned to the sad, dumbfounded look of before. Seeing Marwin's pained expression helped Jackson construct the mental puzzle correctly. Pain ripped through him as he realized how Marwin must feel.

"Dr. Montgomery, is everything all right?" Bradley asked.

"Yes; I was just wondering if you could come over. I found something that I need to show you."

Damn, Bradley thought, looking to his right. He saw Destiny gazing at him, but his head quickly wrested control of his tongue from his heart and nether regions. With a sigh, he said, "What time would be good for you tomorrow?"

"Oh, anytime, I guess. I was really hoping you could stop by tonight," Jackson replied, disappointment evident in his voice.

Shit, Bradley thought again. He glanced at Destiny, who was sipping her wine. Gazing at him with a look that made his stomach tighten, she carefully put the glass on the coffee table. He had already signaled to her that everything was fine with Dr. Montgomery, so she had poured another glass of wine.

"OK," Bradley agreed grudgingly. "Can you give me about an hour?"

Checking his watch, Jackson suddenly realized that the time didn't matter, since he wasn't going to work the next day anyway. "Sure, see you in an hour," he answered.

"He'll be here in an hour," Jackson told Marwin.

Marwin didn't reply. He returned to the bar, where he poured another three fingers of bourbon, "forgetting" to add the water.

Eyeing Marwin closely, Jackson cautioned, "Easy, buddy. I know what you're thinking. I'm sure you're making too much out of this."

"You think so? Well, I'm the one who should be at Destiny's tonight. Not some 'old friend,'" Marwin replied hotly, before draining most of his drink.

Marwin's words stung Jackson, and he stepped back as if slapped. "You're right," he said slowly. "I should have insisted that you go to Destiny's. I'm sorry."

Marwin looked at his friend and sighed. "No, if anyone should be sorry, it is me. I didn't mean to snap at you. I want to help you and by God, I'm going to. Everything else will take a backseat until we find some sort of solution. Besides, she's the one who decided on a replacement for me."

"I doubt she's planning on replacing you. Don't go buying trouble," Jackson protested gently.

"Yeah, I know," Marwin said with a sigh.

Both men sipped their drinks in silence; neither could think of anything to say.

***

Bradley hung up and sat back down on the couch. "He found something that he wants to show me, so he wants me to come over tonight," he explained to Destiny. "I told him that I would be over in an hour."

Destiny scooted down the couch until she was again resting against Bradley with her head on his shoulder. She looked up into his eyes and said, "Well, can you hold me for an hour?"

Bradley draped his arm around her shoulder and she shifted her head onto his chest. Bradley was at first tense, but finally relaxed as the minutes passed. They sat in silence for several minutes before Bradley asked, "Do you want to tell me what's wrong?"

"Uh-uh," Destiny murmured. She lifted her head and kissed him softly on the neck. Bradley immediately tensed again, and he felt her draw even closer to him. She continued kissing his neck, moving slowly upward. Bradley could feel her breath hot on his skin as she flicked her tongue lightly into his ear. A soft moan escaped him and he turned his head to meet her lips. The kiss was at first tender, somewhat tentative. But as the heat rose between them, the kiss intensified; lips quickly parted and tongues darted. Bradley could feel Destiny's breasts pressing against his arm and chest, and another moan escaped. As Destiny's tongue became more and more aggressive, Bradley began to unbutton her flannel shirt. Something in Bradley's brain shouted, alarmed. Stop it! This isn't right. She's drunk and doesn't know what she is doing. She's your friend. Don't let her do something that she'll regret. Besides, you have to go to Dr. Montgomery's. Bradley summoned every ounce of his willpower and pulled his hand away from Destiny's shirt.

"This isn't right. We can't do this, now, Des."

"Why? Is something wrong with me?" she hissed.

"No, of course not. It's just..." Bradley looked at Destiny with sorrow in his eyes. His heart ached to see the hurt on her face. "Look, Des, I don't know how to explain this. I've wanted you for a long time now, but I wanted you to want me, too. Obviously, something has happened between you and Marwin. I know you have been drinking, so I think it is best if we stop for now. Hopefully, we will pick up where we left off someday, except we will be doing it for the right reasons—and sober."

Destiny stared at Bradley, obviously furious. "Get the hell out of here! I never want to see you again!"

Bradley backed toward the door cautiously. "OK, Des. Try to get something to eat and get some sleep. We can talk tomorrow."

"Fuck you!" Destiny screamed, hurling her wine glass past Bradley's head to shatter against the front door.

Bradley looked forlornly at Destiny, then walked slowly out of the door.

**

Exactly fifty-eight minutes had elapsed between the time Bradley ended the conversation with Jackson and the time that he rang the doorbell. Neither Jackson nor Marwin had much to say during this period; both had been lost in thought. Marwin had mentally pummeled himself for how he had handled his relationship with Destiny. Jackson had been silently praying that the detective would be able to make some sense out of Madeline's death. Marwin tried briefly to focus on Jackson's findings, but his mind wouldn't focus. He kept thinking about Destiny. *How could she do this to me? What have I done to deserve this? She was the one who insisted I try to help Jackson, then she calls up an "old friend!" Actually, when I think about it, I haven't done shit. She is the one who weirded out on me last night. She is the one who has been acting crazy lately,* Marwin thought, growing steadily angrier.

Marwin's reverie was broken when Jackson escorted Bradley Jinswain into the room. An immediate rush of jealousy swept over Marwin, and his face glowed red as he turned to greet Bradley.

"Detective Jinswain, this is Marwin Gelstone," Jackson said awkwardly.

Bradley extended his hand to Marwin but let it drop to his side when Marwin just glared at him.

"Well, what can I do for you, Dr. Montgomery?" Bradley asked, turning back to Jackson.

"I, uh... Uh, I found something in Madeline's purse today. It's probably nothing, but we thought you might want to check it out," Jackson replied with mild embarrassment.

"Sure, what did you find?"

"This," Marwin said, holding out the baggie with the packet in it.

Bradley held the baggie up to inspect it. "Any idea what it is?"

"Not really. We're guessing it is some sort of vitamin or herb," Jackson replied, dropping his eyes to the floor.

"I'm the one who wanted you to look at it," Marwin ground out through gritted teeth. Marwin then described the mysterious doctor's appointments with the gynecologist, as well as the vitamins and herbs that Madeline had begun taking. He next related the details of the meeting between Shoehorn and Jackson the previous night. At this point Jackson excused himself, leaving the two adversaries alone.

"Well, that does seem odd, based on what Dr. Montgomery told us about his wife," Bradley mused. "I'll get this run through the lab and see what's in it. Hopefully we'll get the results in a couple of days."

"A couple of days? Why the hell would it take a couple of days to run an assay?" Marwin asked hotly.

Eyeing Marwin closely, Bradley explained slowly, "The contents of a package that likely contains vitamins cannot take priority over DNA fingerprinting. I'm afraid the lab has a few more important criminal cases to work on before they can get to this one."

Furious, Marwin said, "Forget it. If you don't want to help us, I'll find someone who will. I guess you have more important things on your mind right now."

Bradley, immediately picking up on the inferred jab stated, "Look, I don't know what your problem is, but it isn't with me." After a brief pause, he added, "Maybe if you could take care of your own business better, you would be in a better position to help your friend here."

Fists and jaw tightening, Marwin replied, "I don't know who in the hell you think you are, but I am not going to listen to any shit from you."

Taking a step closer himself, Bradley retorted, "I'm not the one who's being shitty here."

Jackson re-entered the room and quickly surveyed the situation. He immediately stepped between Marwin and Bradley. "Guys, take it easy!"

Turning to Bradley, Jackson asked, "Do you think you can help us?"

"Yeah, if they can get around to it," Marwin snapped.

"I'm sure Detective Jinswain will get it taken care of as soon as he can. Mine is not the only case in town," Jackson said, trying to ease the tension in the room.

Staring at Marwin, Bradley said, "I will get this to the lab first thing in the morning. I'm not sure how long it will take, though."

"No problem, thanks. Knowing the contents isn't going to change the outcome, anyway," Jackson concluded sadly.

As Jackson walked Bradley to the door, Marwin appeared to ask, "Did you tell Sherlock here about the asshole posing as the reporter?"

"He contacted you again?" Bradley asked, stopping just short of the door.

"Yeah, just a couple of hours ago, actually," Jackson replied, then relayed the earlier conversation to the detective.

After listening quietly, Bradley stated, "Something is not right here."

"No shit, Sherlock," Marwin interjected sarcastically. "You think it's unusual for someone to impersonate a reporter and harass a man after his wife commits suicide? You must be a genius!"

Taking a breath to retort, Bradley stopped. Visibly restraining himself, through clenched teeth he said, "There is more to this than it appears. I want to go home and put all the pieces together, see if I can make any sense out of everything. I'll call you tomorrow."

An awkward tension filled the room as Jackson closed the door behind Bradley. He and Marwin made their way back to the study. Finally, Marwin apologized. "I'm sorry about all of that. I don't know what got into me."

Jackson turned to face his friend and long-time associate. "Don't sweat it. I know you have a lot on your mind. Why don't you get some sleep? Maybe things will look brighter in the morning."

Eyeing his friend with fondness as well as sadness, Marwin replied, "You don't actually believe that bullshit, do you?"

"No, not really; but it sounded like something a doctor should say."

"Good. I was starting to worry about you. I was afraid you were getting soft in your old age," Marwin said with a smile.

CHAPTER 20

Marwin awakened to brilliant sunshine streaming through his window. Rolling over and glancing at the clock, he jumped straight up with a curse. He rushed first to Bogie's room, only to find it empty. He went to Morgan's room next, finding it vacant as well. Marwin called his children's names with increasing panic as he headed down the stairs.

"Down here, Dad," the reply drifted to him from below.

Breathing a huge sigh of relief, Marwin entered the kitchen to find Bogie and Morgan already dressed for school and just finishing breakfast.

"Why didn't you wake me?!" Marwin yelled.

"We thought you needed to sleep," Morgan replied shyly. "When we went into your room to wake you up, you were tossing and turning and mumbling in your sleep. We figured you needed to sleep some more."

Regretting his yell, Marwin proclaimed with a chuckle, "You two are the best. I'm sorry I yelled at you. I'm impressed that you guys are responsible enough to get ready on your own. I don't care what your mom says about you two, you guys are all right."

After both kids got on the bus, Marwin poured a large cup of coffee and went to the study, thinking he would try to sort out the previous night's events. Resisting the strong urge to call Destiny, Marwin instead focused on the information Jackson had shared with him. He began going through the findings, listing them one by one: the calendar with all the doctor's visits, the mysterious START notation, the calls from the imposter reporter, the supposed suicide rate increase in Knoxville women, Madeline's sudden interest in vitamins and herbs, and Jackson's violent meeting with Shoehorn. How did they all fit together? Why were there so many unanswered questions surrounding what appeared to be the routine suicide of an upstanding citizen?

Marwin felt the beginning of a headache behind his eyes. He wondered briefly if it was the puzzle of Madeline's death or the beer and bourbon from last night. Deciding it was likely due to a combination of the two, he closed his eyes and rubbed his temples, trying to recall some of the information he'd found on the herbs the other night. Eventually, he remembered that he found nothing of use and decided to shower and get ready for work. As he passed the phone, he again fought the urge to call Destiny.

***

Destiny was suffering through one of the longest days of her life. She had awakened with a raging hangover in the foulest of moods. She showered and went through the drive-thru at McDonalds for some fries and a diet Coke, just barely making it to court on time. The molestation trial was in its most difficult day; the child had taken the stand and relayed how her father had visited her at night. It was almost too much for Destiny to stomach, especially considering her hungover condition. She finally caught a break when the judge began feeling ill around lunchtime and dismissed everyone until the following day. Destiny called her office and told them she was going home, but she was informed the man who had threatened the police chief's wife had been arrested. Due to this development, she was required to go to the office to investigate that issue. After three hours, the idiot finally pleaded guilty to a lesser charge, and Destiny was finally able to go home.

Once home, Destiny changed into sweatpants and checked her answering machine. She had thought about Marwin often that day and the mess that was their relationship, but had been unable to call him. She silently prayed that he had left her a message; she desperately needed to see him and get things straightened out. The machine showed seven messages. The first three were from her mother, whom she had forgotten to call back. These were followed by three hang-ups and a neighbor wanting to borrow some flour. *Dammit*, thought Destiny with a weariness entirely too vast for someone of her age. She curled up on the couch, hugged herself tightly, and allowed the tears to flow as the last light of a shitty day began to fade.

***

Marwin's day was like Destiny's: long and frustrating. Apparently, Knoxville was besieged with an unusually early outbreak of influenza. Marwin spent the day counseling patients and physicians on the necessity of beginning antiviral therapy within the first 48 hours of the onset of symptoms. Many of his patients had taken his advice and visited their doctors, so he eventually ran out of Tamiflu and amantadine and was left with only a few rimantadine tablets. He hoped his order would replenish his stock tomorrow. If his wholesaler was out of stock also, it would be a long day.

As he drove home, he decided to call Destiny and get things worked out, one way or the other. He had called her office once, but was told that she was unavailable. He didn't get the chance to call her again due to the onslaught of sick patients.

***

Detective Bradley Jinswain awoke from a fitful night's sleep still feeling tired, both mentally and physically. His mind had whirled for most of the night with thoughts of Destiny. He couldn't believe the way she had acted. He also couldn't believe that he'd turned down her offer of sex. He had tossed and turned until 2 a.m., when he finally gave up and went into the kitchen to make a banana smoothie. He took the smoothie to the living room and sat in the dark for two hours before he finally dozed off. Thanks to his awkward sleeping position on the couch, his back ached and his neck was horribly stiff. Stumbling into the kitchen, he found he had not set the automatic coffee maker and so, had no waiting java. Checking the clock, he saw it was already past nine and thought, *I'd wanted to get to the lab early.* Deciding to skip the coffee, he headed to the shower with his caffeine-deprived mind screaming incoherently.

MOON OVER KNOXVILLE

After a quick shower, Bradley pulled on a pair of tan trousers and a blue sweater. Opening the door to too-brilliant sunshine, he trudged toward his beat-up Honda Civic. Turning the key, he was greeted by the *rur-rur-rur* sound of a dead battery. *Shit*, he thought, climbing out of the clunker. Fifteen minutes later, he had jump-started the battery and was flying down Middlebrook Pike. Weaving in and out of traffic, he was greeted by many people honking and signaling that they thought he was number one.

Finally arriving at the Knox County Police Department, Bradley saw it was almost eleven o'clock. He had hoped to be at the lab by seven to get a jump on things. He'd hoped to convince Vince Atkins, the director of the lab, to process his sample ahead of the items already logged in. He rode the elevator down to the basement, where the lab resided with the morgue.

As the elevator doors opened, he was assaulted by a blast of cold, damp air and a musty smell that reminded him that he hadn't eaten anything yet. Considering the way his stomach was doing flip-flops, Bradley was silently thankful he didn't have to go to the morgue. He tried to assemble the story he'd present to Vince while walking down the dimly-lit hallway. He knew he should log the sample in officially, but the paperwork alone could take days and the results would take forever. Knoxville's crime rate had doubled in the previous fifteen years. When he first became a detective, the lab was minimally used, mostly to identify drug substances. However, now it had become constantly flooded with DNA samples from all sorts of different tissue types.

Entering through the stained-glass door with the word LAB etched into the glass, Bradley saw Vince Atkins seated at a desk, peering into a microscope.

"Close the damned door," Vince snapped without looking up.

Vince Atkins was 45 years old and had been the director of the Knox County Lab for twelve years. When he was promoted at the age of 33, he was the youngest person to ever hold the title of director. He had graduated summa cum laude from Duke University and had taken a job at St. Jude's Children's Hospital as a pathologist straight out of school. Vince quickly showed his knack for unraveling pathological mysteries and soon became the most requested pathologist by the Memphis Police Department. Born and raised in Knoxville, Vince longed to return to the "right end of the state." He was terribly devoted to the University of Tennessee and desperately wanted to get back to his home. When the former director suffered a myocardial infarction while in the throes of passion with his children's (barely) eighteen-year-old babysitter, Vince applied for the job. Based on extensive, glowing recommendations from the Memphis Police Department, he was given the position. It also didn't hurt that the other applicant, the head pathologist at Baptist Hospital, was once found urinating in the street after a night on the town. Vince was given the job with a wary eye; however, in three months' time, his hard work and likeable, although somewhat grouchy attitude won over the doubters. The Knox County Lab was more organized than it had ever been, and the number of convictions lost due to lab error was almost non-existent.

"Mornin', Vince," Bradley said, closing the door behind him.

"What the hell do you want?"

"I just came by to see if you wanted to go to lunch. You hungry?" Bradley said lightly.

"Yeah, right—and my mother is a virgin. Just cut the crap and tell me what you want," Vince grumbled, finally looking up.

Bradley extended his hand, but seeing the nitrile gloves, realized the gesture would be wasted. "I need a favor," he admitted.

"No shit, Dick Tracey. I thought you came down here to freeze your ass off and then wait for me so we could go eat caviar and drink champagne. I'm crushed."

Ignoring Vince's sarcasm, Bradley stated, "I need you to analyze some powder for me." Before Vince could fire off another retort, Bradley continued, "It's important. I wouldn't ask if it wasn't."

"Do you have an order?" Vince inquired, already knowing the answer.

"Uh, no. I really didn't want to have to wait that long. My boss wouldn't sign off on this anyway. He thinks this is a complete waste of time." Bradley invented this last part on the spot, hoping Vince's disdain for his boss would work in his favor.

"So, the old asshole thinks you're wasting time and money, huh? Tell me what you've got and give me a reason not to believe him."

Bradley studied Vince silently, trying to decide how much to divulge. "Save the horseshit story. I know you aren't going to tell me the whole story anyway. Just tell me why I should do this for you," Vince commanded.

"Because I think the powder is important to a case of mine. I'm not sure why; I just feel it."

"This a murder case?" Vince asked.

"No, suicide," Bradley confessed.

"What the fuck? A suicide? Why would I put my ass on the line for a suicide case? I think you're losing it, Jinswain," Vince said, turning back to the microscope.

"Vince, I promise it's important. I wouldn't ask if I wasn't sure that it is crucial." Hesitating, Bradley added, "Plus, you owe me."

Raising his eyes slowly to meet Bradley's, Vince asked, "If I do this, will we be clean?"

"Yes," Bradley responded.

"What guarantee do I have that you won't pull this shit again?" Vince asked.

Smiling, Bradley said, "No guarantee. There are only two guarantees in life—death and taxes. But, I will give you my word that we are square now."

"You're willing to call things square for a fucking suicide? Man, I can't believe you," Vince said incredulously.

"So, does that mean you will do it?" Bradley implored.

"Yeah, just leave the shit here and I will run it tonight."

"Tonight? Can't you get to it before then?"

"Look, you ungrateful fucker, I'm going to stay after hours to do it on my time—and use the county's resources, which could get my ass fired. So take it or leave it!"

Sensing that he has pushed as far as he could, Bradley backed toward the door and said, "Tomorrow is cool. I'll stop by in the morning. Thanks."

"Yeah, eat shit before you come," Vince suggested, turning back to the microscope.

As Bradley headed to his office, he thought about Vince Atkins. He first met Vince at his introduction to the Knoxville Police Department, shortly after arriving back in town. He'd had no personal dealings with Vince until the previous November. Bradley had been part of an undercover investigation of a local deli owner who was supposed to be making book in the back. Starting in early September, Bradley had been posing as a gambler who played football parlay cards dispensed by the owner of the deli. Bradley played parlay cards every week—but he never won, so the owner never had to pay him. However, he gladly accepted Bradley's money every Friday night. On the Friday night before the deli was to be raided, Bradley went in to drop off his cards just like he had been doing for several weeks. As he entered, he saw the owner give a roll of cash to a man in a trench coat. The man quickly stashed the cash in his inside pocket and turned to leave. Bradley locked eyes with the man on his way out, and they instantly recognized each other. The man in the coat was Vince Atkins.

Bradley never mentioned seeing Vince take the cash to anyone, not even to Vince himself. Still, Vince knew that Bradley had seen him taking money from the owner, who was arrested and jailed the following day. Bradley hoped the analysis of the powder would be useful, since he was letting Vince off the hook for it.

***

Based on the workload Marwin faced the next day, the flu outbreak had apparently reached epidemic proportions. Fortunately, he had received several boxes of Tamiflu in his order. Unfortunately, it had all disappeared by 2 p.m. The day was a whirlwind of people coughing, the phone ringing, and of course, the ubiquitous arrogant doctor who didn't have a clue and wouldn't listen to reason. By mid-afternoon, Marwin was out-of-sorts, shaky, and had a headache because he didn't have time to eat lunch. Just as he tried to eat the cold cheeseburger that his technician had brought him almost three hours earlier, he was informed that the phone was for him.

Damn, Marwin thought. "Can you take it?" he asked the technician. "I have got to eat something or you're going to be completely unsupervised, since I will be in a hypoglycemic coma on the floor."

"Uh, no, I tried. He said he will only speak directly to the pharmacist. Sorry," the technician replied.

"Shit," Marwin said aloud, and reached for the phone for what seemed like the thousandth time that day.

"This is the pharmacist," Marwin said gruffly.

"This is Dr. Ernie Shoehorn," the voice replied, then spouted off a phone number. "I want to give Madge Wilson some Tamiflu seventy-five milligrams. She is to take one tablet daily for ten days to treat flu symptoms. Thank you."

"Whoa, whoa, whoa!" Marwin virtually yelled into the phone.

"Is there a problem?" Dr. Shoehorn said tersely.

"Actually, there are a few problems," Marwin snapped. Before the doctor could reply, Marwin continued. "First, I'm not a damned Dictaphone. Second, the dose is not correct. The dose to treat influenza is seventy-five milligrams twice daily for five days."

"That is not the dose that I wish to prescribe. I want her to take one tablet daily for ten days," Shoehorn said with venom.

"Well, that will be impossible too, since they don't make tablets. The adult dose only comes in capsules," Marwin barked.

"Look, I am the doctor and that is the dose that I want her to take. So just fill the prescription without giving your opinion."

"Listen, you egomaniac, unless you can show me that she has severely impaired renal function, I am not filling that dose. Even if she does have impaired renal function, the duration is still only five days, not ten!"

"You will fill whatever dose I prescribe because I am the doctor, and you are just the pharmacist!" Shoehorn declared pompously.

Red creeping all the way around his field of vision, Marwin said, "You can just call it in somewhere else, because I am not doing it that way."

"What is your name and license number?" Shoehorn demanded

"Marwin Gelstone. That's G-E-L-S-T-O-N-E. Make sure you spell it right. My license number is one-six-one-zero-two. Make sure you get that right, too!"

"I will be calling Mrs. Wilson and telling her that I am phoning this and all future prescriptions to another drugstore," Shoehorn threatened.

"You can phone it wherever you like. However, Mrs. Wilson is a life-long customer, so I will be counseling her on the correct way to take her medicine. You can have them label it with whatever asinine directions you want, but I promise you she will take it the correct way."

"Who the hell do you think you are?" Shoehorn thundered.

"I am a pharmacist who knows drugs and is concerned about my patients. Goodbye, Dr. Shoehorn."

Marwin slammed down the phone and mumbled obscenities under his breath all the way to the breakroom, where his ice-cold cheeseburger waited. Marwin tossed the burger in the microwave and returned to the counter to find four phone lines on hold, and three patients in line at the pharmacy register. On his computer terminal was a stack of new prescriptions waiting to be filled. Marwin took a bite of his burger, burned his mouth, and surveyed the scene before him. With a deep sigh, he headed to the counseling area to talk to customers, chewing as he went.

Before he could reach the counseling area, the phone rang again. With all employees busy, Marwin answered the phone while signaling to a waiting customer with an upraised finger. "Professional Pharmacy," he said.

When no response came, Marwin shouted into the phone, "Can I help you?! This is the pharmacist!" Still hearing only silence, Marwin was about to hang up when he finally heard Destiny say, "Hey, it's me."

CHAPTER 21

The phone rang at the Montgomery residence at 7:10 a.m. Jackson, who had been awake until after 4:00 a.m., fumbled for it sleepily. "Hello," he said groggily.

"Good morning, Boss!" Helen exclaimed cheerfully.

"Helen, what are you doing? Is something wrong?" Jackson asked, trying to quickly shake the cobwebs out of his muddled brain.

"Nope, nothing is wrong. I just thought it was time that you got back into your old routine. Maybe start thinking about coming back to work?"

"Uh, I don't think so, Helen. It's only been a couple of weeks. I don't think I could concentrate right now."

"Dr. Montgomery, your patients need you. I know it has only been a short time, but the healing needs to start—and it can't start until you get back into your old life and try to move forward."

Sadness suddenly overwhelmed Jackson. He whispered, "Maybe I don't want to move forward."

Her voice softer, yet still firm, Helen replied, "I'll be there in twenty minutes. Have some coffee ready, and I'll pick up some bagels and fruit."

"I don't think that's a good idea, Helen. I appreciate what you are trying to do and all that you've done, but I'm just not ready," Jackson said despondently.

"I'll see you in nineteen minutes. Bye," was Helen's response. She hung up before he had a chance to argue.

Shit, Jackson thought, falling back on the pillows. *Maybe I'll just stay in bed. I don't care if she comes over or not. I'm just not ready to start life* back without Madeline. Fuck it; I'm going back to sleep. Jackson pulled the covers up over his head.

Five minutes later, Jackson found himself in the shower, letting the scalding water beat down on his back in hopes of loosening some muscles. He had decided to get up so that he could explain how he felt to Helen, make her understand that he wasn't ready to move on.

After stepping out of the shower, he wrapped a towel around his waist and padded downstairs to make coffee; he had neglected to set the coffeemaker the night before. Just as he hit the bottom step, the doorbell rang. Glancing at the clock on the mantle, he saw it was 7:32. Damn Helen and her punctuality. Opening the door, he was greeted by a blast of cold November wind, along with Helen.

"Nice to see you dressed up for me," Helen remarked.

"Uh, yeah. I'm moving a little slow this morning."

Striding into the kitchen energetically, Helen ordered, "Go get dressed while I set up breakfast. Oh, and dress warm. It's cold outside today."

Staring at her and feeling he had completely lost control, Jackson trudged back upstairs to get dressed.

When he returned, Jackson found Helen at the table with a plate of kiwi, fresh pineapple, and honeydew melon. A second plate contained bagels of at least three varieties.

"Wow, maybe you coming over wasn't such a bad idea after all," Jackson admitted.

"Me or the food?" Helens asked playfully.

Feeling as if a weight had been lifted off him, Jackson said, "Both, I think. Both."

Helen and Jackson talked idly about the office and what had transpired over the last couple of weeks. As they talked, Jackson realized that he had indeed missed his patients. Finally, there was a lull in the chatter; they finished their breakfast in silence.

Abruptly, Helen said, "Jackson, you need to come back to work. We need you. Your patients need you. And most of all, you need your patients. I know you have suffered a terrible tragedy, and I'm not trivializing it, but it is time to move on."

After a brief pause, Helen added, "Madeline would want you to move on, not just sit at home and mourn her."

Hurt and anger immediately rose up within him. Jackson retorted, "If she didn't want me to mourn, why the hell did she kill herself?"

Looking Jackson straight in the eye, Helen responded, "I don't know. I wish I could answer that. What I do know is that the woman that I knew and that you loved would not want you to crawl in a hole and become a hermit. She would want you to be happy and live the life you deserve."

No immediate reply came to Jackson, but a tear slowly leaked down his face; he tried for the thousandth time to understand what had happened to his life.

Wiping his tear away, Helen took both of Jackson's hands in hers and said, "I'll clean up when we get back. Get your coat and meet me in the car. I'll drive."

Staring dumbly at her and again feeling like a puppet, Jackson walked to the closet for his coat.

***

Marwin, caught completely off-guard, could only stammer, "Uh, hey, Des."

"Are you busy? Do you have a minute?" Destiny asked.

Looking at the chaos around him, Marwin said, "Nah, not any busier than normal. Besides, I wanted to talk to you anyway."

"I know. We need to talk. Could you come by tonight after work? I should be home by the time you close."

"Sure. Do you want me to pick up some food, or a bottle of wine?" Marwin asked, his spirits immediately lifting.

"No, not really. Why don't we just snack on some shrimp and cheese or something...?"

Marwin's stomach growled with hunger, but he replied, "OK, cool. I'll see you around six-thirty, or I'll call if it looks like I'll be any later."

"OK, see you then," Destiny replied.

"Des? I love you."

For a brief, agonizing moment, Marwin heard no response. Finally, Destiny said, "I know. I love you, too. Bye."

Marwin hung up and walked trance-like toward his waiting patient, his cheeseburger with one bite gone growing cold yet again.

***

When Jackson and Helen returned home, the sun was sinking low in the southwestern sky. They had spent the entire day just riding through the surrounding countryside. Helen had driven and Jackson had talked, intermittently at first. Later, the tension seemed to ease and they were able to enjoy the beautiful, but frigid, day. They had talked of work at great length; Helen brought Jackson up to date on all the patients. The conversation eventually turned to Madeline's death. Jackson told Helen about the suicide letter, calendar, and mysterious packet. He did not mention the imposter from the Sentinel.

Helen listened as Jackson's story rolled out. He was so engrossed that he didn't notice that Helen had driven to the cemetery where Madeline was buried.

Finally realizing where he was, Jackson asked, "What are you doing? Why are we here?"

Ignoring his questions, Helen asked one of her own. "Have you been here?"

"A couple of times. Mostly right after she died, not so much in the last week or so."

"Well, I think you need to go talk to Madeline," Helen opined.

Jackson looked at Helen strangely, opened his mouth to protest, then thought better of it and opened the car door. Jackson didn't wait to see if Helen was getting out too; he suspected she wasn't. As he approached the slightly sunken, uneven gravesite, his mind reached out to his wife. He sank to the cold ground and traced Madeline's name with his finger, quietly talking to his lost love, and the God he'd left behind years ago.

When Jackson's eyes finally focused on his surroundings again, it was almost completely dark. Startled, he rose stiffly and turned to look for Helen. He could barely make out her shadowy outline behind the wheel of the car. As he walked slowly toward the car, Helen opened the door, getting out to meet him halfway.

"Feel better?" she asked.

"I don't know. I can't believe it's dark! How long was I over there?"

"Almost two hours."

"I'm so sorry, Helen. I didn't mean to be here that long. I guess I just lost track of time," he replied bashfully.

"It's OK; I brought you here, remember?" Gazing into his eyes, Helen put her arm around Jackson. "Let's go home, Dr. Montgomery."

***

Detective Bradley Jinswain's phone rang at 6:30 a.m.

"Hullo," he answered groggily.

"Good morning, Detective. Rise and shine," an overly cheery voice said.

"Who is this?" Bradley asked, trying to orient himself.

"Vince Adkins, from the lab."

Instantly awake, Bradley said, "What did you find?"

"I'm not exactly sure, yet. I ran the normal tests, and all I can tell you right now is that it's an organic compound. It is not any vitamin or mineral, nor is it an illicit drug that's in our database."

"Well, what the hell is it?" Bradley asked, frustrated.

"I don't know. I have a friend at the FBI in Langley, Virginia. I'm going to send it to him. They have more sophisticated equipment there, so he should be able to identify it with no problem."

"OK," Bradley answered, disappointed. "Uh, are you going through official channels?"

"No. He and I go way back, so he's going to keep it off the record—for now."

"OK, good. Maybe you should just send him half; keep half in case we have to run this through officially, later," Bradley suggested.

"Don't worry. I'll take care of all the red tape, if needed."

Laughing, Bradley said, "I don't care what the chief says about you; you're all right."

"Yeah, yeah... I'll call when I have the results," Vince replied.

CHAPTER 22

With the coming of darkness came swiftly plunging temperatures. Marwin shivered as he started his car. He turned on the heat, which immediately blasted cold air in his face and up his pants. Cursing, he turned the heat off and headed toward Destiny's. His stomach was in knots; he dreaded and anticipated the upcoming meeting in equal measures. He played out scenarios in his head as he drove toward her apartment.

Should I be mad? Grateful? Excited? Horny? No, not horny; that wouldn't be well received, I'm sure. He wanted to just be himself, but there was a problem; he wasn't sure how he felt, exactly. He had too many emotions swirling through his mind. Shaking his head with dismay, Marwin wondered why he bothered trying to play out a scenario anyway. How many times had he planned out an evening, only to have it turn to shit within the first five minutes? Reaching his destination just as this realization came to him, he pulled into Destiny's apartment complex.

Destiny answered the door dressed in loose-fitting jeans and a sweatshirt.

"Hey, come on in," she invited him, with what Marwin perceived as a genuine smile.

As Marwin stepped into the entryway, Destiny moved close. He immediately engulfed her in his arms. They remained this way, her head on his chest, for several minutes. Neither one wanted to break the embrace or the moment, both enjoying the comfort of familiarity. Destiny finally pulled back but didn't release Marwin's hand. They walked silently into the living room together.

"Thanks, I needed that, "Marwin admitted

"Me, too," Destiny agreed.

"I've missed you so much, Des. I was afraid that I'd lost you."

"Shh, you haven't lost me. I'm right here, and I'm not going anywhere."

With tears welling up in his eyes, Marwin reached for Destiny again and kissed her softly on the lips.

"Thanks; I needed that!" she said, laughing.

"Me, too," replied Marwin.

They sat together closely, talking softly. Destiny finally told Marwin tearfully about Bradley.

"Do you hate me?" she asked timidly.

"No, of course not. I love you. I'm not happy, but I appreciate your honesty."

They sat in silence for a few minutes, sipping chardonnay, eating shrimp cocktail, and nibbling on Munster cheese with whole-wheat crackers. Marwin ate ravenously at first, then finally slowed to a more civilized pace. Destiny rose and went to the refrigerator to fetch more wine. She returned holding some sort of long, sausage-looking product.

"Whatcha got there?" Marwin asked with interest.

"Some Cajun smoked sausage that I picked up today. The guy at the store said it has a pretty good kick to it."

"Cool, let's give it a try now," Marwin suggested.

Destiny sliced the sausage, popping a thin piece in her mouth. She handed Marwin a slice, too.

"Mmm, that's good," she moaned.

"Yep, but it doesn't seem that spicy to me," Marwin said.

"Yeah, you're right," Destiny began, but stopped abruptly. "Holy shit!" she stammered, her eyes widening.

"Holy shit!" she repeated, reaching for her glass. "This stuff is hot as hell!"

Marwin laughed as he began to feel the Cajun spices burn.

Wine not relieving the burn, Destiny headed to the kitchen for ice water. Following her, still laughing, Marwin asked, "You OK?"

Panting, Destiny replied, "Yeah, I think so. Damn, that was hot."

Just then, Destiny let out a massive sneeze, followed closely by another. "God bless you twice," Marwin offered.

Destiny kept sneezing: three times, four, five. "Did you inhale the sausage or eat it?" Marwin teased.

"I ate it, but something has really set me off. Could I be allergic to it?" she gasped.

"I doubt it. First, food allergies usually present as rashes and itching or trouble breathing, not sneezing. Second, it is way too soon for the reaction to occur. The stuff barely hit your stomach, so I don't think it had time to cause that large of a dump of histamine into your system."

Continuing to sneeze, albeit less frequently, Destiny said, "Well, maybe I have become allergic to you."

Marwin didn't comment but looked at Destiny intently.

"Hey, what's wrong? I was kidding," she said.

"Nothing. I know... It isn't that, it's something else." Walking toward the door distractedly, Marwin said, "I gotta go. I need to look into something."

"Go? I was only kidding! Please don't leave."

Coming back to take her hands into his, Marwin said, "I know. I'm not leaving because of that. I just had a wild idea about Madeline's death, and I need to go look some stuff up."

"Madeline's death?" Destiny asked, perplexed.

"Yeah, I'll explain later. It is probably a wild goose chase, but your sneezing fit triggered something deep in my brain."

"What?" Destiny asked.

"I don't want to say now, because it's probably nothing. Let me check into it first; then I will tell you, one way or another."

Pulling Destiny close, Marwin kissed her deeply and said, "I love you. I'll call you later."

"OK... You better," Destiny said, before kissing Marwin one more time.

***

On the drive home, Marwin tried to focus on Destiny's sneezing attack. Seeing her sneeze repeatedly had triggered something in his brain. He remembered a drug that produces sneezing as a major side effect. He couldn't quite remember the name, but thought it was a sedative.

He drove blindly, not really seeing the red lights or stop signs, just stopping and starting when appropriate. His mind continued digging for the drug name, but without success. Frustrated, he turned his thoughts to Madeline's death. Jackson had said that she'd been ill with allergies prior to her suicide. They had found several partially-full boxes of allergy medications in her bathroom. It appeared she might have tried several different ones; apparently the other ones hadn't worked.

What else had Jackson said? Madeline had uncharacteristically bad breath that had spontaneously resolved along with her allergies. What was the timeline involved? Thinking hard, Marwin remembered Jackson saying the halitosis and allergies had begun about six weeks prior to her death. He'd said they both lasted a couple of weeks, then just disappeared.

I assumed it was ragweed, Marwin thought. *But ragweed isn't gone in two weeks, so that isn't likely.* Before he could give it any more thought, he realized he was home.

Marwin entered the house and headed straight to the computer in the study. Just as he was beginning his search, Bogie came in. "Hey, I'm glad you're home. I wanted to go hit in the cages tonight."

"Uh, not tonight, bud. It's too late," Marwin replied distractedly.

"No, it's not. The cages are open until eleven."

"Yeah, but you don't need to be out that late on a school night," Marwin countered.

With anger and hurt in his voice, Bogie said, "I should have known you wouldn't take me. You never do what you say!"

As Bogie stomped from the room, Marwin said, "Hey, wait a minute. Come back here."

Ignoring Marwin, Bogie continued to the stairs.

"Bogie, stop!" Marwin commanded.

"Forget it, Dad. I don't want to go anymore anyway," Bogie said, still ascending the stairs.

MOON OVER KNOXVILLE

Hearing the hurt in Bogie's voice, Marwin said, "Come down here, please."

Bogie stopped and retreated a few steps to look defiantly into his father's eyes. "Look, Dad, just forget it. I probably couldn't hit shit, anyway."

With a huge pang of guilt stabbing his heart, Marwin said quietly, "Go get your stuff. I'll call Mrs. Walker next door to let her know we're gonna be out for a while, and that Morgan will be here alone."

"You sure, Dad?" Bogie asked doubtfully.

"Yeah, Bud. Get your stuff, and I will meet you in the garage."

"Ok, cool!" Bogie replied, bounding up the stairs.

***

The ride to The Hitting Zone was, for the most part, quiet. Marwin tried to draw Bogie into conversation with questions about school, girlfriends, etc., but to no avail. Bogie repeatedly answered in a dull monotone: "Yeah," "No," or "I don't know." Marwin finally gave up; Bogie switched incessantly from one rap station to another in an apparent search for the Rapper's Holy Grail.

Marwin tried to focus on the elusive drug that causes sneezing, but was unable to concentrate. His mind continually returned instead to Bogie, and he reflected on what a huge mess he was making out of his children's lives. *What a rotten father I am*, he thought. *Maybe the kids should spend more time with Lindsey. She probably wouldn't screw things up the way I have.*

The atmosphere in the batting cages was strangely quiet. Marwin had never been here this late at night, and he was surprised to find only two employees on site. The usual cacophony was replaced only by the sound of a radio blaring some classic Ted Nugent on Rock 104.

"Is it too late to get a cage?" Marwin asked the disinterested teenager at the register.

"No, but I can only let you have a half hour, since we close in forty minutes."

"A half hour is fine. My arm will be shot before then, anyway."

"Would you rather have a cage with an Iron Mike?" asked the teenager, referring to an automatic pitching machine.

"Nah. I'll throw, so any cage is fine. Thanks."

"OK, cool. Just take cage one, then," the boy instructed.

After paying the teenager, Marwin and Bogie climbed into the batting cage. Marwin windmilled his right arm several times. "Warm me up, will you?" he asked Bogie.

"Sure," Bogie replied, grabbing his glove.

Once Marwin's arm was loosened up, he said, "OK, we'll start with straight fastballs. Make a good strong swing every time."

Bogie hit the first few pitches weakly, then missed the next one completely.

"Shit!" he exclaimed. "I told you I can't hit!"

Marwin leaned on the L-screen and said, "Relax, will you? There is nothing wrong with you. You're just not getting your hands in front of the ball, so your wrists are breaking too early and you're rolling over the top of the ball, instead of driving through it."

Marwin walked to Bogie and held a ball over the center of home plate. "Show me in slow motion how you would attack this pitch," he instructed.

Bogie reluctantly feigned a swing, but Marwin stopped him just as the bat head reached the ball.

"Stop; look at your hands. See how your right hand has already rotated before impact? Your right hand should have the palm facing up at impact. For that to happen, you have to get your hands out in front and inside the ball. Don't let them fly out, or you will swing around the ball. Let's do a couple of soft-tosses until you get the feel back."

Dropping to one knee in front of his son, Marwin tossed a ball at Bogie's mid-section. Bogie reacted quickly and drove the ball into the left side of the cage netting.

"No, you swung around it, again. Throw the knob of the bat at the ball like you are trying to hit the ball with the knob instead of the bat head."

Bogie hit the next toss straight ahead into the L-screen.

"Good! Do it again," Marwin said.

Again and again, Bogie drove the ball straight into the L-screen.

"Now you're driving the ball!" Marwin exclaimed. "Let's see you do it off of live pitching."

Marwin retreated behind the L-screen and fired a fastball over home plate, which Bogie hammered straight back into the screen that Marwin had ducked behind. "That's the way to get your hands there first!" Marwin shouted.

"Way to rip the ball! Your dad is right; that was a shot!" a voice coming from behind Bogie declared.

Bogie stared at the stranger. Marwin asked, "What the hell are you doing here?"

"I come here most nights," Bradley Jinswain replied.

"What? Are you some kind of pedophile?" Marwin spat venomously.

Ignoring the jab, Bradley said, "Actually, I came here to find you. Your daughter said you might be here."

Momentarily ignoring the fact that Morgan was still awake and had talked to a strange man without an adult at home, Marwin asked, "What do you want with me? Is something wrong with Destiny?"

"No, this doesn't have anything to do with Destiny. This is related to Madeline Montgomery's death."

Marwin stared at Bradley, wondering what the detective had found.

"Uh, Dad, are we going to hit or not?" Bogie asked, breaking Marwin's thought process.

"Yeah... I guess we have time for a few more swings."

"Hey, you can't quit now; he was starting to really drive the ball," Bradley said.

Marwin returned behind the screen and resumed pitching, but his accuracy was poor. He couldn't keep his mind focused on the ball.

"Dad, I need some strikes," Bogie lamented.

"I'm trying, I'm trying," Marwin responded lamely.

After three consecutive pitches that would have required a ten-foot pole to make glancing contact, Bogie said, "Why don't you let him pitch?" pointing his bat at Bradley.

Silently, Marwin tossed his glove into the bucket and exited the cage.

"Is that OK with you, Mr. Gelstone?" Bradley asked.

"Just make it quick. It's getting late," Marwin said disgustedly.

Bradley worked with Bogie for a few more minutes, occasionally stopping to give instructions. As they left the cage, Bradley remarked, "You have a nice stroke. You just need to focus on letting the ball get deeper so you can drive it. You have a tendency to break your wrists too soon and roll over the ball. Next time out, try to hit every pitch to right field. That will make you wait a little longer and allow the ball to travel a little more."

"OK, thanks!" Bogie replied with a grin.

"What did you find about Madeline's death?" Marwin asked abruptly.

"Why don't we go back to your house and talk about it?" Bradley suggested.

"OK, fine. I need to get Bogie to bed, anyway."

"I'll follow you," Bradley said, holding the door for Marwin and Bogie.

CHAPTER 23

Jackson and Helen sat on his back porch in front of the ceramic fireplace, talking occasionally. They had picked up some fried chicken and potato salad; Jackson had opened a decent bottle of Riesling. At first, Jackson was embarrassed for spending the whole afternoon at the cemetery. However, Helen convinced him that she had intended for him to do just that. Helen had not tried to force Jackson to talk. Instead, she made small talk, waiting until he was ready.

Pouring them each another glass of wine and throwing their paper plates into the fireplace, Jackson finally said, "I really appreciate what you did today. I needed to go to the cemetery. I had stopped going. I don't really know why; I just couldn't make myself go. I felt like a real asshole, but I wasn't strong enough to make myself go visit her. Madeline deserves so much better than me. She always did."

"OK, stop," Helen said. "I will not sit here and listen to you throw yourself a pity party. I took you to the cemetery in hopes of you finding some closure for her death. It is time to move forward, Jackson. It has been over a month; you need to start living your life again. I'm sorry if you don't want to hear it, but Madeline left you. She decided to leave you and the life you shared, so it is time to stop feeling sorry for her—and yourself, as well."

Rising, Helen walked to where Jackson was seated and kneeled directly in front of him, so that their eyes were on the same level. Taking both of his hands into her own, she looked directly into his blue eyes and said, "Your patients need you."

After a slight pause, she added, "I need you."

***

After parking at the curb in front of Marwin's house, Bradley followed his host through the garage and into the kitchen.

"Help yourself to something to drink," Marwin called over his shoulder.

To Bogie, Marwin said, "Head on up to bed, Bud. I'll see you in the morning. Oh, good job tonight, too."

Halfway up the stairs, Bogie stopped to reply, "Thanks, and thanks for taking me."

Eyeing his son with a refreshed feeling of love and admiration, Marwin responded, "No problem. Now get some sleep. I love ya."

"Good night," replied Bogie, heading upstairs.

Grabbing a beer, Marwin asked, "So, what did you find out?"

"Well, the lab wasn't able to identify the powder," Bradley answered.

"So, you don't know shit?" Marwin asked, exasperated.

"I didn't say that. I said the lab hadn't been able to identify the powder."

Glaring at Bradley, Marwin said icily, "Couldn't you have called and left a message or something? Why did you have to track me down at a batting cage, where I was trying to spend some quality time with my son, just to tell me that you haven't found out shit?"

"I apologize for interfering with your time with your son, Mr. Gelstone. But I wanted you to know what the lab told me—and I also need to ask you some more questions," Bradley explained.

"OK, you've told me that they don't know what it is. What kind of questions do you have for me? I'm suddenly very tired, and I just want to go to bed."

"First, let me tell you what we do know. The powder is not a vitamin or mineral. It is also not any illicit drug in our database."

"Are you sure? I would have bet it was a vitamin mixture."

"Not according to the lab. They ruled out all known vitamins and minerals. They were able to tell me that it is an organic compound, but they haven't identified it yet. They are sending it up to Langley."

"Langley, Virginia?" Marwin asked incredulously. "Like, where the FBI lives?"

"Yep. One and the same," Bradley replied.

Sipping his beer, Marwin tried to compute what Bradley had just told him. "So, what do you want with me?"

"Is there anything you can think of that you didn't tell us? Anything at all?"

Marwin considered telling Bradley about his mystery drug and Destiny's sneezing attack, but ultimately decided not to; he really had no idea what he was talking about, anyway. "No, not that I can think of. I've told you everything we found."

"Has Dr. Montgomery found anything else? Has he spoken to Mrs. Montgomery's doctor again?"

"Not that I know of. I doubt he will be talking to that asshole ever again, not if he doesn't have to," Marwin opined.

"Do you know her doctor?" Bradley inquired.

"Only via the phone. In fact, I just had a run-in with him over the phone today at work. What a stupid prick he is," Marwin marveled.

Bradley listened as Marwin related the details of his run-in with Shoehorn.

"So, you think he might be a quack?"

"Hell, yes. First, he apparently believes in weeds as therapeutic medications. Second, he obviously doesn't know how to use real medications."

"So, why would Mrs. Montgomery be seeing him if he is a quack?" Bradley asked.

"That is a great question. I wish I knew the answer."

Both men were silent, each lost in their own thoughts. Finally, Marwin said, "You know, I think I'll pay the good doctor a visit. I would love to meet this dickhead in person."

Picking his words carefully, Bradley responded, "Be careful how you handle him. You don't want to do anything stupid that could jeopardize your career."

"Don't worry; I can handle myself. I think I'll stop in to see him tomorrow."

"Do you really think he'll tell you anything useful?" Bradley asked doubtfully.

"I doubt it, but you never know until you try."

"OK. Let me know if you find out anything," Bradley instructed as he turned to leave.

"I will. Des told me what happened between you two," Marwin blurted.

Bradley stopped, but didn't turn around. Marwin continued, "I just want to thank you for not taking advantage of her in a weak moment."

Acting as if he hadn't heard Marwin's words, Bradley walked out into the cold November night.

***

Marwin awoke with newfound energy and bounded to the shower. Feeling better than he had in weeks, he sang along to some Def Leppard blasting from Rock 104 as he showered. He wasn't sure if it was the upturn in his relationship with Destiny or the prospect of facing off with that prick Shoehorn, but something had seriously brightened his mood.

After showering, Marwin grabbed a cup of coffee and a bagel. Then he phoned Sam to let him know that he would be in around noon.

"Glad you called," Sam said. "I had a strange call last night from a patient. Can I run it by you?"

"Sure, shoot," Marwin agreed brightly.

"OK. Mrs. Sampson called the answering service last night after we closed. I called her back immediately, right after the service called me. She told me that her eyes had turned yellow. I thought she had jaundice and might be having some liver toxicity from one of her meds. So, I pulled her up in the computer, but all she's on is citalopram 20mg daily, propranolol 40mg TID, and lansoprazole 30mg at bedtime. None of these jumped out at me as being hepatotoxic. I asked if she had started any new meds that I didn't know about, and she said that she hadn't. I then asked if she was taking any herbal supplements and she said she takes calcium with D, some vitamins for her eyes, and just recently she started taking some red yeast rice for her cholesterol. I told her that I wasn't sure what the cause might be, but that she should not take any of her meds until she saw her doctor. I strongly advised her to see her doc this morning. You see anything that I didn't?"

"Well, more than likely, she is experiencing lovastatin-induced hepatic enzyme elevation," Marwin explained.

"How can that be? She isn't on Mevacor," Sam said, perplexed.

"She is if she's taking red yeast rice," Marwin said. "Red yeast rice contains lovastatin, which is why it is effective in lowering cholesterol. Unfortunately, it isn't a standardized dose and isn't regulated by the FDA, so most people have no idea they could be taking a potentially toxic substance."

"Damn; I had no idea," Sam said dejectedly.

"Don't sweat it. Call her doctor to let them know, and make sure they know to stop the red yeast rice until they know exactly what is going on. Also, try to find out her lipid profile and recommend something besides that red yeast crap."

"OK, will do. Thanks."

After looking up Shoehorn's office address, Marwin decided to try to be at Shoehorn's when the office opened, so he could hopefully see Shoehorn before he started mistreating his patients.

The drive to Shoehorn's office was agonizingly slow; traffic was crawling, at best, on I-40. This gave Marwin plenty of time to work through the upcoming meeting in his mind. After running several scenarios through his mind, all of which ended with him kicking Shoehorn's ass, Marwin turned his thoughts to Destiny. He decided to try to catch her before she headed to the office.

Although dialing a cell phone while driving can be hazardous, Marwin assumed he'd be safe as he was at a complete standstill. All five lanes of I-40 East resembled a parking lot.

"Hello..." Destiny answered, sounding harried.

"Hey, Des," said Marwin.

"Oh, hey Baby. What's up?" she asked.

"I'm stuck in traffic, so I thought I would see how you are. See if you ever quit sneezing."

Laughing, Destiny said, "Finally! I sneezed and blew my nose all night. I wonder where all that snot comes from."

"That's a pleasant thought so early in the morning," Marwin said.

"Isn't that what you love about me, my feminine side?"

"Your feminine side that I love has nothing to do with snot," Marwin said mischievously.

After a few moments of small talk, during which Marwin moved approximately 50 feet, he told her of his upcoming meeting with Shoehorn. They eventually made plans for a late dinner at Marwin's and said their goodbyes. Traffic finally opened up once Marwin passed the Strawberry Plains exit, and he was able to make the last of the drive quickly.

Marwin entered the parking garage and pocketed his ticket. As he walked across the catwalk leading to the professional building, he again tried to play out some scenarios in his mind. He really wasn't sure what he hoped to gain from this meeting, but he always loved a good confrontation with a quack doctor who thought he or she knew more than they really did.

Marwin found Shoehorn's office on the directory and rode the elevator to the 3rd floor. With a deep breath and a focused mind, Marwin pulled open the door to Shoehorn's office. He was greeted by four sets of curious female eyes, staring at him and most likely wondering what a man was doing alone in an OB/GYN office. Marwin nodded to the women and strode to the frost-covered window where the receptionist sat. He waited patiently for her to slide the partition over. She asked, "Can I help you?" Marwin informed her that he would like to see Dr. Shoehorn.

"Uh, do you have an appointment?" asked the woman, in a confused tone.

"No. I am Dr. Marwin Gelstone, and I would like to speak to Dr. Shoehorn about a private matter," Marwin replied calmly.

"You're a doctor?" the receptionist asked, taking in Marwin's attire of khaki pants and a well-worn sweater.

"Actually, I'm a pharmacist," Marwin responded.

"Oh," said the receptionist, immediately dismissive. "The doctor is seeing patients now; he won't be free until lunch time."

"The office just opened. He can't possibly be seeing patients yet. I suspect he is in his office drinking coffee and reading the paper. Could you please ask him if he could spare just a few minutes out of his busy day to speak to a lowly pharmacist?"

"Sir, I'm afraid the doctor is booked. I will take your name and number and ask him to call you when he has time," she offered.

"Look, I drove an hour to get here to see him, and I am not leaving until I do!" Marwin stated in an extra-loud voice.

As the receptionist opened her mouth to reply, Dr. Ernie Shoehorn appeared and asked, "Is there a problem, Tasha?"

"Yes. Doctor, this man wants to see you, but I explained that you are busy seeing patients. I offered to take his number and have you call him later, but he refuses to leave," she explained meekly.

"OK, no problem, Tasha. I will take care of it."

Turning to Marwin, Shoehorn said, "I'm Dr. Ernie Shoehorn. What can I do for you?"

"I'm Marwin Gelstone, and I want to talk to you about Madeline Montgomery," Marwin said, taking the bull by the horns.

Staring at Marwin, Shoehorn said, "I'm afraid I don't know you—and even if I did, I would not discuss one of my patients with you. That information is confidential."

"I'm aware of doctor-patient confidentiality and all the HIPAA bullshit. I'm a pharmacist," Marwin said.

Recognition finally dawning, Shoehorn asked, "What did you say your name is?"

"Gelstone. Marwin Gelstone. That's G-E-L-S-T-O-N-E. I spelled it for you yesterday on the phone, too. You must have a poor memory," Marwin spat sarcastically.

"You!" Shoehorn thundered. "Get out of my office right now!"

"Nope; not until you answer some questions," Marwin replied calmly.

"I have nothing to say to you, other than I will never send another patient to your pharmacy. Now, get the hell out of my office before I call security."

"Well, I would appreciate you not prescribing any more drugs incorrectly, so I don't have to spend all of my time correcting what you have screwed up," Marwin said in a voice easily heard throughout the waiting room.

Shoehorn's face turned red and he all but screamed, "Get out of here, now! I will be reporting you to the pharmacy board before you reach your car. You can expect a notification from them by the time you get to work. I am a prominent physician, and I will see to it that the board investigates your practice."

"Yeah, I am sure the board will jump when you contact them. I wouldn't give myself quite so much credit, if I was you. You're just another doctor who doesn't know anything about drugs and is too proud to admit it, much less try to correct it. Don't think the pharmacy board cares what you have to say, because I assure you, they don't give a shit."

Taking a step toward Marwin, Shoehorn said, "You arrogant jerk! Get out of here! I'm calling security."

Sensing that he'd gone as far as possible for the moment, Marwin said, "OK, but I'll be back; you haven't answered my questions yet. You could save us both some time if you would just take a few minutes right now."

"I'll have you arrested for trespassing if you come back here again," Shoehorn threatened.

"Ooh, I'm scared," said Marwin, like an older kid to a younger one on the playground. Marwin turned and walked out of the office, again nodding to the waiting women, who were all gaping at him.

CHAPTER 24

Westbound traffic was somewhat lighter than the earlier commute, so Marwin was able to travel along at almost the speed limit. Reflecting on his visit to Shoehorn, Marwin smiled to himself. Although he realized that he only succeeded in pissing the doctor off, not actually obtaining any information, Marwin was still pleased. *What a pompous ass! I bet I raised his blood pressure*, Marwin thought with satisfaction.

His earlier bright mood returned and Marwin cranked up the stereo, which was belting out an oldie from The Who. I guess all their songs are oldies now, Marwin mused to himself. As Marwin was preparing to exit I-40, the DJ said, "That was 'Won't Get Fooled Again' by The Who on WIMZ, Rock 104. Man, will there ever be another drummer like Keith Moon? Neil Peart may be a distant second, but no one pounds the drums like Keith Moon does. Or did, I guess I should say. Too bad he liked to party just a little too much; so much so that he OD'd on the medicine that was supposed to help dry him out! Bummer."

As the DJ faded to a commercial for a local dance club, Marwin's brain jolted wide awake. What did the DJ say about Moon's death? Something about overdosing... Marwin tried to replay the DJ's words, something in the back of his mind beginning to itch like the night before, at Destiny's.

Dammit, why can't I remember anything anymore? Marwin thought angrily. As he continued along the familiar route to his house, Marwin suddenly remembered the story of Keith Moon. Moon had been an incredible drummer for the English rock band, The Who. He was often imitated by scores of would-be rockers, but never duplicated. No one had his flair, or his lightning-fast hands. Unfortunately, his career was cut short by drugs and alcohol. He supposedly had a violent, destructive side, especially when he was loaded. Numerous attempts at rehabilitation failed; Moon had finally died due to an overdose of the drug Heminevrin, which was a U.K. brand sedative used during alcohol detoxification.

Marwin recalled this story from pharmacy school. It had been part of a lecture in the class, The History of Pharmacy, which was boring as hell and taught by a fruitcake. The only reason that the story stuck with Marwin was due to his love of rock and roll. He normally slept through most of those classes, but he remembered thinking how ironic it was to OD on a drug that was intended to dry you out. Pleased with himself for finally extracting something from the dark recesses of his failing mind, Marwin smiled and continued to his pharmacy.

Marwin arrived at the pharmacy a little before eleven and walked into the usual chaos: phones ringing incessantly, people waiting in line, and loyal customers sitting in the small coffee area shooting the breeze. Having grabbed a burger on the way in, Marwin dived into the scene and instantly became engulfed in the day. After answering hundreds of calls and filling over 200 prescriptions, Marwin finally looked at the clock above the door and saw that it was almost closing time.

With things finally beginning to settle down, Marwin instructed the staff on what was needed for the next day, then retreated to his office to perform the end-of-day activities. Grabbing a Mountain Dew from the fridge, Marwin checked his cell phone and discovered he had a message from Destiny. Feeling like a lovesick puppy, Marwin's heart rate increased as he listened to the message.

Destiny wants to get together tonight, he thought excitedly. He quickly dialed her number, beginning to form a plan in his head as he listened to the rings. Finally, she picked up on the fourth ring.

"Hello," Destiny said.

"Hey, Gorgeous!" Marwin replied.

"Oh, hey, Baby. Did you get my message?"

"Yep! What would you like to do tonight?"

"I don't really care. Why don't we pick up some food and just hang out?" Destiny suggested.

"Would you rather I cook something? I'm not sure what I even have available at home, though."

"Nah, let's just pick up something. In fact, I'll pick up the food and meet you at your house."

"OK, cool," Marwin said, even though he'd been expecting to go to her house.

"Do you have beer or wine?" Destiny asked.

"Does a bear shit in the woods?" Marwin replied.

"Great; I'll see you when you get home. How long do you think you will be?"

"I should be home by seven."

"OK, see you then. Love ya."

"Love you, too" Marwin answered, with a huge smile.

The ever-present traffic snarl on Kingston Pike failed to deflate Marwin's mood. He reflected idly that it had been a very satisfying day. First, his early morning encounter with Shoehorn; now a late-night date with Destiny. He briefly entertained the possibility of sex but quickly discounted it, as both Bogie and Morgan would be home. It was unlikely that he and Destiny would have much time alone. Still, his mood was bright and upbeat. Marwin began to sing along with the radio while sitting in the immense gridlock. WIMZ was having a Four for Thursday, when they played four songs in a row by a certain artist. They were in a block of REO Speedwagon songs when he started singing. Marwin belted out the lyrics right along with Kevin Cronin, the group's lead singer. As the last notes of "Ridin' the Storm Out" faded, the DJ said, "Up next, we have four from The Who, followed by four from the Stones, and finally, we'll finish this set up with four from Rush. Be right back, after we pay some bills."

Hearing The Who reference, Marwin again thought about the Keith Moon story and vowed to research it more. *When and if I ever get home I need to look up two things tonight: the Keith Moon story, and a drug that has sneezing as a side effect*, Marwin thought. Not long after, he finally saw his street up ahead.

When Marwin finally arrived home, daylight had completely succumbed to the dark, blustery night. Shivering, Marwin glanced skyward as he stepped out of his car. Solid blackness appeared above him, as the stars were absent on that night. A cold, northwesterly wind whipped his face, a few pellets of sleet stinging him as he walked toward the door. Being a lover of winter, Marwin smiled contentedly.

Opening the door, Marwin was assaulted by a wonderful aroma. "Wow, something smells amazing!" he exclaimed.

"Thanks, it is my new perfume, Eau de Garlique," replied Destiny with a smile.

"Ooh, that sounds delicious. You know how I love to eat garlic," Marwin said playfully.

"Ugh, gross, Dad," said Morgan from the kitchen table, with a look of disgust.

"Oops, sorry Baby," Marwin apologized as he approached Destiny from behind. Grabbing her shoulders, he spun her toward him and kissed her deeply. They embraced for several seconds before Bogie finally recommended, "Get a room, will ya?"

"That's a great idea!" Marwin said, casting a mischievous look toward Destiny.

"Ugh, gross again!" Morgan chimed in.

Pulling away from Destiny, Marwin asked, "Have you guys finished your homework?"

"Yes," they replied in unison.

"Good job, you two. Looks like dinner is ready, so I'll open some wine and meet everyone at the table."

***

Jackson sat at his kitchen table, a TV dinner growing cold in front of him. He was exhausted, both mentally and physically. At Helen's insistence, he had returned to work that day and was met by numerous sad-looking staff members who were unable to meet his eyes. All the well-meant condolences had quickly worn thin, and he had retreated to his private office. Soon, the onslaught of patients began and his day had deteriorated rapidly. Many of his patients were also unable to look at him, appearing embarrassed for him. Jackson tried to focus on the various ailments that confronted him, but he was engulfed by the pity that surrounded him instead. The day passed agonizingly slowly, but he somehow made it through without having a nervous breakdown, and left the office shortly after 6 p.m. Thank God for Helen, who had quickly recognized that the day was becoming too much for Jackson and shuffled some of his patients around. He had driven home mindlessly and sat at the table in a daze, wondering how in the hell he'd be able to go back to work the next day. The mere thought of doing it again smothered him.

Jackson was jarred out of his funk by the ringing of the phone. He momentarily considered letting the machine get it, but finally reached for the handset. Seeing Cody's number on the caller ID caused Jackson's spirits to immediately ascend. Jackson and Cody chit-chatted for several minutes before Jackson asked, "How is Sandy?"

After an ever-so-slight hesitation, Cody replied, "Well, that's why I'm calling; Sandy is pregnant, Dad."

First shock, then joy washed over Jackson. He exclaimed, "That's great, Son! When is she due?"

"Mid-July, her OB says. We think she conceived while we were staying with you," Cody said, voice dropping as if he was ashamed they'd sex while home for his mother's funeral.

Sensing his son's unease, Jackson said, "Well, at least something good will come out of your mother's death." His voice cracking, Jackson continued, "I just hate that she won't get to see her grandbaby."

"I know, Dad. Me too."

They chatted for a few more minutes about sports, work, and the upcoming shotgun wedding before Jackson said, "I'm really happy for you guys, but I am deliriously tired and need to get off of this phone before I pass out."

"OK, Dad. Take care of yourself, and we will check on you in a few days."

"Don't waste your time worrying about me. You just take care of Sandy and the new baby. They're your main concern now."

"I love you, Dad," Cody said.

"I know. I love you, too." Jackson responded.

***

With the food demolished and the chardonnay reduced by three-fourths, Marwin and Destiny sat sipping their wine and talking easily. Morgan had gone down the street to study with a friend, and Bogie was upstairs working out. Marwin looked contentedly at Destiny and not for the first time, realized how much he loved her. "You are incredible, Counselor," he said.

With a warm smile, Destiny responded, "Well, thank you, Doctor. I think you're pretty incredible, too."

"You know, I never did get to look up that sneezing attack that you had last night. Let me clean up the kitchen and we can look for some stuff on the computer."

"OK, but I think we may need a little more wine. Digging can be a thirsty job," Destiny said.

"No problem; there's another bottle already chilled."

"Well, let's get started then," Destiny said, gathering up salad plates and heading to the kitchen.

Remaining seated, Marwin watched her walk away and admired her swing. "What are you doing? You're supposed to be helping me," Destiny chastised.

"Oh, I was just thinking about dessert," Marwin said with a smirk.

"You are bad. B-A-D, bad." Destiny replied, with a throaty laugh.

Coming up behind her, Marwin pulled Destiny's hair to the side and kissed her neck. Shivering, Destiny forced Marwin backward with her butt. "You better stop that, before you start something that you can't finish."

Eyeing Destiny's taut nipples, Marwin said, "It looks like I've already started something."

Stepping toward Marwin, Destiny replied, "Maybe you have; maybe you have."

Marwin pulled Destiny to him and bent to meet her lips. Destiny willingly parted her lips, and Marwin's tongue quickly explored familiar territory. Destiny ran her hand down Marwin's back to his buttocks, and she pulled him tightly against her. Feeling him grow against her, Destiny softly moaned and sucked on Marwin's tongue and lips. Gradually, the kiss subsided. Marwin said, "That was amazing. I love kissing you. In fact, I wish I could kiss you all day, every day."

"It feels like that isn't all that you would like to do," Destiny teased, eyes dropping to the bulge in Marwin's pants.

"Well, I guess I could do more than kiss," Marwin breathed.

"Why don't you show me what you can do," Destiny purred, rubbing against him.

"I would love to—but what if Bogie comes downstairs, or Morgan comes back early?"

"They would get quite a show," Destiny offered, but she realized Marwin was right. "Shit, we should have gone to my place," she added, disappointed.

Kissing Destiny tenderly on the lips, Marwin promised, "We'll work something out tomorrow, or this weekend at the very least."

"But I might be out of the mood by this weekend," Destiny protested, grabbing Marwin's still semi-rigid bulge.

"I doubt it. I know you, you horndog," Marwin said, giving her one last squeeze on the butt.

Marwin and Destiny moved into the study, each having traded the chardonnay for a glass of hearty burgundy. Marwin pulled up a chair for Destiny and fired up the internet. They searched through various search engines, looking for drugs that induce sneezing. They came across hundreds of drugs that listed sneezing as a minor side effect, but none that highlighted it as a prominent effect.

"Dammit! Why can't I remember it? I know we learned about a drug in school that produces sneezing as a major side effect."

Sipping her wine, Destiny reached between Marwin's legs and said, "Maybe the blood is trapped down here and your brain isn't getting the necessary oxygen to help you remember."

Already starting to stir again, Marwin said, "My, aren't you the horny one tonight?"

Feeling his response, Destiny said nothing but continued rubbing. Marwin closed his eyes and took his hands off the keyboard as a soft moan escaped his lips. Destiny moved to the edge of her chair, opened her legs, and placed Marwin's knee in her crotch. Completely rigid by this point, Marwin could feel the heat through Destiny's jeans. He pushed his knee against her mound.

"Dad? Where are you?" Bogie called, bounding down the stairs and into the study.

"Shit," Marwin said, pushing away from Destiny's chair just as Bogie entered the room.

Surveying the scene, Bogie smiled sheepishly. "Uh... Sorry, guys. My bad."

"We were just looking up some stuff on the computer," Marwin stated stupidly.

Before Bogie could say anything else, Marwin asked, "What's up, bud?"

"P.C. just called and said he and his dad are going to the Homerun Zone, and he wanted to know if I could go with them."

"You've already finished your homework, right?" Marwin inquired.

"Yes, Sir."

"Well, I don't see why not. Do you need a ride?"

"No, P.C.'s dad will pick me up on the way."

"OK. Get some money off my dresser and get your bag ready."

"OK, cool! Thanks dad!" Bogie exclaimed.

As Bogie turned to leave, Marwin said, "Just remember what we worked on last night—and remember to try to do what Mr. Jinswain said."

"Will do. See you later."

Marwin turned to find Destiny looking at him curiously. "Mr. Jinswain?" she inquired.

"Yep," Marwin replied. He told her about meeting Bradley at the batting cage the previous night. He also disclosed the findings, or lack thereof, of the lab on the powder from Madeline's purse. He finished by telling Destiny about how Bradley had helped Bogie with his hitting.

Destiny seemed quietly reflective for a moment. She said, "That's great. Bradley was a great baseball player until he was injured. There was even speculation that he could have played pro ball."

"That's a shame," Marwin said. "I guess he still loves the game, and that's why he hangs around the batting cage offering help to kids to try to improve their game. That, or he's secretly a pedophile."

"Marwin! Bradley is a great guy. I can't believe you would even say such a thing."

"Easy, easy. I was just kidding. I know he must be a solid guy, because he didn't take advantage of you when he easily could have." After a brief pause, Marwin added, "I even thanked him for taking care of you."

Destiny took Marwin's hands in hers and looked him in the eye. "I love you, Marwin," she said simply. "Now, let's get back to what we were doing."

"Really?" Marwin said, reaching for her rear.

"Not that, you horndog. The computer," she said, but allowed his hands to linger.

"Oh, yeah. What were we looking for again?"

After countless fruitless searches, Marwin became frustrated. "Fuck it!"

"Why don't you come back to it later? Didn't you say there was something else that you needed to look up?" Destiny suggested.

"Yeah, I was going to research Keith Moon."

"Keith Moon? The drummer for the Stones?" Destiny asked.

"No, the drummer for The Who," corrected Marwin. "And, yes, that is who I am talking about."

Marwin related the story of Moon's overdose. Destiny appeared intrigued.

"Wow, he actually OD'd on the drug that was supposed to detox him?" she asked incredulously.

"That's the way I remember it. Let's see what we can find."

A Google search yielded over eleven thousand results for Keith Moon's death. They skimmed numerous articles before finding one that described Moon's death in detail.

"Heminevrin? I've never even heard of that drug," Destiny said, referring to the drug that Moon OD'd on.

"I'm sure not. It isn't available in the U.S. It is only available overseas," Marwin explained.

"Well, how do you even know anything about it, then?"

Marwin recounted the story of his class from pharmacy school, and how Moon's suicide was used in the example. "How do you remember all of that stuff?" Destiny asked.

"I remember what I need to," Marwin answered. "Truthfully, I don't really know anything about the drug. I just remember what it was used for, and that Keith Moon overdosed on it. Otherwise, I don't know anything about it."

Seeing a link to the drug, Marwin clicked on it and was taken to a page where a detailed description of the drug listed everything about it. As Marwin was scanning the information, he suddenly exclaimed, "Holy shit! I can't fucking believe it!"

"What?" Destiny asked, having lost focus on the computer and drifted into a buzzed, dream-like state.

"Look," Marwin directed, pointing at the screen.

Destiny followed Marwin's finger and began to read the side effects of Heminevrin. There, highlighted with bold print, was one word: Sneezing.

Destiny was talking, but Marwin barely heard her as he became engrossed in the drug's side effects. In addition to sneezing, halitosis and increased mucus production were also listed as prominent adverse effects. Continuing to read, Marwin grew cold as he came across a box of large, bold text. WARNING: abrupt discontinuation has led to suicidal ideation, as well as both unsuccessful and successful suicide attempts. Heminevrin must never be stopped abruptly and must always be tapered slowly, under the careful supervision of a qualified physician who is well-versed in the actions of Heminevrin. In addition, the concurrent use of alcohol is extremely dangerous. Heminevrin should only be prescribed to a patient who is committed to maintaining abstinence.

Marwin jumped up from his chair, asking, "What is Bradley's cell number?"

"Bradley's number? Why do you want Bradley's number?" Destiny asked, perplexed.

"Because I know what the powder that was in Madeline's purse is," Marwin replied.

CHAPTER 25

"No, that isn't it. You took your right hand to the ball, not the left. You have to take your left hand and the knob of the bat directly to the ball," Bradley instructed Bogie.

"I know. I just can't seem to do it," Bogie complained.

"Don't say you can't do it, because you can do it. You have to believe in yourself before anyone else will."

Bogie dropped his eyes downward and Bradley realized he'd hit a nerve. Seeing the boy's obvious lack of self-confidence, Bradley said, "Look, dude, I know your dad believes in you. Your friend's dad also believes in you, too." After an ever-so-slight pause, Bradley added, "And I believe in you, too."

"You can't believe in me; you don't even know me," Bogie protested defiantly.

"You're right, I don't know you. But I do know baseball, and I know that you have the potential to be a devastating hitter. I've never seen you field, but if you have even half the fielding ability that you have as a hitter, you should easily play college ball."

Staring at Bradley, Bogie let his words sink in. "You really think so?" he finally asked.

"No doubt in my mind. Now turn around and do what you know how to do."

Bogie hesitated slightly, then nodded and gave Bradley the smallest of grins before turning back to the pitching machine. "Ok, Iron Mike, bring it!" he said to the pitching machine.

As the pitching machine whirred to life and Bogie tensed for the delivery, Bradley's cell phone rang. The phone distracted Bogie; he hit the ball weakly into the net. "You pulled your head out," Bradley said, ringing phone in his hand. "You can't hit a baseball traveling at eighty miles per hour if your head is moving."

"Sorry, your phone distracted me," Bogie said meekly.

"Hello," Bradley finally answered.

"Detective Jinswain, this is Marwin Gelstone. I need to see you right away."

"Hey, Mr. Gelstone. Can you hold on for just a minute?"

"Sure," Marwin said, and heard Bradley telling someone, "That's an excuse. Quit making excuses and do your best. That is all anyone can ask of you. Just do your best."

"But...your phone," Bogie began to retort, but thought better of it. "Yes, Sir," he said, and turned back to the machine.

Returning his attention to his phone, Bradley said, "Sorry about that. What's up?"

"Was that Bogie I heard in the background?" Marwin asked.

"Well, actually, it is. I'm at the Homerun Zone, and he and a friend are here hitting. I was just giving him some pointers."

Thinking that what he had just heard had nothing to do with hitting, Marwin started to ask Bradley what the hell he thought he was doing. As he replayed Bradley's words in his head, he stopped. How many times had he told Bogie the exact same thing? No excuses! Marwin had told his son. Be responsible for your actions, both successes and failures.

"Mr. Gelstone?" Bradley asked, bringing Marwin back to their conversation.

"Uh, yeah. Just call me Marwin, OK?"

"Sure, if you'd like. What can I do for you?"

"I think I know what that powder is, the stuff from Madeline's purse," Marwin stated bluntly.

"You do? How?"

"I'll explain when you get here. Could you just give Bogie a ride, too, please?"

"Sure, his time is almost up anyway. We'll see you in fifteen minutes."

While Bogie was finishing up his time hitting, Bradley stepped outside to call Vince Atkins. He wanted to see if there had been any word from Langley on the composition of the powder. Vince said there had been no word, but he would check again in the morning. Bradley explained that Marwin thought he knew what the powder was; this led to an expletive-filled tirade from Atkins. Apparently pathologists, like doctors, don't put much stock in what pharmacists know. Wishing to put an end to the unpleasant conversation, Bradley told Vince he would call again in the morning. He collected Bogie and headed to Marwin's house with his mind full of curiosities.

***

Destiny stood there, dumbfounded, watching Marwin walk away. She eventually followed him into the kitchen, where she found him pouring cognac into two snifters. "Are we celebrating something?" she asked, perplexed.

"I'm not sure. I think so, but even if I'm right, I don't understand what it means."

"Whoa, I'm lost. What are you babbling about? You said you know what the powder is. What is it, and how do you know?" Destiny asked.

"Let's just wait until your detective friend gets here. Then I will explain everything."

"Bradley's coming here?" she asked slowly, reaching for her snifter.

"Yep. He should be here any minute."

Eyeing Marwin, Destiny took a long gulp of her cognac and silently wondered how the next hour would play out.

Exactly twenty minutes later, Bradley followed Bogie into the kitchen, where he found Marwin and Destiny seated at the table. "How did it go, Bud?" Marwin asked Bogie.

"Great! I was crushing the ball tonight. Right, Mr. Jinswain?"

"That's right. Bogie's swing is coming around pretty well. We need to get his weight a little further back to increase his power, but he is making solid contact and driving the ball well right now." After a brief pause, Bradley added, "There are some drills that I can show him to help with his balance and weight transfer, if you'd like."

"Wow! That would be awesome! Can you show me some right now?" Bogie asked excitedly.

Eyeing Marwin, Bradley answered, "No, not tonight. But if your dad says it's OK, we can go to the cages this weekend."

"Cool! Can we go this weekend, Dad?"

Slightly uncomfortable with the idea of Bogie becoming best buddies with Bradley, Marwin hesitated. But seeing the excitement on Bogie's face, Marwin agreed—and silently wondered what he was doing. After Marwin sent Bogie up to bed, the three adults moved to the study.

"So, what's up?" asked Bradley.

Marwin didn't answer, instead asking a question of his own. "Have you heard from the lab?"

"Actually, I talked to the guy before I came over here. He hasn't heard from Langley, but I'll be talking to him again in the morning. Maybe he'll have some info then."

Shit, Marwin thought. He had been hopeful that the lab report would be in and he wouldn't have to share his wild idea. He'd wanted to amaze the detective by being able to guess what the powder was. Since the report wasn't back, he'd have to go out on a limb and share his theory—which he admitted to himself was far-fetched, at best.

Realizing Bradley and Destiny were both staring at him expectantly, Marwin took a deep breath and asked, "Have you ever heard of Heminevrin?"

Frowning, Bradley said, "No, I don't think so."

"It's a sedative-hypnotic that is sometimes used to detox alcoholics. It isn't available in the U.S., but it is—or was—available in the U.K. Keith Moon, the drummer from The Who, overdosed with it and died."

Looking completely confused, Bradley said, "What does any of that have to do with the powder in Madeline's purse? Are you suggesting that this Heminevrin is in the powder that we found in her purse?"

Deciding to take the plunge, Marwin answered, "Yes." After the briefest of pauses, he added, "I'm pretty sure that's what the lab in Langley is going to find."

"But, you said the drug isn't even available here, right? How would she even get the drug?"

"I'm not sure, but I bet a certain dickhead physician might be able to fill in some blanks for us," Marwin suggested, going all-in.

"Who? Her gynecologist?" Bradley asked, bewildered.

"Yep, Mr. Weed and Seed himself."

Bradley started to say something, but instead stopped and stared at Marwin, obviously trying to make sense out of what Marwin had suggested.

Finally, Bradley said, "OK, before we ask Doctor...uh..."

"Shoehorn," Marwin supplied.

"Yeah, Doctor Shoehorn. Before we start asking Doctor Shoehorn about a drug used to detox alcoholics in Britain, maybe you should tell me how you arrived at this conclusion. And also, why we should care."

Taking a deep breath and understanding that there was still time to pull back from this foolish endeavor, Marwin looked first to Destiny, then to Bradley. He finally said, "OK, hear me out before you start inundating me with questions that I probably don't have the answers to. When I heard The Who on the radio today, it brought back memories of Heminevrin. Don't ask me why. My brain makes strange connections sometimes. Anyway, when I decided to look up some info on Heminevrin, I found some very interesting facts. First, it causes repeated sneezing as a common side effect. Increased mucus production and halitosis are also very common among patients. Madeline was plagued by all of these symptoms in the six weeks leading up to her death. The symptoms abruptly resolved, according to Jackson, shortly before she died. I think she stopped taking the drug and the symptoms went away."

"So, you think she was taking this sedative and then abruptly decided to stop taking it?" Bradley asked.

"I don't know for sure, but I think her doctor abruptly stopped it," Marwin hypothesized.

"What basis do you have for that? And honestly, so what?" Bradley asked again, still perplexed.

"Because Heminevrin has another side effect that I haven't mentioned yet—suicide attempts," Marwin stated solemnly.

"What?" Bradley stammered, wide-eyed.

"Yes. There are reports of suicidal ideation and suicide attempts upon abrupt discontinuation of the drug following a titration from a low dose to a high dose."

"My God!" exclaimed Bradley. "That would mean that Madeline's suicide was coerced. It would then be murder!"

Having been a quiet spectator until then, Destiny finally chimed in, "Yeah, but it would be a bitch to prove."

CHAPTER 26

The clock on the bedside table showed it was slightly past 6 a.m. No light emanated from the blinds, but the tinkle of snow bouncing off the window provided the start to the day. Marwin stared at the clock for what seemed like the thousandth time since going to bed the night before. He had slept fitfully at best; his mind whirled all night between brief dozing sessions. He had replayed the previous evening's events numerous times, including the part with Destiny. As he tossed and turned, he repeatedly chastised himself for calling Bradley and laying out his wild theory. He knew it was a completely crazy idea, but it felt right to him. A hundred questions remained unanswered. How did Madeline get the Heminevrin? Was Shoehorn involved? Could he really have planned to kill her? And, of course, why would he want to harm one of his patients?

The answers were not to be found in his bed, so Marwin plodded downstairs to the kitchen only to see that he had—again—forgotten to set the automatic timer on the coffee pot. Cursing quietly the entire time, he started the coffee and sat down heavily at the table, waiting impatiently for the coffee to brew. The lack of sleep, coupled with the wine and the cognac, had left Marwin with a fuzzy brain and a slightly queasy stomach. *God, who shit in my mouth?* he wondered. He headed to the bathroom to brush the fur from his tongue. Feeling queasier than ever, he poured a cup of coffee with a slightly shaky hand and returned to the table. *Damn, I must be getting old*, he thought, recalling numerous times when he drank more and slept less, with no ill effects.

The java finally punched through the fog, and Marwin's thoughts returned to Madeline's death and his cockamamie theory. *Should I call Jackson? And tell him what, exactly? That Madeline's gynecologist poisoned her with a drug from Europe, and it made her commit suicide? Jackson will think I'm the one who's unstable*, Marwin thought.

Realizing it would be foolish to even broach the subject with Jackson yet, Marwin turned his thoughts to Destiny. They really were great together, he admitted. When they were fighting a couple of weeks back, Marwin had felt as if a huge hole had suddenly appeared in his being. Since they had seemingly been back on the right track, Marwin felt whole again, and he was happier than he could remember. As his thoughts again returned to the idea of proposing to Destiny, just as they had before Madeline's death, Bogie and Morgan bounded down the stairs and into the kitchen, breaking his reverie.

Seeing that both were dressed and ready for school, and that it was after 7 a.m., Marwin realized he needed to get his butt in gear and get ready for work. He kissed Morgan and tousled Bogie's hair, then headed to the shower, hoping to remove the last of the chardonnay-induced cobwebs.

After a longer-than-normal shower, Marwin dressed in grey slacks and a dark green sweater. He grabbed a bagel and headed off to work. As he sat in his car flicking the white flakes of snow from his clothes, his phone rang.

Destiny chirped, "Good morning!"

Seeing the number on the caller ID, Marwin said, "Wow; you're already at work?"

"Yep! Been here since seven," Destiny replied brightly.

"Damn, that's early. How are you feeling this morning?" Marwin asked, secretly hoping she felt like crap, too.

"I feel great!" Destiny exclaimed.

Ah, youth, Marwin thought.

"Well, I do have this ache in my stomach," Destiny admitted. "Actually, it isn't exactly in my stomach; it's farther down, more between my legs," she teased. "What do you think I should do about it, doctor?"

Smiling as he remembered Destiny's randy behavior from the night before, Marwin replied, "I'm not sure. Maybe you need an exam."

"Ooh... When can I get one?" Destiny purred.

"I'm not sure. I think I have a full schedule already booked ahead of you," Marwin answered mischievously.

"You asshole! If that is the case, you can forget ever giving me another exam," Destiny retorted.

"Easy! I was just kidding. I'm not sure what's going on tonight. I will have to check the kids' schedule and see when we can get together. Maybe tonight or tomorrow night at your place, if they don't have anything going on."

Returning to her former playful self, Destiny said, "That sounds like a plan. Just call me this afternoon, so I'll know if I should shave my legs or not."

Their conversation finally became more serious, turning to Marwin's theory about Madeline's death. "Do you really think Shoehorn made her kill herself?" Destiny asked incredulously.

"I don't know. I know it sounds crazy. The guy is a tool and a quack, for sure, but that doesn't make him a murderer. Let's just wait and see what Bradley hears from Langley."

"OK; let me know what he finds out," Destiny instructed Marwin.

"Will do. I'll call you later. Love ya."

"Love you, too," Destiny replied sincerely.

***

Marwin's day quickly dissolved into a flood of phone calls, patients, and prescriptions. The whirlwind of activity prevented him from eating lunch, as well as thinking about Bradley's phone call—which had yet to come. As 2 p.m. came and went, Marwin's hunger and developing hypoglycemia forced him to pick up the deli sandwich his tech had picked up over two hours ago. Marwin ate the soggy, slightly stale sandwich with one hand and typed, counseled, and dispensed with the other. Eventually, the frenetic pace slowed down and Marwin was able to clean up the counter somewhat. Realizing he hadn't heard from Bradley yet, Marwin decided to call him.

"Marwin, you have a patient here to see you. They're in the counseling room," said the technician.

Briefly considering making the patient wait until after he called Bradley, Marwin changed his mind and headed to the counseling room. Upon entering the room, Marwin saw a lady with a tote bag containing what looked like a hundred different prescription drug bottles. *Fuck*, he thought. *I should have called Bradley first.*

***

Bradley Jinswain had slept poorly last night, too. The late-night meeting at Marwin's house had left numerous unanswered questions. The Montgomery suicide had stunk from day one. First, Madeline was a well-known socialite who was heavily involved in the community. She had no history of depression or psychiatric disorders. Second, the victim's husband had received phone calls from a fake reporter. Third, the suicide note seemed completely fake.

Bradley's years of experience had caused him to leave this case open on his desk even though, technically, there was no case—the coroner had signed off on suicide as the cause of death. Something in his gut told him that everything wasn't as it seemed. So, unable to sleep, Bradley had driven to his office a little before 6 a.m. Realizing it was far too early to contact Langley, he decided to dig into Dr. Ernie Shoehorn. Much of the information Bradley found was generic in nature. Shoehorn had graduated in the bottom third of his class at Duke University, then he had done his residency at the University of Michigan, in obstetrics and gynecology. Here again, he appeared unremarkable. After finishing his residency, Shoehorn returned to Knoxville, where he established his private practice. Shoehorn had no criminal record, just two traffic tickets over the previous ten years, both paid.

After glancing at his watch like a kid in Science class, Bradley scrolled down the list of students in Shoehorn's graduating class at Duke. A very interesting name occupied the top of the list, making the detective's thoughts race: *Jackson Montgomery. So, Shoehorn attended the same medical school* as Jackson Montgomery. Undoubtedly, they must have known each other. Madeline had just recently started seeing Shoehorn as a physician, yet Jackson knew nothing of it. What significance does this carry? Obviously, this connection had nothing to do with Marwin's theory from the night before, but it was still a connection between Shoehorn and Jackson Montgomery.

Seeing that enough time had elapsed to call Langley, Bradley did one more search before shutting down his computer. He checked to see if Shoehorn had been issued a traveling VISA. Interestingly, Shoehorn held a current VISA and had taken a week-long trip to the Italian Alps in March. No other trips were found, so Bradley shut down the computer and called Langley.

Waiting for the phone to be answered five hundred miles away, Bradley wondered if Marwin's theory could be accurate. Finally, the phone was answered. "Lab."

"Hey, it's Detective Bradley Jinswain in Knoxville."

"Vince Atkins asked me to call you directly about the little investigation you are helping him with. You got any news for me?"

After a long pause, the scientist said, "Uh, yeah. I've got the analysis. Where exactly did you get this stuff?"

Ignoring the question, Bradley asked, "So, what is it?"

Taking his turn to ignore a question, the scientist said, "This is some strange shit. You will never guess in a million years what that powder is."

His mouth speaking before his brain could stop it, Bradley heard himself say, "Chlormethiazole—or Heminevrin, as it is commonly called."

Stunned silence was followed by the lab contact saying, "I'll be damned. How did you know?"

"You mean that really is what you found? Chlormethiazole?" Bradley asked, disbelieving.

"Yep, sure is. I didn't even know what it was. I had to run it through our computers to find any information about it. You do know this isn't available on the American market, right?'

Bradley's mind was racing after the initial confirmation, so he barely heard the man's question. "Uh, yeah, actually I did," he finally stammered. "Look, I gotta run. Thanks for everything. I really owe you."

"Hey, wait a minute! You can't just leave me hanging like this. I want to know what you have gotten into down there."

"I can't get into that right now. Thanks again. I owe you, big time."

"You sure as hell do. I better hear from you soon," the lab tech said, his voice fading away as Bradley slowly replaced the receiver.

I'll be damned, Bradley thought. Gelstone was right.

***

"Marwin Gelstone, please," Bradley requested when the phone was answered.

"I'm sorry. Dr. Gelstone is busy. Can I take a message?" the technician replied.

"No. Tell him Detective Jinswain is on the phone. I need to speak to him right away."

"Oh, OK. Just a moment."

Less than a minute later, Marwin picked up the phone, "Hey, Bradley. Did you get the results?"

"Yes, and you were right. The powder in Madeline's purse was chlormethiazole."

"Holy shit! I can't believe it," Marwin said.

"I know, it's pretty wild," Bradley agreed.

"So, what do we do now?" Marwin asked.

"I'm not sure, really. Let me think things through, then we can formulate a plan as to what to do with this information and how to pursue it."

"OK. Just keep me up to date, please," Marwin said.

"Sure, no problem. If it wasn't for you, we wouldn't have had a clue," Bradley said with amazement.

"Well, you still found out what the powder was," Marwin reminded him.

"True, but we wouldn't have had a homicide investigation quite as quickly. We would still just have had an open-and-shut suicide case."

Stunned by Bradley's implication, Marwin asked, "Homicide? You really think so?"

"Marwin, I'm not sure—but I'm damned sure gonna find out."

After hanging up, Marwin was forced to return to the madhouse that paid his bills. Finding it difficult to concentrate, Marwin became increasingly short-tempered. Soon, he was snapping at technicians and patients alike. This action further frustrated him, and he wondered if the day would ever end. When 6 p.m. finally arrived, Marwin was mentally and physically drained. He quickly dismissed his employees and retired to his office, where he found a large stack of faxes from Jackson Montgomery's office. *Shit*, he thought. He quickly scanned the consults as he thumbed through the pages. Almost all of them were routine hypertension and dyslipidemia consults. Realizing he wasn't in the right fame of mind to deal with them, Marwin grabbed his coat, slapped off the light, and vowed to come in an hour early the next day.

On his way home, Marwin dialed Destiny's home number, but got no answer. After leaving her a message, he called his house and got Bogie. Bogie informed him that he had a project to do, and he might need some help. *Fuck!* Marwin thought. "When is it due?"

"Uh, tomorrow," Bogie said sheepishly.

"Tomorrow? How long have you known about this?" Marwin asked angrily.

"A few days, I guess," Bogie responded vaguely.

"Well, I hope it's almost done," Marwin said, still steamed.

"Not exactly, Dad. I actually haven't started yet," Bogie confessed.

"What the hell—" Marwin started. Bogie quickly interrupted him.

"I mean I haven't started putting it all together yet. I have done some research, though," Bogie said.

Seething, Marwin declared, "You better have. What is this project about, anyway?"

"I have to make a travel brochure about The Odyssey."

"Shit! I hate mythology," Marwin proclaimed. "I hope to hell you know what you're doing."

"Yeah, I do. Don't worry. I just need some help," Bogie said.

"OK, we'll finish it up tonight after dinner. Do as much as you can before I get home, please. I'll see you in about twenty minutes or so."

Hanging up, Marwin thought, *Shit, shit, shit!*

CHAPTER 27

The ringing of the telephone interrupted Jackson, who was hard at work on his second Scotch of the evening. Cursing silently to himself, he looked at the phone and debated if it was worth expending the energy required to answer it. Finally, after four rings and just prior to the answering machine engaging its dutiful self, Jackson answered wearily.

"Hello."

"Hey, Dr. Montgomery, it's Bradley Jinswain. Did I catch you at a bad time?"

"Nah, I was just emptying some things out," Jackson replied, eyeing his glass and the half-empty Scotch bottle. "What can I do for you?"

"I wanted to let you know that I have the test results back from the powder you found in your wife's purse."

This news caused Jackson to put his tumbler down with a thump and sit up straighter in his recliner. His heart rate edged northward, toward tachycardia. Not sure why he was suddenly feeling so anxious, he asked, "So, what was it? Some sort of vitamin?"

"No, Sir. The powder was chlormethiazole, a sedative-hypnotic. Did you know she was taking sedatives?"

His anger exploding, Jackson yelled, "Hell, no! I had no idea she was taking sedatives! Besides, I've never heard of that drug."

Rising, Jackson walked to his study, where he kept a Facts and Comparisons. Most physicians use the PDR, but Marwin had suggested he get a Facts and Comparisons, because he said the PDR was outdated when it was published; Facts and Comparisons was updated monthly.

"How about Heminevrin?" Bradley inquired.

"Hemi- what?" Jackson asked.

"Heminevrin. It's a sedative that is sometimes used to detox alcoholics," Bradley explained.

"Whoa; I don't know what the hell you're talking about," stammered Jackson. "I have never heard of Heminevrin, or chlormethiazole. We use chlordiazepoxide to detox drunks and keep them from having seizures."

"Heminevrin isn't available in the U.S.," added Bradley.

"Well, no damned wonder I've never heard of it. Madeline hasn't been out of the country, so where the hell did she get it?" Jackson asked himself, thin air, and Bradley simultaneously.

"I don't know, but I'm going to find out," Bradley replied, with fierce determination.

***

Marwin awoke to a brilliant November day. The sunshine cascading through the blinds had roused him from his slumber. His sleep the previous night had been minimal, but he had, of course, been out like a light when Sol decided he should get up. Rubbing the grit from his eyes, he pulled on a pair of UT sweats and a tee shirt, then headed to the kitchen to get some much-needed coffee.

Seeing no sign of the kids, he made a mental to-do list: 1) get his gambling stuff in order, 2) make plans with Destiny, 3) get the kids to clean up the house, 4) call Bradley to see if any further developments had occurred, and 5) try to get Bogie to the batting cage. Checking the clock, Marwin saw he only had about three hours before he had to call his bookie and place his bets.

Feeling slightly more awake, Marwin took his coffee into the study and fired up his football program, beginning work on a full slate of games. He had been unable to get to his gambling stuff earlier during the week due to work, Madeline's mystery, and Bogie's project on The Odyssey.

Marwin's mind still ached from the late night he and Bogie had spent working on the project, two nights before. Bogie, like himself, hated mythology and had done very little research, contrary to what he had told Marwin on the phone. They had spent hours researching Odysseus, Cyclops, the Scylla, and Calypso's Island. It was pure torture for both Marwin and Bogie. Finally, just after 2 a.m., they had finished what Marwin hoped was at least a passable brochure on Homer's world of The Odyssey.

Having finished his calculations on all the games, Marwin returned to the kitchen for another shot of Joe and a bagel. Upon entering the kitchen, Marwin found Morgan seated at the table, reading one of the Harry Potter books.

"Hey, Baby, how long have you been up?"

"About an hour or so, I guess," Morgan replied distractedly.

"How's the book?" Marwin asked.

"Good, but Sirius just got killed!"

"Who is Sirius?" Marwin asked.

Sighing, Morgan replied, "Dad, Sirius is Harry's Godfather. He was Harry's dad's best friend."

"I guess I'm supposed to know that, huh?"

"Sure, you know everything," Morgan replied sweetly.

Marwin smiled and ruffled Morgan's hair before grabbing his coffee and returning to the study to place his bets.

Hanging up with his bookie, Marwin dialed Destiny's number. Instead of the expected ringing, he heard a voice. "Uh, hello?" he said, confused.

"Hey Marwin, it's Jackson."

"Oh, hey. I... The phone didn't even ring here, so I didn't know you were on the line. I thought I was dialing Destiny."

"Well, I've been trying to call you for twenty minutes, but your line was busy. Why don't you have call waiting?"

"I was on the phone with an associate," Marwin explained.

"Associate, my ass. I know you were talking to your bookie."

"I don't know what you're talking about," Marwin claimed, grinning. "Besides, if you knew what time it was, you shouldn't have been calling anyway."

"Again, about that call waiting thing…" Jackson said.

"Nope, not interested. I talk to people all day at work, so I rarely talk on the phone at home. I sure as hell don't want to talk to two at one time."

Chuckling, Jackson admitted, "I can understand that; I don't use the phone much at home myself."

Knowing the answer, but asking anyway, Marwin inquired, "So, what's up?"

"I got a call from the detective letting me know they had identified the powder in Madeline's purse. He said it was chlormethiazole; apparently, it's a drug used to detox drunks. I've never heard of it, and I have no idea how she might have gotten it. Have you ever heard of chlormethiazole?"

Marwin recounted how he came up with the chlormethiazole theory about the powder, also admitting that Bradley had already notified him.

"Wow; I'm impressed, Dr. Gelstone," Jackson said with admiration.

"Ah, sometimes you get lucky. You know, like when a blind hog finds an acorn to eat occasionally," Marwin replied.

Ignoring his friend's modesty, Jackson asked, "So, what do you make of this whole thing? I didn't even know that Madeline was taking a sedative, much less one from another country. How the hell do you think she got it?"

"Well," Marwin began cautiously, "I suspect she may have gotten it from Dr. Asshole; he is the only doctor she'd been seeing, right?"

"I guess, but I didn't even know that she was seeing him until after she died," Jackson replied, dumbfounded.

Picking his words carefully, Marwin said, "Did Bradley give you any specifics about the drug?"

"No, not really. He just said it's a sedative used in some foreign countries to detox alcoholics. Why?"

Searching for the best approach, Marwin finally settled on the straightforward one. He said, as gently as he could, "One of the side effects of abruptly discontinuing chlormethiazole is suicidal ideation."

Stunned silence filled the line as Jackson processed what Marwin had just told him. Finally, he whispered, "That son of a bitch. He killed my wife."

After hanging up with Jackson, Marwin showered, got the kids off to their destinations, and settled onto the couch to watch some football. His only plans for the day were to watch football and count his winnings.

After just a short time, the telephone interrupted his game. Grudgingly, Marwin answered it. "Hey, it's me," purred Destiny.

"Oh, hey, what's going on?" Marwin asked, his mind already shifting from football to another kind of contact sport.

"Not much. I was heading to the grocery store, and I thought I'd see if you wanted to go with me. I thought you might want to come over tonight, too. We can decide on the menu as we shop, if you want to go."

"Uh, OK. Sure. Do you want me to pick you up, or are you coming here?"

Hearing the slight hesitation in Marwin's voice, Destiny asked, "Are you sure? You don't have to go. We just haven't seen much of each other this week, so I thought we could hang out and do some domestic stuff."

"No, that sounds good. I'll pick you up in fifteen minutes."

Marwin pulled on some broken-in jeans and his favorite UT hat, then headed out the door. As he was backing out of the driveway, he remembered that he'd failed to brush his teeth. He made a mental note to do so at Destiny's, first thing.

The drive quickly became frustrating. Once again, I-40 was a parking lot. Marwin tried jumping on Kingston Pike, but that was even worse. He resigned himself to a slow, crawling trip with a halfhearted curse. Stuck in traffic, he turned his thoughts to Madeline's suicide/murder. *Is it really possible that Shoehorn intentionally murdered Madeline? Could it have been an accidental side-effect of her therapy? If that quack did murder her, what was his motive? Plus, if he was smart enough to engineer Madeline's death, maybe he wasn't a quack after all.* Marwin had too many questions and not nearly enough answers.

Looking up, Marwin realized he had traversed the entire route to Destiny's with little or no memory of having done so. When Marwin knocked on Destiny's door, she greeted him in a silky hunter green robe with a hungry look in her eyes.

"Whoa, I thought we were going to the store to get something to eat," he stammered.

"We are, but first we are going to have an appetizer here," Destiny said, closing the door behind Marwin.

Destiny led Marwin into the living room, where the shades were drawn and several candles were burning brightly. Pillows had been scattered around, and a game board was in the middle of the floor. On the coffee table sat a can of whipped cream, a squeeze bottle of chocolate syrup, a bowl of grapes, a tin of mints, and two candy bars. Taking in the scene, Marwin said, "Man, you sure work fast. I just talked to you like thirty minutes ago, and you didn't even know that I was coming with you."

"I knew you would come over," Destiny replied with a devilish grin.

"Oh, yeah? You think you control me, huh? One of these days I will resist you."

Untying the robe so that Marwin got a glimpse of the lacy lingerie underneath, Destiny said, "Maybe, but not today."

"Damn, I hate it when you're right," Marwin said. "I'll be right back; I need to go to the bathroom."

"OK, but don't take too long. I might be out of the mood if you take too long."

"I doubt it," Marwin said, walking away.

"Asshole," Destiny fired at his back.

When Marwin returned with fresh breath, he found Destiny had opened two Amstel Lights and poured them into frosty glasses. "I guess it's five o'clock somewhere," Marwin said, taking a sip.

"Yep. That's what Jimmy Buffett always says," Destiny replied, taking a sip of her own beer. They sipped contentedly for a few moments in silence.

"OK, let's go. What are we playing for?" Destiny asked.

Thinking for a minute, Marwin finally answered, "If I win, I get the forbidden fruit."

"No way," Destiny replied, immediately knowing what Marwin was referring to.

"Yes way," Marwin retorted.

Looking Marwin in the eye, Destiny said, "OK, you're on!"

Stunned, Marwin said, "Really? What do you get if you win?"

"You will be my slave for a whole day," Destiny replied immediately, obviously having already thought this part out.

"OK. Let's do it, then," Marwin agreed.

Marwin and Destiny sat facing each other on the floor. Destiny began by rolling the dice and moving the corresponding number of spaces. The spaces asked questions about relationships, then directed the players to perform some intimate act.

"I think I would like to have a child of my own," Destiny said in response to a question.

"Are you sure?" Marwin inquired.

Looking directly at Marwin, Destiny said, "Only with you."

Marwin and Destiny locked eyes for several seconds. Destiny finally broke eye contact and drew a card from the pile on the board. Reading it, she smiled and instructed Marwin, "Take your shirt off and lie down."

After Marwin had done as she instructed, Destiny leaned down and kissed him lightly on the lips. Her lips then traveled to his neck, where her kiss intensified. As Marwin began to visibly react, Destiny grabbed the whipped cream and sprayed it around his nipples, then made a trail down to his navel. Destiny licked the whipped cream from both of Marwin's nipples, then sucked hard on each one until they become taut. After leaving Marwin's chest, Destiny slid down to his beltline and rested her chin on the bulge in his pants. Looking directly into his eyes, Destiny began to lick the whipped cream from his navel, slowly swirling her tongue. As Marwin reached for her, she pushed his hands away and said, "You lie back. I'm in charge now."

As Destiny continued licking northward, she placed her pelvis directly over Marwin's bulge and began to grind slowly. Moaning, Marwin grabbed her butt, but Destiny simply said, "No."

Destiny finally made it all the way to Marwin's face; she kissed him hungrily for several seconds, then said, "OK, your turn."

Marwin, trying to regain some composure, rolled the dice and moved his game piece accordingly. Studying the square intently, Marwin read the directions aloud. "Describe three qualities of your partner that you find attractive. Well, let's see. I love your breasts, ass, and beaver."

"You butthead," Destiny chastised. "I don't think that is what they mean."

"Oh, OK. How about your incredible spirit, your kindness, and your loving heart?"

Smiling, Destiny said, "Thank you. Now draw a card."

Marwin did as he was told and read a card slowly to himself. Rising, he said, "Get undressed," reaching for the bowl of grapes.

Destiny disrobed and settled back on the pillows. Marwin took a small purple grape and touched it lightly to Destiny's lips, then popped it into his mouth. Reaching for another grape, he traced her face with it, moving it across her lips, chin, and closed eyelids, then down her nose, and finally back around to her slightly-parted lips. Marwin placed the grape between her lips and gently inserted it into her mouth. While Destiny slowly chewed the grape, Marwin instructed, "Keep your eyes closed."

Marwin took another grape from the bowl and put it in his mouth. Removing the grape, he then traced Destiny's left nipple and areola. Re-inserting the grape in his mouth, he repeated the act on the right breast. As Destiny's nipples hardened, Marwin again wetted the grape with his saliva, then traced a path downward to her black patch. Wetting the grape once more, he rubbed it lightly over her lips. At first he rubbed very gently, then with more fervor. As Destiny began to move her hips, Marwin slipped the grape into her opening. "Uh, oh," he said innocently. "I guess I'd better get that," he added huskily, and lowered himself down to Destiny's mound. Marwin licked Destiny's lips slowly, then opened them slightly with his finger to find the throbbing bud inside. As Marwin worked his tongue across Destiny's clitoris, he lifted her butt and placed a pillow underneath so that her pubic mound was angled up. Marwin left the bud and worked downward to the opening, where he plunged his tongue deep inside. Probing, he finally located the grape. Pushing her legs up and back toward her chest to afford deeper penetration, Marwin locked his lips around the opening and sucked. The grape popped out of Destiny's vagina, causing her to gasp. Marwin rose, still chewing the grape, and saw the fire in Destiny's eyes. He covered her body with his and their mouths locked. Destiny broke the kiss and rolled Marwin on his back, then greedily removed his pants. She engulfed his engorged member even before his pants hit the floor. After several seconds, Marwin withdrew from Destiny's mouth and said, "Turn over."

Without a word, Destiny turned over and placed her pelvis over two pillows stacked on the floor. She looked back over her shoulder and licked her lips, then spread herself for him. Marwin easily slid into the waiting opening and they began to buck wildly. Destiny moaned loudly, tensed, then went still. Marwin continued to pound from behind for a few more strokes, climaxed massively, and they both collapsed to the floor.

Sometime later, they sat fully dressed on the couch, sipping their somewhat-warm beers. Marwin finally said, "Thanks, Des. That was incredible."

"Thank you, Dr. Gelstone," she replied. "So, are you ready to go to the store now?"

"Sure. Let's go by my house and see what the kids are into tonight, then we can figure out what we're doing. Maybe we can finish our game."

"You perv!" Destiny said, laughing.

After stopping at Marwin's they headed to Kroger. Neither said much on the drive, both basking in the afterglow of their tryst. As they strolled the aisles of the grocery store, Marwin abruptly asked, "How hard is it to get a body exhumed?"

"What? What are you talking about?" Destiny asked.

"I was just thinking that we need to know if Madeline actually took any of the chlormethiazole. We know she had a packet of the drug in her purse, but we don't know if she ever consumed any," he explained.

"I don't think we can get a judge to issue an exhumation order just because you want to know if she has any amount of some drug in her system. Especially since the drug isn't available in the U.S. and she hasn't been out of the country. You need some evidence that strongly suggests she did ingest the drug, as well as some evidence suggesting foul play was involved in her death. Otherwise, I don't see a judge letting someone dig her up."

"Well, I guess we'll just have to get that evidence," Marwin said flatly.

CHAPTER 28

Jackson sat on the couch, idly switching between four different football games, his half-eaten sandwich on the table beside him. He had been trying to concentrate on football, but his mind kept wandering to the mysterious powder found in Madeline's purse. He'd convinced himself that Shoehorn was to blame for Madeline's death. His first inclination was to drive to Shoehorn's office and confront him. Unfortunately, the office was closed. He was in the process of Googling for Shoehorn's home address when the phone rang. Seeing Marwin's number, he answered.

"Hey, what's up?"

"Not much. Destiny and I just went to the store and picked up some things for dinner. We got to talking about the powder in Madeline's purse. There are a lot of unanswered questions."

"Yeah, like how the hell did she get ahold of the stuff? Actually, I was just looking up the asshole's address. I thought I might pay him a visit and see if I can get some answers to all these questions," Jackson said.

"I'm not sure that is a good idea," Marwin protested.

"Why the fuck not?" Jackson asked hotly.

"I don't know, I just think we should talk it all out with Bradley and see what he says. We don't want to do anything that might mess up the investigation."

"What investigation? The cops ruled her death a suicide!"

"Bradley said he's going to look into it," Marwin explained.

"I don't give a shit! I am going over there, and I'm not leaving until I get some answers."

Oh, shit, Marwin thought. "Give me a half hour, and I will go with you."

"Hey, are you sure?" Jackson asked.

"Yeah. It'll give me something to do besides watching my money fly away. I'll see you shortly."

***

Marwin dropped Destiny and the groceries at her apartment, then hopped on I-40 heading to Jackson's house. The earlier traffic congestion had completely cleared, and he rolled along at 75 mph wondering if he and Jackson were about to make a huge mistake. Finally deciding it would be fun to confront the quack doctor again, Marwin switched the radio to the local sports talk station, hoping to catch up on the scores before he reached Jackson's house.

Jackson opened the door and climbed into Marwin's car before it came to a complete stop. "Damn, you in a hurry?" Marwin asked.

"Yeah, I want to get to that asshole as quickly as possible," Jackson spat.

"And what exactly are you planning on doing, when you do see him?" Marwin asked cautiously.

"Whatever it takes to get the answers we need!"

"OK, we'll get some answers, but please promise me you won't do anything crazy," Marwin pleaded.

"I guess that depends on the answers we get," Jackson replied solemnly.

Turning into a modest neighborhood, Marwin said, "Are you sure this is the right place? All the doctors I know wouldn't even let their servants live in such poverty."

"Very funny, asshole," Jackson retorted. "Turn left at the next street. His house should be about halfway down the block."

Marwin again wondered if they were making a huge mistake. Before he came to a conclusion, Jackson said, "There it is."

Pulling up to the curb in front of a two-story brick house, Marwin asked, "You ready?"

"Hell, yeah. Let's go!" Jackson replied.

Reaching for the doorbell, Marwin said, "You know, this could get ugly."

"Damn right it could," Jackson said in a serious, troubled voice.

Marwin pushed the back-lit circle and listened as the doorbell chimed inside. *Ah, hell,* Marwin thought. *Maybe we'll get lucky and the jerk won't be home.*

"Where is that asshole?" Jackson said, reaching past Marwin to repeatedly ring the doorbell.

Getting no response, Jackson started banging on the door and shouting, "Open up, you piece of shit!"

"Well, that should get him to open the door and serve us beer and pretzels," Marwin said sarcastically.

Ignoring Marwin, Jackson continued ringing the doorbell while simultaneously banging on the door with his fist. After what seems like a ridiculous amount of time to Marwin, Jackson finally admitted, "I don't think the fucker is home."

"Are you sure? Maybe he didn't hear you," Marwin said.

"Shit," Jackson responded dejectedly. All the previous venom had disappeared from his voice, replaced by a sadness that hurt Marwin's heart.

"Hey, come on, let's go. Maybe it's for the best, anyway. You look like you were ready to kick some ass and take some names."

"Yeah, I was, but just one name: Asswipe Shoehorn," Jackson said sadly.

"You know, we could snoop around here and see what we can find," Marwin offered.

"What are you, Alex Cross or something? You're a pharmacist, and I'm a doctor. All we could find would be the way to the Knox County jail, arrested for breaking and entering. I know you love the color orange, but I don't really want to see myself in a big orange jumpsuit, about to be bent over by a murderous weightlifter who happens to be fresh out of KY," Jackson said.

Chuckling at the visual that just formed in his head, Marwin said, "I wasn't talking about breaking into his house. I thought we might talk to some of his neighbors to see if we can get any information that way."

"What's so funny?" Jackson asked.

"Oh, nothing, I was just picturing you in that bright orange jumpsuit with the weightlifter."

"Asshole," Jackson retorted, turning for the car.

"Yep, that's where he was going," Marwin fired back. "Come on, let's see what the neighbors know about Doctor Weeds and Seeds."

Marwin and Jackson spent the next two hours going door to door through Shoehorn's neighborhood like a pair of Jehovah's Witnesses. The only thing accomplished was Marwin learning more people must read the HIPAA notices than he'd previously thought; several people had refused to tell them if they were a patient of Shoehorn's or not. "Who knew people actually read those HIPAA notices?" Marwin quipped.

"Certainly not me, that's for sure. I assumed everyone just signs them and forgets about them," Jackson answered.

"There's one more house on the block. Should we even bother?" Marwin asked dejectedly.

"May as well. Worst thing they can do is tell us to get lost," Jackson offered.

"No, the worst thing would be if they call the cops," Marwin suggested.

"True story," Jackson said. "Come on, let's take a chance like Columbus did."

"But he's dead now. Let me do the talking this time," Marwin said, walking to the door of a single-level house with lights glowing in two rooms.

"Why? Have I been asking the wrong questions?" asked Jackson.

"Well," Marwin began, "I suppose there's nothing technically wrong with barking 'Do you know that sonofabitch Ernie Shoehorn,' but it hasn't worked too well so far."

"OK, smartass, you take charge," Jackson said, ringing the doorbell.

They waited patiently as someone pulled the curtains aside to peer out at them, obviously sizing them up as potential axe murderers or IRS agents. Apparently satisfied that they were neither, a lady of approximately seventy opened the door and said, "Can I help you?"

"Sorry to bother you, Ma'am—" Marwin began.

"Joanie? Is that you?" Jackson interrupted to ask over Marwin's shoulder.

"Well, I can't believe it! Jackson Montgomery, on my doorstep," the lady said, as she embraced Jackson in a huge bear hug. "Come in, come in! Let me get you some coffee—or maybe something stronger, if you'd like."

"Thanks, Joanie, that would be great," Jackson said. He stepped inside, leaving Marwin standing on the stoop in confusion.

Turning back, Jackson asked, "You comin'? Or you just gonna wait out here for curb service?"

Marwin followed Jackson inside and found himself in a home comfortably decorated in country décor.

"Aren't you going to introduce me to you friend, Jackson?" the lady asked.

"Of course. Marwin, this is Joanie Ayers. She was my neighbor before we moved into our new neighborhood. Joanie, this is Marwin Gelstone. He's a pharmacist whom I work closely with."

"Pleased to meet you, Marwin," Joanie said, extending her hand.

"Likewise, Mrs. Ayers," Marwin replied, gently shaking her hand.

Jackson listened as Marwin and Joanie discussed her aches and pains and the laundry list of medications with exorbitant prices that she took before finally butting in. "Do you know that slimeball who lives around the corner, Ernie Shoehorn?"

Face instantly blackening, Joanie exclaimed, "That sonofabitch! I not only know him, I detest him! Every day, he walks his mutt past my house and lets it crap in my yard and then doesn't even have the decency to pick it up. He says I should be grateful, as he is providing natural fertilizer for my lawn, free of charge."

Pleasantly surprised by Joanie's venom, Jackson asked, "Have you ever seen him as a patient, or know anyone who has?"

"Are you crazy?" Joanie asked incredulously. "I wouldn't let that slimy bastard get within ten feet of my beaver."

Taking her candor in stride, Jackson responded, "Well, I'm glad to see someone else shares my opinion of the good doctor."

"Good doctor, my ass. He's a fricking quack! It isn't safe to be his patient, 'cause you might just end up dead," Joanie opined.

***

Bradley Jinswain sat at his desk, gently rubbing the grit from his eyes. On the desk in front of him were the police reports from twenty-two suicides over the last three months. Knoxville wasn't a small town, but twenty-two suicides in three months seemed off to Bradley. He had researched the suicide data from the previous five years and found that Knox county averaged sixty-seventy suicides per year. So, twenty-two in three months was very high. Bradley had examined the reports carefully for three hours, searching for a link to Madeline Montgomery's case. So far, the only commonality he saw was that most of the suicides were female.

After ten minutes of trying to rub the answers out of his head—without any satisfactory results— Bradley decided the best course of action would be to personally interview family members of the individual cases. Unfortunately, all twenty-two cases were closed, so his interviewing of the families would not be supported by the department. Realizing he would have to tread lightly and do all the legwork on his own, Bradley sighed and dialed the contact number for the first case.

A dull voice finally answered after the third ring. "Mr. Jacobson?" Bradley inquired.

"Yes, how can I help you?"

"This is Bradley Jameson from the Suicide Support Association," he said, making up a last name on the spot. "I was wondering if this was a good time to ask you a couple of questions?"

An audible gasp escaped the man, followed by a hoarse, cracking voice, "What do you want? Why would you call here?"

"I'm sorry, Mr. Jacobson. I know this is difficult for you, but we are looking into suicides in your area and your wife's name is on our list. Would you be able to answer a couple of quick questions?"

A lengthy silence ensued and Bradley was sure the call had been disconnected. Finally, Jacobson said, "I have nothing to say to you. Goodbye."

Cursing under his breath, Bradley hung up. He continued to work his way down the list of suicide victims for a frustrating two hours; then Bradley finally got a break.

"This is Bradley Jameson from the Suicide Support Association," Bradley began as the phone was answered. "I was trying to reach a family member of Cora Elbertson."

"Oh, I'm Amy Wycliffe, and Cora was my mother."

"I'm sorry to bother you. I was hoping you might be able to answer a couple of questions for me."

"The Suicide Support Association, you said?" she asked.

"Yes, Ma'am. We are looking into suicides in your area, and your mother's name appeared on our list."

"Can I ask you what you hope to find, Mister... I'm sorry, what was your name?"

"Jameson. Bradley Jameson," Bradley said, the lie rolling easily off his tongue. "We are investigating an unusually large number of suicides over the last few months, hoping to find a link between some of the cases," Bradley continued, relieved he didn't have to lie about that.

"Oh. OK, I see. I'm not sure I'll be able to help, but I will be happy to answer any questions that I can."

"Thank you, Mrs. Wycliffe," Bradley responded.

"Might as well call me Amy, if I'm going to be divulging family secrets to you," she said with a faint laugh.

"OK, Amy it is, then. Did your mom have a history of depression, or had she been ill for a long period of time?" Bradley inquired, following his previously invented script.

"Nope, my mom was as healthy as a horse. It was all I could do to get her to go to her gyno once a year."

"Would you mind telling me her gynecologist's name?" Bradley asked hopefully.

"Sure, she and I go—uh, went—to the same office. We both see...uh, saw, Dr. Ernie Shoehorn, over in east Knoxville," Amy supplied. "Why do you ask?"

As the name exploded in Bradley's ear, his mind raced to come up with a plausible explanation.

"Mr. Jameson? Are you still there?" Amy asked.

"Uh, yeah, sorry. I just recognized that name from another victim," Bradley stammered.

"Huh, that's a little weird," replied Amy. "But it is a large practice. I think there are about six or eight doctors in the group, and Dr. Shoehorn oversees all of them. I guess he's kinda like the director or something."

"I see," said Bradley, trying to figure out how best to proceed.

Coming to his rescue, Amy volunteered, "It was really my idea that mom go to Dr. Shoehorn. He's one of the leading researchers in natural medicine. He doesn't believe in filling your body with all that crap that the pharmaceutical companies put out. I just love him. Plus, he is very gentle and thorough."

Deciding that he needed to think this through, Bradley stammered, "Uh, thanks for your help, Amy. Would you mind if I contact you again, if I need any more information?"

"Sure, no problem, Mr. Jameson. Just call me here. I'm here most of the time, since I have to take care of Dad now. He isn't doing too well since Mom's death."

"OK, thanks," Bradley said again.

"Do you have a number that I can reach you at, Mr. Jameson?" Amy asked. She heard nothing but the dial tone in reply, as Bradley had quietly disconnected.

CHAPTER 29

"What do you mean by that?" Jackson asked, as a bolt of fear and excitement shot through him.

"Well, I know—or rather, I knew—two perfectly healthy women who went to him. In less than two years, they were both dead," Joanie stated, matter-of-factly.

Sensing Jackson's fear, Marwin asked, "What happened to them? Were they elderly? Did they have cancer, or a heart attack or something?"

"No, they were both in their late fifties or early sixties, I believe. As far as I know, neither one of them had any serious medical problems. I think they just went for routine gynecologist stuff. Tragically, they both committed suicide," Joanie explained.

"What?!" Jackson all but screamed, visibly stumbling backwards.

"Yeah," Joanie began, noting Jackson's extreme reaction. "One of them jumped into the Tennessee River, and the other became severely depressed and swallowed all of her antidepressants."

"My God! Oh, my God!" Jackson exclaimed.

"What's wrong, Jackson?" Joanie asked, reaching for his arm.

Seeing Jackson was coming apart, Marwin said, "Mrs. Ayers, Jackson's wife, Madeline, committed suicide recently; she also went to Dr. Shoehorn."

"Sonofabitch," Joanie said. "I'm so sorry, Jackson. I had no idea about Madeline. You poor, poor man."

For one of the few times in his life, Jackson Montgomery was unable to speak. He stared wildly at Joanie with tears welling up in his eyes. "I think I need to get us all something to drink, and then we need to sit down and do some talking," Joanie stated, leaving the room.

Turning to Marwin, Jackson said, "I can't believe it. I blamed Shoehorn for Madeline's death but deep down, I didn't really think he could be responsible—especially with the method that she chose."

Trying to block out that horrific image, Marwin suggested, "Why don't we talk to Joanie and see what we can put together?"

"OK, let's find out what's going on with that quack," Joanie said, entering the room with a bottle of Courvoisier and three snifters. "Tell me what happened, Honey," she said gently to Jackson.

At first, Jackson said nothing, instead just swirling the cognac round and round. Finally, he downed the smooth liquid and began to relive his nightmare.

***

Bradley had replayed his conversation with Amy Wycliffe multiple times. He was unable to determine the significance of Amy's mom being a patient of Dr. Shoehorn's at this point. How uncommon would it be for a doctor to have more than one patient to commit suicide in a single year's time? For a shrink, it probably wouldn't be that uncommon—but a gynecologist? That seemed a bit bizarre to Bradley. Unable to decide what to make of the information, Bradley grabbed his coat and headed to the batting cages, hoping to clear his head.

***

Joanie and Marwin sat in silence as Jackson spun his tale of horror. At first, neither touched their cognac—but eventually, both drained their glasses as Jackson's pain became more evident. After Jackson finished his grisly story, Joanie said, "Oh, Jackson. I am so, so sorry. I cannot imagine losing someone like that."

"Thank you," Jackson said.

"Joanie," Marwin began, somehow having progressed to a first name basis after the snifter of cognac. "Could you give us the names of the other two ladies? We're working with a detective, and I'm sure he will be interested in any information that you can supply."

"Sure. One was a good friend of mine, Cora Elbertson. The other was Millie Kellogg's daughter-in-law—Millie lives just a few doors down. Her name was Catherine Rice. I believe she may have lived out near Farragut."

"Thanks, Joanie. Would it be all right if the detective contacted you?" Marwin asked.

"Absolutely. I will do anything in my power to see that asshole get what he deserves!"

***

"Dammit!" Bogie swore under his breath. He had just hit a weak ground ball into the left side of the cage netting. Stepping out to re-focus, then settling back in at the plate, Bogie drove the next pitch deep into the back of the cage.

"See the difference?" Bradley asked from outside the cage. "The first swing, you tried to muscle up; your right hand and shoulder took over, so the big end of the bat went first and you rolled over the pitch. On the second swing, you kept your hands back and stayed inside the baseball. You led with your left hand and allowed your right hand to drive through the ball. That ball would have been a bomb into the left field gap."

"Uh, yeah, I guess. Sometimes I get frustrated and just try to kill the ball, if I'm not hitting well," Bogie admitted.

"Yeah, and how does that work for you?" Bradley asked with a smirk.

"Not worth a damn," Bogie conceded.

"OK then, stop trying to make something work that you already know doesn't. Instead, trust what you know works, and focus on perfecting it; keep doing it, over and over. Even if you don't get a hit every time, continue working on your mechanics. And don't ever think you've mastered the game, either. Work hard every day. Strive to get better every day."

"OK. Thanks, Mr. Jinswain."

"Need a ride home?" Bradley asked. "I was actually going to see your dad anyway."

"Sure; just let me tell Josh's dad that he doesn't need to take me home, and I'll meet you outside."

"All right. We can work on some mental drills in the car," Bradley offered.

"Awesome!" Bogie exclaimed, running off.

***

The ride back to Jackson's was quiet. Both Marwin and Jackson were busy ruminating about their visit to Joanie's house. Finally, Jackson asked, "How are we going to prove that Shoehorn killed all these women?"

"Whoa; we aren't going to prove anything, since we are both healthcare professionals. I suggest we turn everything over to Bradley and let him do the investigation," Marwin answered.

"But the Knoxville PD has already closed the case as a suicide," Jackson countered.

"I know, but Bradley is already interested and doing some digging on his own. Our new information will surely stoke his interest even more."

"But..." Jackson started to retort, trailing off when the truth of Marwin's statement sank in. "OK, you're right. Let's see what Bradley has to say," Jackson said, resigned.

"I'll call him right now," Marwin replied, digging in his pocket for his cell phone.

"Huh," Marwin said, after hanging up with Bradley. "That's funny."

"Please tell me what's so funny. I could use a good laugh right about now," Jackson said.

"Bradley said he was on the way to my house. He apparently has some new information about Madeline's death."

Without another word, Jackson's grip on the wheel tightened and his right foot instantly became heavier as he changed course to Marwin's house.

***

Jackson and Marwin arrived at Marwin's house to find Bradley and Bogie waiting for them. Upon entering, Bogie headed to his room. The three adults retired to Marwin's den, where he turned on his large flat-screen TV, changed it to a sports channel, and muted the sound. Seeing Jackson's scowl, Marwin said innocently, "I just want to see some scores roll by. I'm not really going to watch TV."

"Yeah, right, you degenerate," Jackson quipped.

Turning to Bradley, who had been watching their exchange with a quizzical look, Jackson asked, "OK, Detective, what did you find out?"

"Well, I found another suicide victim who was also a patient of Dr. Shoehorn's," Bradley answered without preamble.

"Well, that is pretty good, Bradley, but we found two suicide patients who were victims of Dr. Shoehorn's," Marwin stated, intentionally switching the nouns.

"Damn! You're kidding, right?" Bradley said incredulously. "How exactly did you find these victims?"

"Some good, old-fashioned detective work," Marwin replied with a grin.

"All right, Detective Gelstone, why don't you tell me what you've done."

Marwin and Jackson took turns telling their story, each interjecting points of interest that carried special significance for them. Bradley quietly took notes on a pad that he produced from his pocket. As Marwin finished up by divulging the names of the two patients, Bradley wrote them down and placed a star beside one of them, Cora Elbertson.

"I spoke to Cora Elbertson's daughter today," Bradley offered. "She was very understanding and is willing to help in any way she can."

"Does she suspect Shoehorn in her mom's death?" Jackson asked.

"No; in fact, she loves the good doctor. She's actually the one responsible for her mom going to see Shoehorn. Apparently, she's a health nut and wanted her mom to be treated with all the natural products that Shoehorn promotes."

"Damn. If it turns out that Shoehorn is responsible for her mom's death, that will be a huge burden for her to carry—knowing that she led her mom to him," Marwin said solemnly.

A minute passed as the group silently reflected on Marwin's words. Then Jackson said, "OK, Bradley, where do we go from here?"

"I'm not really sure, to be honest. I don't think I have enough to go to my boss and ask for the investigation to be re-opened. I think we need more than just three patients who committed suicide and just happen to see the same gynecologist."

"It's not just a fucking coincidence!" Jackson exploded.

"I agree," Bradley said quickly. "I don't believe in coincidence anyway."

Calm returning, Jackson said, "Sorry, I didn't mean to rip your head off. I'm just so frustrated."

"It's fine, no big deal. Let's just try to come up with a plan on how to proceed," Bradley consoled Jackson.

"I know how we can trap the bastard," Marwin said, reaching for his phone.

"How?" Jackson and Bradley asked simultaneously.

Marwin didn't answer. Instead, he said into the phone, "Hey, Des, how's Bonnie doing?"

"Uh, well... I believe she's fine, but you were the last one to see her," Destiny replied, easily understanding Marwin's nickname for her private parts.

"Actually, I think you need to have her checked out immediately," Marwin responded.

"Why? I'm not due for my yearly for about three more months. What is going on, Marwin?" Destiny inquired, perplexed.

"I need you to make an appointment to see Dr. Shoehorn as soon as possible."

"Shoehorn? Wasn't that Madeline's doctor? Why in the world would I want to see him? Didn't you say he was a quack?" she protested.

"To help us put that son-of-a-bitch away for good. I'll explain later. I've gotta go now, but I'll call you tomorrow and we can work out the details."

Accepting his request, Destiny responded, "OK, see you tomorrow. Goodnight."

"Goodnight, Baby. I love you," Marwin said, then hung up.

"What was that all about?" Jackson asked. "And who is Bonnie?"

Ignoring the questions, Marwin said, "We can get Destiny to go see Shoehorn. Maybe he'll give her chlormethiazole, too."

"You've been reading too many James Patterson books, Sherlock," Jackson quipped. "Things aren't that easy in real life."

"Destiny is about twenty years too young to fit the profile of the other victims," Bradley suggested.

"True, but she can fake it. I can coach her on the symptoms of menopause, and she can express an interest in natural remedies. I guarantee you that quack will give her a bunch of vitamins to take and probably won't even do bloodwork to check her endogenous hormone levels," Marwin explained.

Mulling it over, Jackson finally said, "I would hate to have Destiny be examined by that slimeball."

"Oh, shit. I didn't think about that," Marwin said, immediately distressed. "No way that asshole is touching her!"

"It's OK, we'll come up with something. I appreciate you trying," Jackson said, genuinely grateful.

After Jackson and Bradley left, Marwin retired to his study. Kicking off his shoes, he sank heavily into a chair. As the energy flowed out of him, Marwin began concocting a plan to snare Shoehorn. The one stumbling block that continued to stump Marwin was the pelvic exam that Shoehorn would surely insist he conduct upon Destiny.

Unable to find a mental solution, Marwin turned up the volume on the TV. It was still set to the sports channel, which was running the day's scores across the bottom of the screen in a loop. He grabbed the notepad that contained the day's wagers and went down the list, placing checks by the winners and an x by each of the losers. Calculating pluses and minuses in his head, Marwin realized the day had shaped up to be awful, all around. *Fuck!* Marwin thought. *Today has been a blood bath!* With that thought, however, Marwin suddenly forgot the lost wagers and sat back in the chair, smiling at the solution to his problem.

CHAPTER 30

Marwin woke up to the sound of country music and a hairdryer. Glancing at the bedside clock, Marwin realized he had to get up immediately, if they were going to make it to church on time. Undoubtedly, Morgan was already up—hence the racket coming from her room. As the war began to rage between the go-to-church angel and the stay-at-home devil sitting fictitiously on his headboard, Marwin started to plan out his day. He had to talk to Destiny and bring her up to date on his plan. He needed to look at the pro football game schedule in hopes of salvaging some of yesterday's financial disaster. Briefly, he considered taking the day off from gambling, maybe just paying his bookie on Monday instead of possibly digging an even larger hole. He quickly disregarded this foolish thought, got out of bed, and made his way to Morgan's bathroom, where he found her curling her hair and singing along to the Top-40 countdown.

"Hey, Baby Girl," Marwin said, taking in Morgan's outfit of skin-tight jeans (complete with numerous holes), a tight sweater that stopped about four inches north of her jeans, and a pair of purple tennis shoes. "You know we're going to church this morning, right?"

"Aw, no, Dad! I have plans with Patrick today."

"Well, after church, if your homework is done and your room is cleaned and you ask me, then maybe I can take you over to Patrick's house."

"No, dad, I'm not going to church. Patrick's mom is picking me up and taking us to the movies," Morgan replied matter-of-factly.

"Who the hell said you could go to the movies?!" Marwin exploded. "You don't get to decide to do whatever you want to do, whenever you want to do it. Now, I suggest you put on some more church-appropriate attire, straighten up your room, and meet me in the kitchen in thirty minutes for breakfast."

"Argh, Dad!" Morgan screamed as she slammed the bathroom door.

Ignoring her, Marwin said, "I will see you at the table in thirty minutes, or you won't be doing anything today."

Knowing he was about to receive the same sentiment, albeit with slightly less venom, Marwin moved to Bogie's bedroom. He found Bogie completely under the covers, apparently undisturbed by the cacophony that just erupted from Morgan's bathroom. "Get up, Bud. We're going to church," Marwin instructed.

An undecipherable grunt escaped the covers, so Marwin knew Bogie was alive, at least. "Breakfast in thirty. Be there," Marwin said as he headed off to take a quick shower.

The ride to church was mostly uneventful, with Bogie listening to music through his earbuds, Morgan texting Patrick—no doubt describing Marwin in all kinds of colorful language—and Marwin trying to convince Destiny to meet them at church. Destiny claimed she was covered up with work, but she sounded like she'd just rolled over when Marwin called her.

During church, the kids sat mostly disinterested during the sermon on the Ten Commandments while Marwin's mind drifted from the day's football games to Destiny's upcoming visit to Shoehorn. He was hoping his idea of the night before would be the best way to get Shoehorn to implicate himself in Madeline's death without subjecting Destiny to a physical exam.

As the sermon closed and the benediction was given, Marwin selfishly asked the Lord for the wisdom to pick winning teams. He gathered the kids, and they all headed out to meet Destiny and Jackson for lunch.

Marwin settled Bogie and Morgan in a nearby booth, then joined Jackson and Destiny at the mahogany bar.

"Good morning, Sunshine," Destiny said as Marwin walked up.

"It's a better morning now," Marwin replied, leaning down to kiss her.

"Get a room," Jackson advised.

"Wow, thanks Dr. Gelstone," Destiny said, smiling.

"Anytime, anytime," Marwin responded, returning the smile.

After ordering a fried chicken salad, a seafood pasta salad, and a rack of ribs, the three got down to business. Marwin explained his idea of having Destiny pose as a patient of Shoehorn's in hopes of gathering incriminating evidence.

"Do you really think he'd give me that weird drug that you found in Madeline's purse?" Destiny asked.

"I doubt it," Jackson replied. "James Patterson there seems to think so, though."

"I believe we can help push him into it," Marwin said.

"How?" Jackson asked.

"Destiny just needs to let him know that she is close to me," Marwin said. "I guarantee that will send him over the edge."

"So, you must have made quite an impression on him, huh?" Jackson teased Marwin with a smile.

Ignoring the barb, Marwin told Destiny, "Just don't mention that you know Jackson or Madeline, as that might make him suspicious."

"All right. What exactly is going to be my problem?" Destiny inquired.

"Menopause, of course," Marwin responded.

"Are you crazy? I am nowhere near menopause," Destiny protested.

"You aren't as far away as you might think," Marwin said sweetly.

"Bite me!"

"Is that an invitation?" Marwin asked innocently.

"You two are killing me," Jackson said. "Destiny, if Marwin and I coach you on the signs and symptoms of menopause, do you think you can sell it to Shoehorn?"

"I'm sure I could. After all, I did play Snow White in a play in kindergarten."

***

As Marwin was plowing through the chaos of retail pharmacy on a Monday morning, his technician informed him that he had a call waiting on line two. "This is the pharmacist," Marwin answered, picking up the phone.

"Hello, Dr. Gelstone," Destiny said.

"Oh, hey. What's up?"

"I just made my appointment with Dr. Shoehorn. I'm seeing him Thursday morning at ten thirty."

"Great! I'm really kinda surprised that you could get into see him so soon," Marwin said.

"Well, I told the nurse that my vagina had dried up and that I am unable to have sex anymore," Destiny stated.

"I believe I may have something that can help you with that, Ma'am," Marwin replied.

"I'm sure you believe that, but I think I can handle this on my own," Destiny retorted.

"Well, handling it on your own just might help with that dryness," Marwin quipped.

"Perv," Destiny fired back.

"I'll see you tonight, and we can start going over all the symptoms of menopause. We will put special emphasis on your vaginal dryness."

"Perv," Destiny repeated, then hung up.

***

Thursday morning dawned bright and sunny, yet Marwin woke with a gloomy feeling. His stomach was queasy, and he was sweating as he thought about Destiny seeing Shoehorn. They had been rehearsing her story all week, and Marwin was confident that Destiny would be able to fake it convincingly. She'd even called the night before to inform Marwin that she had started her period, which was perfect: it would keep Shoehorn from doing the pelvic exam. Still, Marwin couldn't shake the feeling of unease. He'd offered to drive her to her appointment, but she said that was stupid and would only make Shoehorn suspicious if he found out. Marwin couldn't argue with her reasoning, so he let her go by herself. Still, he had taken the day off so that he could see her as soon as she was done with her appointment.

He decided to take a shower, grab some breakfast, then crunch some numbers for that night's big college game. Having just paid out $1200, Marwin vowed to get his money back as soon as possible, maybe even by the weekend.

***

"May I help you?" the lady behind the frosted glass asked as Destiny approached the window in Shoehorn's reception area.

"I'm Destiny Lawson, and I have a ten-thirty appointment with Dr. Shoehorn."

"Yes... Ms. Lawson, I need a copy of your driver's license and your insurance card. You'll need to fill out all the forms on this clipboard, too. Dr. Shoehorn had a cancelation this morning, so he is ready when you are."

Destiny took the clipboard and began the arduous process of filling out all the medical information requested. After fifteen minutes, Destiny returned the forms to the receptionist and said, "I believe you know more about me now than my mother does."

"Yeah, sorry about all the forms, but it is vital that Dr. Shoehorn has all of your medical information so that he can provide you with the most current treatments available," the receptionist replied in a bored, canned voice.

"Well, he's got it, so let's get on with it," Destiny said.

Destiny was led down a hallway painted in light, pastel colors to a triage room, where she was weighed and handed a cup to fill. After providing the urine sample, she was taken to an exam room, told to undress, and given a hospital gown with a breezeway in the back. "Dr. Shoehorn will be right in," the nurse said.

As Destiny undressed, she eyed the table with the stirrups at the end, each fitted with funny, fuzzy socks. *Cold feet are the least of my problems if my feet are up there*, she thought. As the butterflies began to take flight in her stomach, Destiny ran through the script again in her mind. Before she had much time to get nervous, the door opened and Dr. Ernie Shoehorn walked in, dressed in a white lab coat and light blue Oxford shirt, open at the collar.

"Good morning, Ms. Lawson. Thanks for coming in today," Shoehorn said, extending his hand toward Destiny.

Taking what she hoped was an unnoticeable deep breath, Destiny replied, "Thanks for seeing me so quickly, Dr. Shoehorn. If I don't get some relief soon, I'm going to go crazy."

"Well, let's see what we can do for you. Why don't you tell me what's going on, and I imagine we can come up with something to help you."

Over the next ten minutes, Destiny recited her story, putting special emphasis on her hot flashes and vaginal dryness. Doing her best Jennifer Lawrence impression, Destiny said, "All of that is bad, but the worst part is that I can't have sex with my boyfriend, Marwin, anymore. It's just too painful. Since he's a pharmacist, he has already recommended all the OTC lubricants, as well as a special mixture that he compounded last week. None of them have helped, though."

Obviously only half listening, Shoehorn stared at Destiny's chest and said, "I see. Well, you are somewhat young to be having these symptoms, so we'll need to get some bloodwork to check your hormone levels. I would also like to talk to you about your diet, and possibly some supplements that I think may help your situation."

"Uh, Marwin said he could do saliva samples to check my estrogen and progesterone levels. Do you really need to draw blood? I have a needle phobia."

"Well, saliva tests are not as accurate as blood tests for hormones," Shoehorn replied. Some of Destiny's hints finally penetrated his attention to her chest and made it into his brain. Shoehorn asked, "Who is this pharmacist? Where does he work?"

Looking sheepish, Destiny answered, "Marwin Gelstone. He owns Community Pharmacy in west Knoxville. Do you know him?"

Destiny watched as Shoehorn's face briefly darkened, then cleared. Shoehorn responded, "Uh, I'm not sure... Maybe. Why don't we get back to your problems? Let's do a physical exam. Then I'll get Linda back in here to draw some blood. We will form a game plan based on the results."

Allowing her ire to flare just a little, Destiny said indignantly, "I told you, I don't want any bloodwork. Marwin can check whatever hormone levels need to be checked. I will have him call you with the results, and maybe you two can work together on a game plan for me. He works closely with most area doctors, anyway."

Unable to control his anger this time, Shoehorn snapped, "No! I will not be taking any test results or having any conversations with that arrogant jerk!"

"What? I thought you didn't know him," Destiny asked, surprised.

Shoehorn didn't respond; he just stared at Destiny. Finally breaking his silence, he said, "Ms. Lawson, I have had some unpleasant, and frankly, unprofessional dealings with Mr. Gelstone. I didn't want my personal experience to cause you to doubt my ability to help you, so I denied knowing him. That being said, I promise to do my best to help you. I will not hold your relationship with Mr. Gelstone against you. I will act professionally, even if he chooses not to."

Trying to find just the right amount of indignation to use, Destiny replied, "I don't appreciate your language, and it seems unprofessional to refer to one of your peers as an 'arrogant jerk.'"

"He is not my peer!" Shoehorn thundered. "He thinks he's so smart, but he doesn't know anything about medicine. Maybe you should see another doctor, Ms. Lawson. Maybe I can't help you after all."

Realizing she may have pushed too far, Destiny pleaded, "No, please, you have to help me! I have done a lot of research, and I know that you are very well-respected in the natural community. I want to be cured, but I prefer to do it naturally, if possible. I am a very health-conscious woman, so I would prefer not to put a bunch of synthetic crap into my body."

As Destiny's use of the key words impacted Shoehorn and stroked his ego, he calmed down. "Why don't we start over? I feel sure that I will be able to get you straightened out."

"OK. Thanks, Dr. Shoehorn."

Shoehorn checked Destiny for a goiter, listened to her heart and lungs, and seemed to linger just a bit too long when the stethoscope was over her breasts. "Just lie back," he instructed. "I'm going to check your breasts for lumps."

"Is that going to help diagnose my condition?" Destiny asked.

"Ms. Lawson, I am the doctor. You came to me for my expertise. Now please, let me do my job."

"All right," Destiny agreed hesitantly.

As Destiny scooted back on the exam table, a large smear of blood appeared beneath her. "Oh, my! I'm so sorry. I must have just started my period," Destiny said, embarrassed.

"Don't worry about it. It happens from time to time," Shoehorn reassured her.

Seeing the large amount of menstrual fluid on the table and gauging the difficulty of the pelvic exam, Shoehorn said, "It looks like it might be best to have you come back next week for the pelvic exam. We can do everything else today, then get you back in next week for the pelvic."

"OK. I'm really sorry, Dr. Shoehorn," Destiny said.

Shoehorn completed the rest of the physical exam and sent the nurse in to draw four tubes of blood. With everything finished, Shoehorn said, "All right. Ms. Lawson, despite your young age, you do have many of the symptoms of menopause. Of course, we'll have to wait for the results of lab tests, but I am pretty sure they will show decreased hormone levels. I would like to start you on some natural supplements in the interim, and we'll see how it goes."

"OK, great! That would be awesome," Destiny said.

After receiving a bagful of medications from Shoehorn, Destiny left the office. She called Marwin as soon as she got into her car.

Answering before the phone finished the first ring, Marwin said, "Hey, how did it go?"

"Fine. I'll tell you about it over lunch. Where are you?"

"I'm at home. I'll meet you at Jack's for a sandwich and a beer."

"OK, that sounds awesome. I'll see you there in about twenty minutes."

"OK. I love you."

"I know. I love you, too," Destiny replied, hanging up.

Exiting I-40 at 17th street, Marwin called Jackson to let him know that Destiny had seen Shoehorn. They agreed to get together for dinner to discuss how to proceed.

"Maybe we should call Bradley and have him meet us, too," Jackson suggested.

"Let's just see what Destiny has to say, first. We can call Bradley if she has anything to add to the details," Marwin said.

"All right. I'll see you around five-thirty, and I'll bring a salad. You come up with the main course and the sides," Jackson advised.

"Yes, dear," Marwin responded as he pulled to the curb in front of Jack's deli.

"Well, well. Look what the cat dragged in," Jack said from behind the counter as Marwin walked through the door. "You come by to pick up some cards?" he continued, referring to the illegal parlay cards that he distributed.

Looking rapidly around to see who might have just heard Jack's question, Marwin said, "Uh, no. Just meeting a lady for lunch, Jack."

"Lady? What lady would have lunch with a dirtbag like you?" Jack asked with a smirk.

"Yeah, I've missed you, too," Marwin retorted.

As Marwin sat down at the Formica-topped table that rocked unsteadily from side to side at the least touch, Jack asked, "You havin' the usual?"

"You mean you can remember what my usual is, as old as you are?" Marwin teased.

"Yep. Ham and smoked cheddar on white, light on the mayo, and steamed to perfection."

"Damn, I guess you ain't as old as you look, Jack. I'd like a Rolling Rock, too, please."

"All right. What for your lady?"

"She's a big girl, so I'll let her order for herself."

Halfway through the beer, Marwin spotted Destiny coming through the door. He marveled at her simple beauty. She was dressed in jeans that accented her rear end and a Tennessee sweater that clung to her ample chest. Marwin waved easily to her.

"Did you order for me?" Destiny asked, leaning down to kiss Marwin.

"Nope, you're on your own."

"Well, you suck. Uh, I'll have a Reuben on wheat with a Rolling Rock, please, Jack."

"You got it, but remind me to tell you some things about that joker you're sitting with before you leave," Jack said.

"How 'bout you make our sandwiches and leave us alone, Dr. Phil!" Marwin snapped.

Turning his attention back to Destiny, Marwin saw the bag of medicine that she had placed on the rickety table. "So, let's see what the quack thinks you need," he said, picking up a bottle.

After inspecting each bottle, Marwin said, "This is just a bunch of herbal shit. There's nothing like the packet that I found in Madeline's bathroom. I guess Jackson was right. It was crazy to think that he would just give you the drug on your first visit."

"Yeah, but I definitely got under his skin," Destiny replied.

"How so?"

"I told him that you were my boyfriend, and that I wanted you to do any testing that needed to be done. Then I told him that I thought it would be a good idea if the two of you consulted together on my treatment."

Choking on his beer, Marwin asked, "You really suggested that? How exactly did that go over?"

"He blew his top and said that he wouldn't be taking anything from you, much less consulting with you. Then he called you a jerk."

"Really? That asshole called me a jerk?" Marwin asked indignantly.

"Yep. I was afraid he was going to kick me out without treating me. I kinda pushed his buttons pretty good."

"Well, apparently he settled down, since you left with all of this crap," Marwin replied, gesturing toward the bag.

"What's actually in there?" Destiny inquired.

"A bunch of weeds and seeds. Kava-kava, cinnamon, glycyrrhiza, vitamins B, E, and D, some valerian, and even some St. John's wort."

"Am I going to get warts?!" Destiny asked, alarmed.

"No, it is w-o-r-t, not w-a-r-t, and you won't be getting anything since you won't be taking any of this crap."

"So, I let that old pervert feel me up for nothing?" Destiny asked with disgust.

"No, I don't think so. I'm not sure where we go from here, but I do think that we pushed him a little ways down his twisted road."

"But what if he decides to kill some other innocent person because we pissed him off?" Destiny worried.

"I don't think he'll do that. I'm not sure why I think that, but I do. Let's hope we can get him before he decides to hurt anyone else. I am going to meet with Jackson tonight to try to decide how to proceed. I think I'd better call Bradley, too. This may be getting too big for a pharmacist, a doctor, and a lawyer to handle."

"My, my, Dr. Gelstone! I've never heard you admit that a challenge was too much for you to handle," Destiny mocked. "Maybe you're getting old."

"Oh, I'm getting old, but not too old to spank the ass of a smart-mouthed kid," Marwin responded with a smirk.

"Maybe that will be your reward after you bring Shoehorn down," Destiny said demurely.

"Shoehorn doesn't know it, but he's really screwed now that I have added incentive," Marwin said, as Jack put their sandwiches on the table.

After leaving the deli, fully sated, Marwin stopped by Kroger to pick up some chicken breasts, peppers, onions, and pepper jack cheese for dinner. Once home, he marinated the chicken in Dale's Steak Sauce, topped it with the sliced peppers and onions, then prepared some parmesan potatoes for the side. As Marwin headed outside to fire up the Big Green Egg, Sam called.

"What's up?" Marwin asked distractedly.

"I just wanted to give you a heads-up. I just had another run-in with that quack Shoehorn."

"Shit! Who's he trying to kill now?" Marwin asked, completely attentive.

"Apparently, Mrs. Dickinson—who is in the hospital wing of the nursing home, with pneumonia. Shoehorn wrote an order for Cubicin, and when I called him to let him know that Cubicin can't be used to treat pneumonia, he went crazy! He said that we need to get our medical licenses if we want to practice medicine, and that he is going to contact the pharmacy board to report us. He also said he would hold us responsible if anything happened to Mrs. Dickinson, because I won't dispense the Cubicin."

"Cool," Marwin said flippantly. "We will probably get a commendation from the board for saving her life. Plus, why is her gynecologist treating her pneumonia? He is a real piece of work."

"I know, right? I told him that I would start her on Zosyn plus tobramycin, and that we would do the kinetics for the tobra and monitor her labs. He wasn't happy, but he agreed to change the orders, so everything is taken care of. I just wanted you to be aware, in case he contacts you or you get a call from the board."

"Thanks for the heads-up—and more importantly, for taking care of our patient. Don't worry about Shoehorn, I'll take care of him."

***

Over dinner consisting of Dale's chicken, parmesan potatoes, Jackson's salad, and a bottle of chardonnay, Marwin filled Jackson in on Destiny's visit to Shoehorn, as well as his conversation with Sam.

"He is a disgrace," said Jackson. "Every doctor learns that you can't use daptomycin in pneumonia."

"Do you know why, though?" Marwin asked, already suspecting the answer.

"Uh... No, not really. But I know not to use it."

"Well, that's the most important part, but you should also know why you can't use it," replied Marwin, topping off their glasses.

"Well, please educate me, Dr. Gelstone. I can hardly wait," Jackson said with a sigh.

"I thought you would never ask," Marwin responded smugly. "Daptomycin—or Cubicin as it is called by the brand name—is inactivated by lung surfactants. It would be completely ineffective for pneumonia."

"No wonder we aren't supposed to use it," Jackson quipped. "Now that Pharmacology 101 is over, what are we going to do about Shoehorn?"

"I'm glad you asked, Dr. Montgomery. I think I have a plan to nail that bastard," Marwin replied.

Jackson sat back sipping his wine as Marwin laid out his plan.

"Hell, it just might work. Let's give it a try," Jackson said after Marwin had finished.

CHAPTER 31

Destiny, dressed fashionably in a plain blue patient gown with her ass hanging out, sat on the exam table waiting for Dr. Shoehorn to arrive. Her palms were sweating and her stomach was in knots as she pondered her mission.

"Good morning, Ms. Lawson," said Shoehorn as he entered and closed the door.

"Thanks for working me in, Dr. Shoehorn," Destiny said politely. "I'm sorry about my, uh, issue last week."

"No problem. It happens all the time," Shoehorn replied. "I have your lab results and all the hormone levels are within the normal range for your age, so I think we can look for other causes for your symptoms. Have you been taking the supplements that I gave you?"

"Yes, I started them as soon as I got home. I haven't seen much difference, except that I am kinda sleepy a lot of the time. In fact, the vaginal dryness and painful sex seem to be worse. Last night, Marwin proposed and we tried to have sex to celebrate—but it was just too painful, so we had to stop. You've got to help me, please! I want to spend the rest of my life with Marwin, but we need to be able to enjoy sex. It is very important to us!"

"Well, based on your labs, there might be a deeper cause for your problems. It is possible that subconsciously you don't find Mr. Gelstone attractive and your mind may be repulsed by his touch. This would lead to extreme dryness and painful intercourse, as mental arousal is responsible for the vaginal secretions that allow for normal sexual activity."

"How dare you!" Destiny accused. "I love Marwin! We have always had a great sex life until just recently. Maybe you aren't going to be able to help me after all. I don't think that I am interested in taking psychological advice from a gynecologist. It seems like you may be trying to practice beyond the scope of your expertise."

As patient and physician glared openly at one another, both seemed to realize that they had pushed too hard to achieve their individual objectives. Slowly, Shoehorn said, "I'm sorry, Ms. Lawson. I didn't mean to upset you. You're right, I overstepped my boundaries. I told you that I don't care for Mr. Gelstone, but I shouldn't allow my feelings to influence your care. I'm afraid that I was acting as unprofessional as... uh, my apologies. I really do believe that I can help you. I have a special treatment regimen for dyspareunia—uh, painful intercourse."

"Marwin did say there was a relatively new treatment. I think he said it was called Osphena?"

"Well, there again, Mr. Gelstone believes that he is a doctor and he is not. Osphena will not help your problem, as the etiology is not hormone-related. However, I do have something that I am positive will take care of your symptoms. It involves a fairly complicated titration over several weeks, and you will need to see me every two weeks so that I can assess your progress. If you follow my instructions, you should see an end to your symptoms," Shoehorn said.

Destiny's mind raced as she tried to process his words. *Could he really be about to give me a drug that could cause me to commit suicide? Holy shit!* Destiny thought. *Maybe we really do have a chance to take him down.*

Trying to put the appropriate amount of gratitude in her voice while still showing her displeasure at his earlier suggestion, Destiny said, "I will do whatever you say, as long as it's safe and will help me have sex with Marwin again. I just want to get married and have a normal, healthy sex life with the love of my life."

"Ms. Lawson, out of respect for you marrying a healthcare professional, I will give you my special regimen that I reserve for only a select few patients," Shoehorn said, smiling. "I'll be right back with your medication, but I still need to do the pelvic exam to make sure there is no anatomical reason for your dyspareunia."

Shit, Destiny thought. Realizing they may be getting close to nailing him, she responded, "Uh, OK, sure. I guess."

In less than three minutes, Shoehorn returned with a small manila envelope, which he laid on the table. "OK, Ms. Lawson. Just lie back and put your feet up in the stirrups."

***

"We've got him!" Destiny announced as soon as Marwin answered his cell phone.

"What happened?" asked Marwin.

"Call Jackson and Bradley, and I will meet all of you at your house in an hour. I will give you all the details then."

"OK, fine... But just tell me the basics of what happened," Marwin pleaded.

"Nope. I'll see you all shortly. Oh, and Mrs. Lawson, I love you," Destiny added cryptically.

With Destiny's last comment still ringing in his head, Marwin called Jackson and asked him to contact Bradley; he told Jackson they would gather at his house for the impromptu meeting. Marwin deflected Jackson's questions as he had no answers, then asked Siri to call his favorite Chinese restaurant. After placing his order for sesame chicken, beef and broccoli, fried rice, and egg rolls, Marwin headed toward the restaurant with his head still spinning like a top.

***

Jackson was the first to arrive, and immediately began peppering Marwin with questions.

"Dude, get a beer or some wine and chill. Des will be here any minute. She is the only one who knows what happened," Marwin said, while spreading the Chinese food out on the table.

"OK, OK," Jackson grumbled. "She needs to hurry up, though."

"As you wish," Destiny said, walking into the kitchen.

"About damned time," Jackson retorted.

"Easy, Buddy. Remember, she is bringing us good news," Marwin suggested.

"Aw, shit. I'm sorry, Destiny," Jackson apologized sadly. "I don't know what's wrong with me."

"No problem, I understand," Destiny replied softly, laying her hand on Jackson's shoulder.

"I'll go let Bradley in," Marwin said in response to the ringing doorbell.

After the food and drinks had been passed around, Destiny said, "I'll be right back."

Destiny returned with a small manila envelope in one hand and a folded sheet of paper in the other. Before anyone could ask any questions, Destiny opened the envelope and dumped out fourteen individually numbered white packets.

"Holy crap," Jackson said. "Those look like the one that Madeline had in her purse."

Speaking carefully, Destiny opined, "I suspect they are identical, Jackson. I believe the good doctor wishes to do me bodily harm. I believe the packets contain varying amounts of Marwin's drug. I have the titration schedule here."

"But, why? Why would Shoehorn give that to you? What did you say to him?" Marwin asked, dazed.

"Let's just say I really pushed all the right buttons," Destiny responded.

Marwin, Jackson, and Bradley all sat silently, mouths agape, as Destiny replayed the events that occurred in Shoehorn's office.

"That fucker," Marwin spat as Destiny recounted Shoehorn's theory on her dryness.

"Maybe he's smarter than we thought," Jackson said with a smirk.

"Eat shit," Marwin suggested.

"So, Marwin asked you to marry him?" Bradley asked timidly.

"Uh, no; I just made that up because I know Shoehorn hates Marwin," Destiny replied, looking directly at Marwin.

Silence filled the room as all eyes turned expectantly toward Marwin.

"Uh, wow, Des. That was a great idea," Marwin finally managed.

"Which part? Me making it up, or you actually asking?" Destiny teased.

After several long beats, Marwin replied, "Both."

Breaking the awkward silence that followed, Bradley said, "I'll get these to the lab at Langley, ASAP. Since they know what to test for now, it shouldn't take long to verify the contents. What exactly do you think they will find, Marwin?"

Obviously still trying to process the fact that he technically just asked Destiny to marry him, Marwin said slowly, "I think the first few packets will have the highest amounts of chlormethiazole, and the amount of active drug will likely decrease until the last couple, which probably don't have any active drug in them."

"OK, let's see what the labs shows. I'll let you guys know as soon as I do," Bradley said, heading to the door.

Being the good fatherly figure, Jackson said, "I'm heading out, too."

After Bradley and Jackson left, Destiny said, "I guess I should go, too. I have a full day tomorrow."

"What? You can't go; you haven't answered yet," Marwin said shakily.

Looking confused, Destiny asked, "Answered what?"

"My proposal," Marwin replied with a small nervous laugh.

Destiny looked at Marwin intently for several seconds, then said, "I believe I was the one who came up with the idea. I'll talk to you tomorrow. Love you."

CHAPTER 32

The cold and flu season continued to rage, and Marwin struggled to keep up. His mind whirled with thoughts of chlormethiazole, Shoehorn, and his relationship with Destiny. As he counted 75mcg Synthroid for the prescription he was filling, his certified technician stopped him. "Uh, Marwin... Mrs. Hickox gets Synthroid one hundred seventy-five micrograms, not seventy-five micrograms."

Looking again at the prescription label, Marwin said, "Shit, I was about to really screw up." Dumping the tablets back into the bottle, Marwin continued, "Thanks, Miranda. I appreciate you checking up on me."

"No problem. You always told us to double-check ourselves and the pharmacists, because no one is perfect and anyone can make a mistake."

"Especially me, right now. Thanks, again," Marwin said with a sigh.

Marwin's days were filled with Relenza, Tamiflu, Zithromax, and Levaquin; his nights were occupied with Destiny, chlormethiazole, Destiny, and more Destiny. There was still no word from the lab and no answer from Destiny yet, either. In fact, he had not seen her and had hardly talked to her since their meeting. She had been as swamped with work as he had.

As Marwin nursed a snifter of cognac at his desk, his gambling stuff spread all over the place, he contemplated calling Bradley again. Bradley had been very understanding, but he did begin to show some irritation after Marwin's third call that afternoon. Sitting mostly in a daze, Marwin started when his phone rang.

"Hey, Marwin, it's Bradley," the detective stated.

"Oh, hey! Did you get the results?"

"Yes. You were right and wrong. It was chlormethiazole, but all fourteen packets contained the same amount."

"Huh, that's weird. To induce suicidal ideation, you'd have to abruptly stop the drug after consistent use."

"Well, maybe Shoehorn will change the dosage later," Bradley suggested.

"Yeah, could be. I remember Madeline's calendar showed visits every two weeks for three months. I guess Destiny will have to go back to see him again. We need to prove that Shoehorn is intentionally stopping the drug abruptly to induce suicide ideation. He's probably breaking the law by dispensing a non-FDA-approved drug, but that would be a minor violation. We need to prove that he is trying to cause her to kill herself."

"OK, let's send Destiny back and see if he gives her some more. If he does, we'll analyze it to see if he changes the dose—or omits the chlormethiazole completely," Bradley said.

"Shit. I was hoping she wouldn't have to see that slimeball again," Marwin admitted.

"Yeah, I know. So was I. Let me know when she sees him again," Bradley said.

After hanging up with Bradley, Marwin called Destiny and informed her that she would have to keep her next appointment with Shoehorn.

"OK," she said resignedly.

"I want you to complain about allergies and bad breath when you see him, so he'll think you're taking the packets. Also, let him know that you feel sluggish and dizzy, at times," Marwin instructed.

"All right. The sluggish part won't be a stretch—and I can eat some onions and garlic before I go," Destiny responded.

"Uh, Des, how about we get together this weekend? I miss you."

"Sounds great! I miss you, too," Destiny replied brightly.

***

The morning of Destiny's appointment dawned cold and snowy. Marwin went to her apartment to help her rehearse the part one more time. He brought a tube of cream with him, which he applied to Destiny's nostrils and upper lip.

"Is this really necessary?" she asked as he applied the capsaicin cream. "Damn, that burns!"

"I know, but we need to simulate some of the symptoms. This will make your nose red, and it will look like you've been blowing it a lot."

"You owe me, after all this is over. This burns like hell!"

"I'll be happy to pay if we can put Shoehorn away," Marwin said.

***

"How are you doing today, Ms. Lawson?" Shoehorn asked, looking up from her chart.

"Well, I actually feel pretty good, I guess," Destiny replied.

"How are your symptoms?"

"They seem to be a little better. We have had sex every day this week, and the pain seems to be a little better each time," Destiny said shyly.

"Oh, w-well, that's good," Shoehorn stammered. "Any problems with the treatment?"

"Not that I know of. I have this terrible cold and I've been sneezing non-stop, but I don't think that has anything to do with the treatment."

Not looking up from the chart, Shoehorn asked, "Anything else?"

"Well, Marwin says my breath stinks and I don't know why. Maybe it's all the mucus that I have right now. I've also been kinda tired lately, and a little dizzy at times, but I don't know if that means anything or not."

"Uh-huh, I see. Well, it sounds like everything is going as expected. I am going to give you another two weeks of medication, then I will see you back after that."

"Thanks, Dr. Shoehorn. We really appreciate all that you're doing for us," Destiny said sweetly.

CHAPTER 33

Destiny and Marwin sat drinking coffee at a small table outside the coffee shop, enjoying the cold but brilliant day.

"I hope we hear from Bradley soon," Destiny declared. "It's already been six days since we gave him the last set of packets, so we should be hearing something. What do you think the results will be?"

"Chlormethiazole, I'm sure. The question is: how much will be in each packet? Something has been bothering me since we got the results of your first batch, but I couldn't figure out what was wrong. It just came to me. Was there a number on the packet that we found in Madeline's purse? How much drug was in that packet? I never asked Bradley how much was in it, or if there was anything else in the powder. I guess I was too shocked at the actual results. Why was there any drug in the packet? If he was withholding the active drug to induce suicide, there shouldn't have been any drug in that packet."

"I don't know. I don't remember anyone mentioning a number on the packet. Maybe Jackson or Bradley will know," Destiny replied, reaching for her phone.

"Hey, Brad, do you know if the packet of Madeline's was numbered like my packets were?" Destiny inquired after Bradley picked up.

"Hang on and I can tell you," Bradley replied. "Yep, there was a number 2 on the packet that they found in Madeline's purse," he said after a short pause.

"OK, great. Do you happen to know the exact drug content of the packet, in milligrams?"

"No idea, but I will check with my guy at Langley and will get back to you."

"OK, thanks. See ya," Destiny said, hanging up.

"Damn, way to just take charge," Marwin marveled.

"Well, since it took you so long to come up with the questions, I didn't want to wait any longer to get the answers," Destiny said, smiling.

***

"Hey, Destiny, you don't happen to be with Marwin, do you?" Bradley asked.

"Well, actually, I am," Destiny replied, glancing sideways at Marwin, sitting next to her on the couch.

"Great. I need his opinion on something," Bradley said.

"Did you get the results?"

"Yeah. Can you just put me on speaker?" he asked.

"Sure. Go ahead, you're on speaker, and it's just Marwin and me here."

"Marwin, the packet from Madeline's purse contained five hundred seventy-six milligrams of chlormethiazole, and four hundred milligrams of cimetidine. What is a normal dose of this drug, and why is there cimetidine in with it? I looked cimetidine up on the internet and found that it's used for ulcers and reflux. What does that have to do with anything?"

"Before I answer, how much chlormethiazole was in Destiny's packets, and did they also have cimetidine in them?" Marwin asked.

"All of the packets that were given to Destiny in the first two batches contained five hundred seventy-six milligrams of chlormethiazole and four hundred milligrams of cimetidine," Bradley answered.

"A normal dose is one hundred ninety-two to three hundred eighty-four milligrams. However, some abusers have taken as much as twenty-five grams. Unfortunately, most of those do not survive; it is usually lethal in large overdoses. The cimetidine is added to inhibit the metabolism of the chlormethiazole, which leads to higher blood levels of the drug."

"Let me make sure I have this right," Bradley began. "The packets contain two to three times a normal dose, along with a substance to boost the levels even higher?"

"Yep, that's it exactly," Marwin affirmed.

The three sat quietly for almost a minute, each lost in their own thoughts. Finally, Bradley said, "So, Shoehorn is providing high levels of this dangerous drug, then stopping it abruptly to induce suicide? That seems sort of risky, to me. Could a person die just from the high levels of the drug?"

"I'm certainly not an expert on this drug, but I would think that not only is it possible, it is likely—especially if they mixed it with alcohol," Marwin opined.

"So, not only do we need to investigate the patients of Shoehorn's that committed suicide, we also need to look into all of his other patients' deaths," Bradley suggested.

"Yep, focusing especially on unexplained causes or patients who died of respiratory failure," Marwin advised.

"OK, I will get right on it," Bradley said, sighing. "Looks like Destiny will need to make another visit to the good doctor."

"Great," interjected Destiny, who had been listening quietly. "Why do I need to see him again?"

"Well, right now we have no evidence that he is trying to harm you. Each packet has the same amount, so he hasn't stopped it abruptly. He can make a case that he is trying to help you by treating your anxiety with the chlormethiazole," Marwin said sarcastically. Doctors use doses that are out of the normal therapeutic range all the time, so that won't cause him any legal issues."

"He really creeps me out," Destiny stated with a shudder. "I don't know if I can continue seeing him every two weeks for much longer."

"Well, let's try to push him into speeding up his 'therapy,'" Marwin said.

"How?" Destiny asked.

"You need to piss him off," Marwin said with a smile.

***

Destiny's next appointment fell the morning after the conclusion of her child molester trial. She was all smiles and had a renewed pep in her step, albeit with a mild post-celebration headache, as she entered Shoehorn's office. As she waited to be called back, she replayed yesterday's guilty verdict for the slimeball child molester. *Hopefully, he'll never be able to molest anyone else. He may even get a taste of his own medicine,* she thought, knowing how child molesters often fare in prison.

"Ms. Lawson," the nurse announced, "You can come back now."

The nurse led Destiny to an exam room and instructed, "Go ahead and get undressed and put your gown on. Dr. Shoehorn will be in momentarily."

"I don't think so," Destiny replied. "I just need my medicine. I don't need an exam."

"I'm afraid that you are scheduled for a pelvic exam today, according to the doctor's notes," the nurse replied.

"The hell I am. I will straighten this out with him when he gets here," Destiny said, taking a seat, fully-dressed, on the exam table.

"Straighten what out, Ms. Lawson?" Shoehorn asked, entering the room.

"Your nurse said that I am scheduled for a pelvic exam today. I just had one, so I am not having another one done anytime soon."

"Well, that is going to be a problem," Shoehorn said sarcastically. "I need to check your vaginal secretions to make sure that the treatment is working."

"The last time, you just asked me questions. You didn't do an exam, so I don't see why you need to do another one when you just did one a month ago," Destiny complained.

"That is exactly why I need to do one today. Is the treatment helping? At the last visit, you said things were improving, but I need to check from a clinical standpoint."

Horrified at the prospect of another pelvic exam by this vulture, Destiny's mind whirled. She had to get him to give her more packets and hopefully, put an end to all of this.

Forming her answer slowly, Destiny responded, "I think the medicine is helping. I feel more mellow most of the time. Things that used to bother me, really aren't that big of a deal now. Plus, the sex has gotten amazing! I am now having multiple orgasms every time that Marwin and I have sex, and we're able to try more adventurous positions, now that it isn't painful. Marwin is truly amazing. I never knew that sex could be so good! Please, just give me some more of the medicine," Destiny begged.

"I'm afraid that there will be no more medicine until I check your vaginal secretions and verify that there is clinical improvement," Shoehorn replied, matter-of-factly.

Oh, shit! What am I going to do? Destiny thought.

Stalling for time, Destiny asked, "How are you going to do that? I doubt I will have much in the way of vaginal secretions with my legs up in the stirrups."

"Don't worry about that, Ms. Lawson, I have a protocol that will assist with that. Now, please get undressed so we can get started."

***

Destiny called Marwin after she left Shoehorn's office and solemnly requested that he, Jackson, and Bradley meet her at Marwin's house that afternoon. Before hanging up, she instructed Marwin to make sure he had plenty of wine, as she thought they were all going to need it.

When Destiny entered Marwin's kitchen, she saw pizza boxes littering the counter top. Marwin and Jackson were both stuffing large slices of pizza in their mouths, while Bradley was eating a salad. Destiny greeted Jackson and Bradley, then gave Marwin a lingering kiss. She pulled him close and whispered, "We have to finish this soon."

Pulling back, Marwin asked, "Are you okay? Tell us what happened."

Skipping the pizza, Destiny poured a tall glass of Merlot and recounted how Shoehorn forced her to submit to another pelvic exam.

"That son of a bitch!" Marwin shouted, spilling his wine. He made no attempt to clean it up. "That's it, you are not seeing him again! I'm sorry, Jackson, but we can't ask her to do this anymore."

"I understand completely. I don't want her to have to be touched by that creep again." Turning to Destiny, Jackson said sincerely, "Thanks for trying. I am so sorry that you had to put yourself through this for me."

"It's nice to see that chivalry isn't dead, but I can take care of myself. If I elect to let some old perv feel me up, then it is my prerogative."

"Des, stop!" Marwin shouted.

"No, you stop, Marwin. We started this; if we don't see it through to the end, then it was all for nothing. We are going to put that bastard away!"

Seeing the determination in her eyes, Marwin knew there was no point in arguing. "OK, Baby. Let's get that fucker."

With the mood slightly lightened, Destiny finished describing her visit to Shoehorn. She told them about Shoehorn having her watch porn so that he could supposedly measure her vaginal secretions.

"Damn, you have to give it to the old quack. That was ingenious," Marwin marveled.

"I don't know about ingenious, but I do know that both you and Destiny have referred to Shoehorn as 'old.' Need I remind you that he and I are the same age?" Jackson asked.

"Oh... Uh, s-sorry Jackson. I didn't mean to imply that you are old," Destiny stammered.

"No, you're an old perv—or just a perv, in general," Marwin offered.

"What great friends I have," Jackson mumbled.

Finally breaking his silence, Bradley asked, "Well, did he give you any more packets?"

"You're damned right he did. No way was he going to feel me up and not give me the drugs!" Destiny added cheerfully, handing Bradley an envelope.

Opening the envelope and inspecting the contents, Bradley said, "I will get these sent off express, first thing in the morning."

CHAPTER 34

As the winter dragged on, the first decent-sized snowfall covered Knoxville with five inches of white powder. Normally, snow energized Marwin. He had always loved the white stuff. From the time he was a kid growing up, he had enjoyed sledding, tubing, skiing, and just playing in the snow. Even as a pseudo-adult, he loved to get out his sled and go sledding down the steep hill in his neighborhood. His play time was much shorter these days than when he was younger; he quickly retreated to his fireplace with a glass of cognac and the latest Stephen King or Dean Koontz novel. Of course, he enjoyed the snow even more if Destiny happened to be "stuck" at his house when it hit.

This snowstorm had done nothing to lift him out of the funk into which he had fallen over the previous couple of weeks.

The Christmas holidays were over and the kids had returned to school. Marwin had been slammed at work during their holidays and had not been able to spend the time that he usually did with the kids. He had not taken Bogie to the batting cages even once over the break and had rarely seen Morgan, as she was usually either at Lindsey's or her best friend's house.

Marwin had seen little of Destiny; she had traveled to Louisiana to see her family over the holidays. Jackson's son Cody and his fiancée had flown in to celebrate Christmas with Jackson, so Marwin hadn't seen him, either.

Marwin also couldn't get the visual of Shoehorn touching Destiny out of his head. The mere thought of it made his stomach churn.

The days seemed endless and the nights longer as Marwin slogged through work, silently waiting to hear from Bradley and the lab at Langley.

Further adding to his depression was the fact that almost all of the NFL future bets that he had placed before the start of the season were now dead. He hadn't totaled them up yet, but he knew it was going to be ugly. He would be paying out very soon.

As Marwin stared blankly out the window in his study, his home phone rang. "Hello," he answered, distractedly.

"Hey, Marwin, it's Bradley."

Immediately snapping out of it, Marwin said, "Hey, what's up?"

"I just got off the phone with my guy at Langley, and I have the results of the latest batch of packets." Not giving Marwin a chance to ask a question, Bradley continued, "These packets didn't contain any chlormethiazole at all. They were also devoid of cimetidine. These packets contained cornstarch and carbamazepine, which my guy said is an anti-seizure drug. What the hell is Shoehorn trying to do now?"

After a long pause while his mind was spinning, Marwin replied, "He's trying to kill Destiny."

"That is what I thought you would say," Bradley said. "Not to be a downer, but you do know that it will be tough to prove that he is trying to kill Destiny, and even tougher to prove that he directly caused Madeline's death?"

"Yeah, I know," Marwin replied. "Look, Brad, I've been thinking about this for weeks. I've even broached the subject with Jackson, and he is agreeable. We'll have to have Madeline exhumed to prove that she ingested the chlormethiazole. Her having a packet doesn't prove that she ever took the drug. The problem is, how are we going to get a judge to issue an exhumation order?"

"Well, she already has issued one," Bradley answered.

"What? How? What are you talking about?" Marwin asked incredulously.

"Let's just say that I am on good terms with a certain judge, and I've been keeping her up to date on our investigation. In fact, she suggested the exhumation weeks ago, when Shoehorn first gave Destiny the packets. She said that we would need to prove that Madeline actually took the drug and even then, we might not get a conviction since the whole scenario is so far-fetched."

"Well, I'll be damned. All this time, I thought you just hung out in batting cages. I had no idea that you were actually working."

"Yeah, well, occasionally I try to be productive. I'll get the exhumation scheduled, then we can get a hair analysis done. If it is positive for chlormethiazole, we'll arrest the bastard," Bradley declared.

Stunned, Marwin asked, "How did you know we needed to do a hair analysis?"

"You're not the only one with a computer," Bradley replied smugly. "I'll be in touch."

***

With Bradley's behind-the-scenes groundwork already in place, the exhumation occurred three days after Marwin and Bradley's conversation. Bradley was the only person to brave the pouring rain for the somber event. The county medical examiner obtained the necessary hair samples and Madeline was returned to her resting place, hopefully never to be disturbed again.

Later that evening, Marwin, Jackson, and Bradley sat in a booth at Ruby Tuesday's, each lost in their own thoughts. The exhumation brought Jackson hope, but a deep sadness came with it. He sat idly swirling his ice cubes and the remnants of his scotch, his mind wandering in and out of memories.

"How long until we hear something?" Jackson asked for the second or third time.

Trying to hide his irritation, Bradley replied gently, "A couple of weeks, probably."

"Damn," Jackson responded, also for the second or third time.

"Let's just make sure we have a plan for what we will do once the results come back," Marwin interjected.

"I agree. We have to be ready to move if the hair analysis is positive for chlormethiazole," Bradley said.

"OK, let's assume the hair analysis is positive. Destiny says she thinks it's unlikely that a jury would convict Shoehorn of murder, even if we get a grand jury to indict him. There is very little data out there concerning chlormethiazole and suicide," Marwin stated.

"I know. I haven't been able to come up with much at all," Bradley confirmed.

Momentarily coming out of his funk, Jackson suggested, "Maybe we can just confront Shoehorn with the evidence and he'll confess."

"Uh, sure. Maybe a rainbow will shoot out of my ass, and I will shit gold," Marwin said dryly.

"You got a better plan, smartass?" Jackson retorted.

"No, not really. I just don't think Shoehorn will confess and go to jail for the rest of his life. I think he knows how difficult it will be to prove that he directly caused anyone to kill themselves. He may have been last in his class at Duke, but this is an ingenious way to kill people with little chance of getting caught."

"Well, all I know is that the bastard is going down, one way or another. Either we find a way to get him convicted, or I take care of him personally," Jackson snarled.

"Easy, Jackson," Bradley pleaded. "Let's get the results, then we'll figure out how to handle this. Don't do anything crazy that would jeopardize you and your family. Your family has suffered enough with Madeline's death; don't make them lose you, too. Think about it; that would be a double victory for Shoehorn."

"I know," Jackson sighed dejectedly. "I just get so angry thinking about what he did to Madeline and what he's trying to do to Destiny that I lose my mind and say shit I don't really mean."

"Hey, that could be it!" Marwin exclaimed. "Anger and alcohol often produce true feelings. I doubt that we can sit down with Shoehorn and get him drunk, but maybe we can piss him off enough to blurt out something that he shouldn't."

"How are we going to do that?" Bradley asked.

"I'm going to pay him a little one-on-one visit. If you can play Dick Tracy and help by recording our conversation, I'll handle the pissing him off part," Marwin replied with a smile.

"Let me check with my judge friend to see if we can record him legally, if it will be admissible evidence. If so, are you willing to wear a wire?"

"Sure. That old pervert won't want to undress me, so there's no danger of getting caught wearing a wire. We still need to know the hair analysis results and the legality of the recording before we do anything. I want it to stand up in court if we happen to get lucky enough for him to admit anything."

"Don't worry about the legal side; I'll take care of that part," Bradley said evenly.

***

A beautiful, sunny, April Fool's Day found Marwin in a far from sunny mood. The unseasonably warm weather and premature spring has caused allergies to explode. He had quickly exchanged Tamiflu and Z-Pack prescriptions for Astelin and Nasonex. The steady stream of sneezing patients with watery eyes who asked, "Why does my nasal spray cost a hundred and forty dollars?" was wearing Marwin down. He hadn't had a good consult in over a week—and hadn't seen Destiny for more than an hour during that time, either. Also, there were still no results from the hair analysis. All-in-all, Marwin thought his life sucked.

"Telephone, Marwin," Sam shouted over the din in the pharmacy.

Marwin's mind was wandering as he checked prescriptions and prepared to give the same counseling spiel he'd already given a dozen times that day, so he didn't hear Sam.

"Telephone, Marwin!" Sam repeated.

"Pharmacist," Marwin said half-heartedly when he picked up the receiver.

"It's about time. I thought you might be in the crapper," Bradley mused.

"Metaphorically speaking, I am," Marwin replied. "Tell me you have some news about the hair analysis."

"Actually, I do. Madeline's hair was positive for chlormethiazole."

"Oh, my God! I can't believe it!" Marwin replied, stunned. "That crazy bastard actually killed her."

"It would appear so, if what you say is true," Bradley responded. "Now, we just have to prove it."

"Did you get me cleared for the wire?" Marwin asked.

"Yep, the good judge said she would sign the warrant if the hair analysis results were positive."

"Awesome! How soon can you set it up?" Marwin asked, with more energy than he had felt in days.

"I have all the stuff we need. I can come by your house tomorrow afternoon and get you hooked up. Can you meet with him tomorrow after he closes?"

"Sure, that will work. I'll see you around three tomorrow afternoon, at my house."

***

In typical Knoxville fashion, the next day dawned cold and blustery. Strong, north-westerly winds had brought plummeting temperatures and a chance of some heavy, wet snow to the area. *Only in East Tennessee*, thought Marwin, as he prepared for the day.

Marwin was restless as the day dragged slowly by. He had rehearsed his part over and over while waiting for Bradley to appear.

The doorbell rang a few minutes before 3 p.m. "What took you so long?" Marwin blurted as he opened the door for Bradley.

Glancing at his watch, Bradley started to reply, but just smiled and entered the house. "You ready?" he asked.

"Uh, I sure hope so. Before, I was sure that I could pull this off. Now, I'm not so sure. What if I get caught? What if he doesn't confess anything? Can't I just beat a confession out of him?"

"Easy, killer," Bradley cajoled. "No way will he know you're wearing a wire, because the wire is in this watch," Bradley said, extending his arm to show Marwin the replica Seiko. "Shoehorn will never suspect a thing."

"Okay, but—," Marwin began.

"I have no doubt that you can piss him off. I'm quite sure you will find the right buttons to push," Bradley interrupted.

"Thanks, but I'm afraid your confidence may be misguided," Marwin said shakily.

"Just focus on Madeline and Destiny, and all the other innocent women he has hurt. You'll know what to do when the time comes. And I'll be right outside with backup, if things start to go south."

"Go south?" Marwin almost whispered.

***

Bradley, Marwin, and Detective Dan Jennings parked just down the street from Shoehorn's office, in the parking lot of an auto parts store. Bradley's listening device had a range of a half mile, so he could easily hear Marwin's conversation inside Shoehorn's office.

Sensing Marwin's trepidation, Bradley said, "We are right here, less than a hundred yards from his office. We can be inside in less than a minute, if you need us." Grasping Marwin's shoulders and looking him in the eye, Bradley continued, "Let's get this bastard!"

Staring back at Bradley, Marwin took a deep breath and slowly exhaled. "All right; let's do this."

As Marwin walked slowly toward Shoehorn's office, Bradley popped the hood on the car to be less conspicuous. Having repeatedly tested the watch, Bradley was confident that the recording equipment would work perfectly. Bradley wanted Marwin to wear an ear piece, but Marwin had refused. He was afraid that Shoehorn would spot it.

"You really think this will work?" Jennings asked.

After several seconds, Bradley replied, "It better."

After entering the building, Marwin checked his watch, then slunk around the corner to wait. Promptly at 5 p.m., a nurse came to the office door and locked it, leaving several staff members inside. Ten minutes later, the door was unlocked and three staff members left for the day. With no sign of Shoehorn and no idea how many staff were still in the building, Marwin began to sweat. He fidgeted in his small area for a moment, then decided to go for it. *It's now or never*, he thought. Just as he stepped out of his hiding place, Marwin saw Shoehorn opening the door for a single nurse. Assuming the nurse was the last one to leave besides Shoehorn, Marwin stepped up to the office door just as the nurse walked out.

Seeing Marwin, the nurse said, "Sir, we are closed."

"I know, that's why I am here," Marwin said, looking directly at Shoehorn. "I need to speak privately to the good doctor."

"I have nothing to say to you," Shoehorn replied, closing the door.

Jamming his foot in the door and pushing it backward, Marwin said, "That's OK. I'll do all the talking."

Startled, the nurse asked, "Should I call the police, Ernie?"

Before Shoehorn could answer, Marwin said, "Sure, go ahead. I think they would be very interested in hearing how your good doctor has been inappropriately touching his patients during his exams."

"What the hell are you talking about? I have done no such thing!" Shoehorn roared.

Backing away, the nurse reached for her phone and announced, "I'm calling the police."

"Fine," Marwin said evenly.

"No, Patty, don't call the cops. I'm sure this is just a misunderstanding that has led Mr. Gelstone to his preposterous accusation."

Opening the door to allow Marwin entry, Shoehorn instructed the nurse to go home. "I will lock up after Mr. Gelstone and I finish discussing whatever it is that he wishes to talk about."

"Maybe I should stay," the nurse replied.

Taking a chance, Marwin said, "That's a great idea! You need to hear what this monster you work for has been doing to his patients."

"That is enough! You will not disparage me in front of my staff," Shoehorn hissed. "I will speak to you privately in my office, and we will settle this once and for all. There is no reason to impose on Patty. She has family to get home to."

"OK. She'll hear about everything soon enough anyway," Marwin said agreeably. "Oh, and Patty, it's Doctor Gelstone, for future reference."

Eyes blazing, Shoehorn locked the door and pulled the blinds down. Turning to Marwin, he said, "You have some nerve, coming here and spouting a bunch of nonsense in front of my staff. I am sick of your constant interference and harassment. If this continues, I will have no choice but to go to the authorities."

"I doubt that you want anything to do with the police, since you've been molesting your patients." After a brief pause, Marwin added, "As well as causing some of them to commit suicide."

Rocking back as if slapped, Shoehorn roared, "You're crazy! Now you're accusing me of harming my patients? What the hell is wrong with you? I am a well-respected physician whose sole goal is to give my patients the best quality care possible. I will not listen to your insulting accusations any longer. I suggest you go home, Mister Gelstone. If I hear any more of your outlandish accusations or experience any more harassment at your hands, I will bring the authorities into the situation."

"I don't think so," Marwin retorted. "I know that you touched Destiny inappropriately because I saw the tape. You also did unnecessary pelvic exams so that you could get your pitiful little dick hard!"

"W-what?" Shoehorn stammered. Taking two steps toward Marwin with his fists balled at his sides, Shoehorn snarled, "Get out of my office! You cannot come in here and make absurd accusations with no proof."

"Oh, I have proof," Marwin said, further closing the gap between the two of them. "Like I said, Destiny had a video recorder in her watch. I watched the entire disgusting office visit. I thought you were just a quack; I didn't realize you were a pervert, too!"

Face reddening and neck bulging, Shoehorn leaned closer to Marwin. "Get out, you son of a bitch!"

"Not until we reach an agreement. I haven't shown the tape to the police—yet. I would prefer not to, actually, since Destiny is the district attorney. I am willing to destroy the tape, if you agree to close your practice. At least that way, you won't be able to molest or kill any other innocent women."

Laughing, Shoehorn barked, "You're insane! First, you accuse me of molesting patients. Then you turn around and try to blackmail me?! I believe blackmail is illegal in Tennessee."

"Actually, blackmail is illegal in all states, dumbass," Marwin replied. "I prefer to think of it as giving you options rather than as blackmail. It sounds so much nicer. Look, Shoehorn, you're finished. You're a shitty doctor, and a pervert to boot. There is no place for you in medicine."

At this, Shoehorn's expression made Marwin think he was about to be punched in the face. With a murderous glare, Shoehorn turned on his heel and stomped down a hallway.

Following Shoehorn down the hallway, Marwin shouted, "You can't just walk away from this. It isn't going away, and neither am I."

Marwin stopped in the doorway that Shoehorn had just gone through.

"Wrong, *Mister* Gelstone. I believe you *will* be going away," Shoehorn said, pointing a handgun at Marwin's chest.

"Whoa, what are you doing? You're going to shoot me now?" Marwin asked, voice shaking. "There is no way that you will get away with shooting me. You will rot in jail."

"Well, you'll never know one way or the other, since you'll be dead," Shoehorn spat maniacally.

Seeing the crazed look in Shoehorn's eyes, Marwin started to tremble. Unsure of how to proceed and fearing for his life, Marwin looked from the black hole of the pistol's barrel back into Shoehorn's dark eyes. *Shit*, Marwin thought.

"What's the matter, *Mister* Gelstone? Cat got your tongue? What happened to the pompous, threatening man who was throwing around those wild accusations? Not so threatening now, are you? You got way out of your league when you decided to take me on. You don't know who you're messing with. I make a difference in my patient's lives, while you just stuff pills in a bottle and perpetuate addict's addictions. I use cutting-edge treatments for my patients—"

"Like chlormethiazole?" Marwin blurted without thinking.

Still pointing the gun at Marwin's chest, Shoehorn cocked the hammer and scoffed, "Like you would know anything about chlormethiazole, mister pill counter."

Afraid his bladder was about to let loose, Marwin shakily said, "Well, why don't you educate me, oh great doctor?"

"I see no need to waste my time trying to educate the likes of you, especially since you won't be here to use the knowledge, anyway," Shoehorn said with a sickening laugh.

Sensing his time was running out, Marwin tried a softer approach. "Look, maybe I underestimated you, Doctor Shoehorn. You're right, I don't know much about chlormethiazole, but I would love to learn. Tell me how you use it in your practice. Is that part of your cutting-edge therapy?"

"Enough of this chatter," Shoehorn said, ignoring Marwin's question. Motioning across the hall with the pistol, he said, "I'm going to need you to lie on the table."

"I don't think I have anything you'll want to examine," Marwin snapped, and immediately regretted it. "Please, Doctor Shoehorn, tell me how you're able to use this strange drug to make a difference in your patient's lives," Marwin implored.

"OK, fine. You lie down on the exam table, and I will explain about the chlormethiazole. Otherwise, I'll just kill you now and you will never learn my secrets."

Wondering where the hell Bradley was, Marwin began to walk shakily toward the exam table in the room across the hall.

"Get up on the table and lie back with your hands behind your head," Shoehorn instructed, still pointing the pistol at Marwin.

"OK, OK. Now, what is so great about chlormethiazole?" Marwin asked, thinking about Destiny. *I'm sorry, Des. I thought I could do this; I thought I could put this bastard away. It looks like he's going to put me away.*

Keeping the gun trained on Marwin, Shoehorn quickly wrapped twine around Marwin's wrists and attached the other end to the door knob. "All right, Mister Gelstone, I am a man of my word," Shoehorn began, after assuring himself Marwin had been secured.

"The best thing about chlormethiazole is that it makes my patients disappear! No more disgusting women asking me to save their sex lives. Perverts, every one of them! Speaking of perverts, your Destiny may be the biggest one that I have ever encountered. She got so wet during my exams, I thought she was going to climax right there on the table."

"Fuck you!" Marwin screamed, struggling against his restraints.

"Sadly, she won't be fucking you any longer, Mister Gelstone. I'm afraid that she is about to commit hara-kari. Your unfortunate demise at the hands of a mugger will further add to the depression that the chlormethiazole is inducing. She will likely be dead before your funeral is complete. Maybe you guys can get a two-for-one deal at the cemetery," Shoehorn suggested with a smirk.

Pulling the pillow from beneath Marwin's head and placing it over the end of the pistol, Shoehorn said, "I'm afraid we must end our intriguing conversation now. I'll have a lot to clean up after we're through, so I really must get on with it."

Staring at Shoehorn and trembling, Marwin said, "You won't get away with this, you—" Marwin's insult was interrupted by the glass door of the outer office exploding inward.

Hearing the explosion, Shoehorn pressed the pillow over Marwin's face and jammed the pistol deep into it. Marwin thrashed his head and tried to kick out with his feet as Shoehorn pulled the trigger and the gun emitted a muffled *pfft*. Shoehorn dashed out of the room as the blood began to seep slowly from under the pillow.

CPSIA information can be obtained
at www.ICGtesting.com
Printed in the USA
LVHW05s1336010918
588583LV00007B/10/P